"Even if you don't entirely mean it at this moment, I have no doubt you'll come to see that this was for the best. Your lover may have shown you that love was fickle—"

Helena would have protested, but Rand put a finger to her lips as he said, "I'm glad he did. Because now I may show you that autonomy and independence are the best gift a husband can give his wife."

She looked at him without masking her skepticism. "Or a wife her husband, my lord?"

"Indeed." He sat back, turning his face up so that sunshine caressed the strong, beautiful lines of nose and jaw. The carriage horses trotted on in a leisurely manner. "Indeed."

Husband. Helena itched to sketch him as he was then. The jumble of her feelings—ire, dismay, admiration, even fear—would give a strength and boldness to her strokes that would capture him perfectly. Elemental male at one with his universe.

She sighed. A sketch of him she could admire. The man himself, as husband, was another matter altogether. "I am not Rosaline, you know."

"I am glad of it. You are much more kissable." He gave no warning at all before he turned his face away from the sun, leaned in toward her, and kissed her soundly on the lips. His body molded against hers, the arm he had rested behind her head becoming a tight band holding her to him, preventing escape as his kiss deepened. . . .

Dear Romance Readers,

In July of 1999, we launched the Ballad line with four new series, and each month we present both new and continuing stories set everywhere from medieval England to the American West—the kind of passionate, romantic stories you love best, written by the most gifted authors. At the back of each book, we tell you when you can find subsequent books in the series that have captured your heart.

First up this month is **With His Ring,** the second book in the fabulous new *Brides of Bath* series by Cheryl Bolen. What happens when a dedicated bachelor who marries for money discovers that his impetuous young wife has married for love—his? Next, Kelly McClymer returns with **The Next Best Bride.** A jilted groom marrying his errant finacée's twin sister is hardly romantic, unless it happens in the charming *Once Upon a Wedding* series.

Reader favorite Kate Donovan is back with another installment of the *Happily Ever After Co.* This time in **Night After Night** a young woman looking for a teaching job instead of a husband finds the key to her past—and a man with the key to her heart. Finally, ever-talented Cindy Harris concludes the *Dublin Dreams* series with **Lover's Knot,** in which secrets are revealed, friendships are renewed . . . and passion turns to lasting love.

Why not start spring off right and read them all? Enjoy!

Kate Duffy
Editorial Director

Once Upon a Wedding

# THE NEXT BEST BRIDE

## Kelly McClymer

ZEBRA BOOKS
KENSINGTON PUBLISHING CORP.

http://www.kensingtonbooks.com

ZEBRA BOOKS are published by

Kensington Publishing Corp.
850 Third Avenue
New York, NY 10022

All Kensington titles, imprints and distributed lines are available at special quantity discounts for bulk purchases for
sales promotion, premiums, fund-raising, educational or
institutional use.

Special book excerpts or customized printings can also be
created to fit specific needs. For details, write or phone the
office of the Kensington Special Sales Manager: Kensington
Publishing Corp., 850 Third Avenue, New York, NY 10022.
Attn. Special Sales Department. Phone: 1-800-221-2647.

Zebra and the Z logo Reg. U.S. Pat. & TM Off.

First Printing: April 2002
10  9  8  7  6  5  4  3  2  1

Printed in the United States of America

*To Yvonne, Kathy, Sylvie, and Lynn—the most insightful, kind, inspiring ladies I know*

# Chapter One

*London, 1849*

The dregs of the evening fetched up Rand Mallon, Earl of Dalby, exhausted but flush. His companion, too, had been successful at cards. Indeed, Mr. Roscue Anderlin had the luck of a man playing with an angel on one shoulder and the devil on the other.

They sat facing each other now, slumped in their chairs, legs outstretched, a glass of brandy each. If any of the night owls who dotted the darkened corners of the men's club had cared to give them anything other than an incurious glance they would have seen nothing more than a pair of incurable reprobates savoring their victories despite the likelihood of tomorrow's hangover.

Only Rand would likely notice that his companion was as tense as an overtightened harp string and had been less than focused on the game this evening. Six hands and twenty pounds to the good was not shameful for an evening's work. But it should have been nine hands and fifty pounds. It was time to find out what was causing the inattention. He had a feeling he would not like the answer, so he sighed before he demanded, "Spill it."

Uneasily, his companion shifted, fingers combing through one stiff sideburn with nervous energy. But there was no prevarication, no claim of innocence. That was one of the reasons for their friendship. "I hate to be the one to tell you this, but your bride-to-be is about to run away."

The news gripped him around the middle, like a boxer's hold. For a moment he struggled for breath. "And where would the fair Rosaline be going, if not to the altar with me?"

"To America."

Rand wanted to curse. To shout. To argue. But he did not doubt the truth of the information. He slumped farther into his chair. "I knew I had a poor reputation, but I didn't expect it would send her to another continent." The amber of his brandy glimmered in the forgivingly dim light of the club as it swirled to and fro with his movements.

His companion leaned back into the plush leather of the chair, relaxing now that the fateful news had been delivered. "You can curse me for bearing bad news, if you wish."

Rand stared morosely into the shadows. "Will cursing you deliver my bride to the altar?" The answer to the question was a foregone conclusion, but all the same he had to ask.

The reply was as certain as he had expected. "No. A stinging string of impolite words might, however, ease some of the temper I see brewing in you."

"What temper? I am calm as a monk at prayer." He swigged down the contents of his glass and held it out, whereupon a servant stepped from the shadows and silently supplied a refill.

"The temper that is turning your earlobes red."

Sometimes a friend could know one a bit too well, Rand reflected. Which was why he did not have many friends. "Do you begrudge me a few moments of indignation? I was planning to be married in two weeks' time, and now I am told my bride will not join me at the altar. No one will spare a jot of sympathy for Markingham's reprobate heir, will they?"

"Sympathy? Why? You are not marrying for love. You've made no secret of it. You face the parson's mousetrap only to secure an heir and wrest control of your funds from your grandfather's hands."

"Only?" Remembering his traitorous earlobes, Rand spent a moment calming his anger. "The reasons seemed important to me when my grandfather promised me control of my inheritance simply for marrying and providing an heir. Why else go to all the bother to find a woman who'd agree to my terms?"

"Perhaps he will volunteer to give you control of some of your funds when he learns you have been jilted, in compassion for your poor, wounded pride?"

Rand laughed aloud, a sharp bark of laughter that carried the sound of his bitterness through the quiet room. "No. He will not. Not until I am married and produce an heir." Even then the old man might have some trick up his sleeve to try to hold on to his control, but Rand had shared that possibility with no one, not even his best friend.

"So, you are still determined upon that course?

Despite"—said with an apologetic sigh, cut by a wicked half smile—"despite knowing that proper young ladies will be wary of the jilted earl?"

"Wary? They will be eager, the foolish children. What is it about a man with no scruples to speak of, that green girls see him with stars in their eyes?"

"I have never fathomed the secret of such idiocy, myself, despite having so many sisters. Though I don't suppose it hurts that you are devilishly handsome as well as a rake. I believe the combination of green eyes and dark curls is almost guaranteed to make women swoon." They both sighed and spent a moment in silent consideration of such behavior, before Rand's companion lamented, "How unfortunate that you do not wish a green girl."

"Beyond unfortunate. Where I shall find a woman who is as agreeable as Miss Rosaline Fenster to living her own life and leaving me to my own disreputable one is a puzzle I do not enjoy having to solve—again," he grumbled, almost completely resigned to the fact now. Amazing how amenable a few glasses of brandy could make him. Tomorrow he'd pay with the devil of a headache.

"Perhaps this time you will just have to settle for the next best alternative."

"And what would that be?"

"Compromise one of the young women who has begun to think she will never find a husband. Perhaps her gratitude will keep her from complaining when you do not reform."

"Such an act would be in keeping with my reputation, I suppose. Do I sound fastidious if I say the idea repels me?"

"Why? You need a wife. Isn't seduction a time-honored way for a rake to acquire one?" There was a faint bitterness beneath the words that made Rand's ears prick up.

"The work involved seems excessive: wooing and seducing a young virgin only to have to deal with her tears before and after the wedding. I much prefer the straightforward bargain that Rosaline and I made."

His companion shifted in the leather chair, as if trying to find a comfortable position, before leaning forward to offer in a casual tone, "Perhaps I have the answer for you."

Rand braced himself for a joke, then noticed his companion once again vibrated with the tension he had noticed earlier this evening. "Let me guess. Myra Wirthsham—squinty eyes, elephant ears, and all."

Instead of an answering grin at his witticism, he received a sharp rebuke. "Miss Wirthsham is too good for the likes of you." Belatedly, Rand remembered that his friend disliked anyone making fun of the less-than-beautiful young women who were forced to compete with those nature had blessed. "I mean Helena Fenster."

Rand would have laughed, but for the pair of serious blue eyes focused on him. There was not a hint of a smile, and he knew the subtle signs of humor in his best friend too well to doubt that he had just been made a legitimate offer. "Impossible."

The only answer to his rejection of the idea was silence. Rand thought of Helena, Rosaline's twin. Though they were identical in appearance, they were immensely different in behavior. He imagined putting the same bargain before the prim Helena as he had before Rosaline. The very idea was absurd.

He ticked off the reasons on his fingers, allowing them to be absorbed into the silent and dimly lit gravity of the club's dark-paneled walls. "She is Rosaline's sister, she is impossibly proper, and she has made no secret of her utter disregard for my rather questionable morals."

"Not as impossible as you think." Reluctantly, his friend added, "She has a secret that makes her vulnerable to an offer from you right now."

The only type of secret he could imagine was a scandalous indiscretion. He could not imagine such a thing in context with Helena, however, try as he might. "What has she done? Allowed a man to kiss her in the gazebo? What young miss worth her salt has not?"

"She took a lover, expecting a formal bid for her hand, but he proved to be a cad."

Rand had thought himself incapable of being shocked anymore. The idea of Helena Fenster with a lover was so farfetched he'd have believed no one else who told him such a thing. "I hope, for her sake, he did not prove as clumsy with her pleasure as he did with her heart."

His comment was rewarded with a flush of color upon his friend's cheeks, to his great satisfaction. "I believed this might put your suit in a new light. I did not intend to spread gossip that might hurt the young lady."

"If no one knows, her reputation is secure. If she marries me, her reputation has a permanent blemish. Ros accepted that."

"Relished it would be more accurate."

"Her sister—"

"She is not so conventional as she appears."

"I will take your word for it. Certainly she has chided me for my drinking and gambling both."

"You are to marry her twin; it is understandable that she be concerned."

"And now you suggest that I exchange one sister for the other at the altar?"

"Exactly."

Rand considered the idea. "Am I expected to blackmail the girl into marriage?" He found the idea distasteful.

"Of course not. You will make the same bargain with her as you made with her sister—in addition, you will promise never to bring up her indiscretion in the future."

"I can see the advantage for me," Rand said slowly. "But for Helena? What does she gain married to a unrepentant rake? Wouldn't she be better off chasing down her lover and forcing him to marry her? Surely the duke has the necessary power."

"Helena is not a fool. She has the sense to see marriage to a willing husband as preferable to being shackled to an unwilling coward. Which benefits you, in that she understands too well how futile it is to attempt to change a man's true nature."

Rand's curiosity rose at the contempt that shaded his companion's words. "Just who was able to breach Helena's formidable propriety?"

"That information is not for me to divulge." A curt, sharp warning that Rand was close to trespass.

His curiosity grew stronger. He wheedled, "If I am to approach the girl to strike a bargain—"

"Let me manage that. Simply decide whether this exchange of brides will suit you."

Rand did not need to think overmuch. The girl was Ros's sister after all; there must be more similarities than were apparent at first. He could, at the very least, be honest with her. "You swear she will leave me to my own devices?"

"Exclusively."

A warning voice in the back of his mind compelled him to be cautious. After all, a wife was forever. "I'll need to speak to her. Can that be managed? Someplace private. I want the truth from her, not you—especially if she's the one to be my bride."

"I'll arrange it. And then you'll see I'm right." His companion swallowed down the remaining brandy before standing to go. The blue eyes that met his shone with candor, and the smile was one of pure relief. "I know my sister."

With a quick glance around, Ros planted a hard kiss on his lips.

Rand pushed him—or rather *her*—away with a harsh exclamation. "You forget yourself, *Mr.* Anderlin. And that after jilting me."

She only laughed, which made the false sideburns glued to her cheeks quiver. "What? Do you worry for your reputation?" And then her expression grew more somber. "I'm sorry, Rand. I don't want to be married, not even to you, who'd let me do as I liked."

He didn't answer. She, of all people, knew the hopes he had pinned to a marriage. An heir. A life of his own that did not depend on his grandfather's approval.

He was glad to see her squirm a bit with guilt. Still, he was not surprised to see that she would not change her mind.

She fingered her whiskers, her gaze full of certainty. "I know my sister. You and Helena will suit. I'm sure of it."

* * *

"It's the perfect solution you know, Hellie." Ros's disembodied voice drifted down from the apple tree. "I can't marry him."

Helena ignored her, concentrating on the sketch she was roughing of Ros in the apple tree. She couldn't see her right now, but she knew her sister had her skirts hiked up in an unladylike way. No doubt she was swinging one leg idly as she spoke of foolish things. America. Why did Ros always wish for adventure? Why could she not simply settle down with the earl, have children, and enjoy tea and gossip with her sisters? Helena brushed away the leaves that had landed on her sketch pad and sighed.

Rosaline moved sharply when Helena did not respond, making the branches sway overhead. "I won't marry him—even if you don't agree to take my place. I shall jilt the poor man in a most humiliating fashion."

Helena could imagine the scene. The duke would be furious at the scandal. His duchess, their oldest sister Miranda, would do her best to soothe the ruffled feathers of family and guests. "Perhaps that is for the best, then. He is a reprobate of the first order. No doubt it will only add to his reputation, to be jilted." Try as she might, Helena could not picture Rand Mallon sad or angry. The earl would doubtless have some wicked quip to offer the embarrassed guests—at Ros's expense as well as his own.

"He is a good man, Hellie, no matter that he seems a little wild."

"Wild as a tiger. Even you had not intended to tame him, Ros. Just to leave him to his own vices while you pursued yours." Helena allowed herself to imagine the earl across the breakfast table. Absurd. The man, no doubt, did not rise until well after noon.

"I've never known him to do harm to anyone."

"He's fought a score of duels." Over cards and over women. Married women.

"Rumors, all."

Helena resisted the urge to screech. "You seconded one, Ros. Do you think I didn't know?"

"Sometimes a man of his reputation ends up in a situation he would rather not. He shot into the air."

"How noble."

"I would not have done so. Lord Melfrom had dealt from a marked deck and fleeced half a dozen green boys before Rand exposed him for it."

"The man I always dreamed of—able to turn up a cardsharp and manage to live through a foolish duel."

Ros's unusual spate of patient persuasion snapped. "He's willing to marry you, knowing why you'd even consider trading places with me."

Helena went still, and cold dread seized her limbs. "You didn't tell him."

"Of course I did. How else could I convince him that you would accept his offer?" Ros was silent for a moment when Helena did not answer, and then she offered tentatively, "He didn't seem to be bothered a bit."

"How reassuring." Perhaps it was a blessing that her sister was going to jilt the man. Facing him again, knowing that he was privy to her darkest secret . . .

"Considering your circumstances, I can't believe you would throw stones."

Helena was stung by her sister's words. "You speak as if my fate is dire if I do not marry your earl. Are you not the one who encouraged me to slip the bonds of propriety?"

Ros threw a wizened apple down, which bounced off Helena's shoulder and rolled down to rest in her lap. "You speak as if you have no fear of scandal or humiliation. And I told you a few moments alone in the garden would give him an opportunity to speak his heart—not lift your skirts."

Helena knew she had been foolish; she did not need Ros to remind her. Her only hope had been to keep that knowledge from anyone else. And now Ros had told the earl, who might gamble the secret away for his own drunken amusement. "You should not have told him. Perhaps no one would have ever had to know. I am not yet certain that I will have a child."

Ros came down from the tree in a shower of leaves. She did not hug—she was not one for embraces—but her hand came to rest warm and strong and steady on Helena's shoulder. "There is always the tea—"

Helena shook her head violently. "No. If I was so stupid to believe William and end up with a child, then I deserve the shame." She closed her eyes. "I cannot believe I thought he would marry me."

"He told you so, with his hand upon his heart. How could you have guessed he lied?"

Helena looked into her sister's blue eyes, the mirror of her own. How could they be so different inside? "You would have known."

"I don't dream the same dreams you do, Helena. I don't want a husband, babies, a home to manage." She pressed, "All things you can have with Rand, if you marry him."

"But not love. Not a husband who will cherish me, or who will make me proud." She imagined an evening in society with Rand: Would he dance with her before retiring to the cards—or would he favor some other woman with that honor? His mistress. One of his many mistresses.

"He will give you your freedom, Helena. Once you've given up your dreams of fairy-tale princes, you will see that you made the best bargain possible. Just think—you will be able to draw and paint. Perhaps spend a year in Italy taking lessons with a master. And Rand will not play the part of disapproving husband. He will applaud you; he will encourage your talents."

"Don't try to wheedle me with your own brand of fairy tale. If I consent to this marriage, I will be much too busy producing and raising his heir to have much freedom to travel to Italy."

Rosaline wrinkled her nose. "That is one reason why I decided America was more attractive than marriage to Rand, freedom or not. But you are not me. You want children."

"I do want children. But I do not want a life of lies. And if the worst happens, I will have to explain an early child—who will no doubt have William's robust health and large size. And I will worry that my husband might speak the truth that would destroy me because he was too drunk to watch his tongue." Or worse, that he would do so cold sober because he could no longer bear to claim her child as his.

"I hope you do not have to. However, if the worst were to happen, Rand will not mind." Her hand tightened on Helena's shoulder and there was a note of iron will in her voice as Ros added, "I will make him swear it. I will not have you or your child hurt. And I will promise you both that he will answer to me if he does not keep his word."

It was perhaps not until then that Helena realized Ros was set on this marriage. Not only so that she could go to America. But so that Helena would be protected from her own foolish actions.

There was truly only one question left to answer: Would marriage to the earl save her—or sentence her to a life of misery?

# Chapter Two

Helena shook off her sister's comforting hand. "Oh, why did I have to be so foolish, Ros? Why couldn't I have been like you—dressing the part of a man and content with gambling and drinking? Why did I think it would be romantic to be alone with him? To let him . . ."

"I don't know, Hellie. It was a mistake. But you can mend it. Marry Rand. He'll be happy to accept your child, if you are to have one. And if you are not, you'll only have to bear his company while you make a child together. I assure you, he will be eager to let you live your life however you wish."

Helena wanted to cry. The offer was much too tempting, and all because she had not been as sensible as she should have been. "One foolish mistake—"

"Two, actually." Ros snapped her mouth shut, as if she realized that she should not have spoken. Sometimes Helena wished she did not always confide in her sister. "He said he would speak to Valentine that very day. I did not know what to do—"

"A simple and firm 'No' would have served, I am certain."

"I'm afraid you inherited all the will for the pair of us, right from the womb."

"You have enough will, Hellie; you're just afraid to use it. You'd rather not have the consequences that sometimes result, such as having to marry Rand. I don't mind them, if the goal is worthwhile enough."

"Do you truly believe America is a worthy goal? Why can't you just stay here? I will miss you terribly." Strong emotion made her sister cross, but Helena could not help herself. Ros had always been there—to talk, to help, to show her how to be strong, and to be strong for her when she could not be.

"I've made up my mind, Hellie; no use pouting about it. After you've had a baby, you can come to visit." Ros smiled with a misplaced confidence that amazed Helena. "I wouldn't be surprised to hear that you'd quite become resigned to your husband by then."

"The earl?" Helena forced away a picture of Rand's lips descending to meet her own as Rosaline tapped the sketchbook she cradled in her lap. Helena was startled to see what her unconscious fingers had laid out on the page. "You've been studying the male form, I see."

Helena curled her knees up, hiding the foolish sketch from sight. "He would truly not mind if I were to come to him already carrying another man's child?"

"He would count it a blessing."

"What kind of man does not mind raising another man's child as his own? What if I had a son?" Helena doubted any man could feel blessed by a cuckoo in his nest. "I must speak with him. Such a matter cannot be left to your word. I must look into his eyes and see that you are right about this."

Her sister smiled widely, and Helena felt as if she had just fallen into a snare with the noose about to snap tight. "Good. I told him you would meet him tonight, in my stead."

Tonight. The immediacy spurred her to panicked argument. "I cannot—the scandal, if I were seen . . ."

Ros snorted in a decidely unladylike manner. "You'll wear my disguise, of course, silly. As a man you can go wherever you please without anyone's notice."

"Ros! Helena!" Ros scrambled up from the ground at the sound of their youngest sister's voice. Helena wanted to protest, but she knew she could not do so now. Kate was not one to give up the search, and they both knew there was no sense in staying silent in the hopes she would go away.

With a sharp motion of her hand, Ros indicated that Helena remain as she was. "I'll go. You stay a moment. You look as if you could cry." With a flash of skirts Rosaline disappeared, leaving Helena alone in the shade of the tree.

Helena thought of bracing the earl in his own lair. He was sure to make a mock of the matter between them. But he needed a wife, and she might very well find herself in desperate need of a husband.

She looked at the couple she had drawn sitting in the tree.

The Adam with the earl's face and the bare chest of David himself, held the apple to his Eve. And an Eve with Helena's face—for Ros could never have managed that expression: a mingling of temptation and trepidation.

"Hold still or you will have sideburns on your chin."

The cleverly padded waistcoat and vest that Ros used to give herself a bulkier, more masculine shape, made Helena's limbs feel heavy and clumsy. "Maybe this is not a good idea. I could speak with him tomorrow, when he comes to dine with us."

Ros continued adjusting the clothing without pause. "With Miranda nearby? Do you want your secret discovered?"

"No." She didn't want another person to know what she had done. That the earl knew was awful enough.

"Then you must speak to him in private, tonight." Ros adjusted her collar and stepped back to survey her work. "You cannot be worried about your virtue, since you no longer possess any."

"Ros!"

"Sorry." Ros made a face at her. "You are the most virtuous of women. One mistake does not make you ready for the dung heap, no matter what some lords and ladies claim."

Helena surveyed herself in the mirror, amazed at the transformation. "You are right never to marry or have a child. Your ability to comfort leaves a great deal to be desired."

"Get the matter settled between you tonight. You will both feel better for it."

Both? Was the earl as reluctant as Helena about

this harebrained scheme of Ros's? She sank onto the tiny stool before the dressing table, turning her back on her unsettling image. "You said he had no doubts."

"For himself, no. But he does not believe you will take a man of such ill-repute as your husband."

"He knows of my circumstances—"

"He wants what you want, Hellie." Ros pulled her up impatiently and led her to the door. "He wants to look into your eyes and see that you mean what you say. He does not want a wife who regrets her bargain after a few months' time. Just as you do not want a husband who goes unhappily into the marriage. You two are more alike than either of you realize."

Helena shuddered. Was she so like the wicked earl? She was sure she was not, despite her lapse in judgment.

Carefully, she followed Ros's instructions on how to hail a hansom cab as if she were a man, not a woman alone. To her surprise, the cabbie seemed to take her gruff voice and masculine appearance at face value. Though she felt uncomfortable at first traveling without a chaperon, she found herself growing to like having the cab to herself.

Before she knew it she was at the door to the earl's apartment. His man greeted her with a familiar, "Welcome, sir. His lordship is awaiting you." Without ceremony she was ushered into the small anteroom that apparently served him as parlor, sitting room, and dining space. Though she doubted that he dined in often.

He did not stand when she entered the room, and for a second she struggled at the offense. Did his knowledge of her indiscretion make him behave so rudely?

Oblivious to her dismay, he asked bluntly, "Well? Did she agree? Or has she more sense than a pea goose and refused you out of hand?"

It struck her then. She was dressed as a man—of course he would not stand. His tone and the familiar way he gazed at her made clear he thought her Ros. She opened her mouth to correct his mistake, and for some reason only said, "She hasn't the sense to say no, under the circumstances."

His expression was maddeningly unreadable. "A lover is not the disaster she seems to think it is. You have told her that, I trust."

At first his comment puzzled her, but then Helena realized with a shock that Rand knew of her lover, but not of the possible consequences. Ros had not told him that, drat her. Somehow, it was easier as Ros, to say carelessly, "It is not the lover she laments, but the possibility that in a few months there can be no doubt that she is no longer a virgin." She threw herself into a chair as she had seen her brother do at his most casual.

He did not seem overly shocked. "Poor mite. Truly worried that her lover left her a parting gift, is she?"

As herself, Helena might have waved her finger under his nose and chided his carelessness over something so important. As Ros, however, she affected a shrug. "The question is, why aren't you?"

"What do I care where the brat comes from, as long as I can wave it under my grandfather's nose and get control of my life at last?"

She could see no sign that he lied. Still, she prodded. "Most men care. What if she bears a son, an heir for you who doesn't share your blood?"

Rand shrugged and looked away toward the fire.

"I won't know, will I? If we're married and I plow my own row, who's to say whose child it is, even were it to come a few weeks before time?"

"Plow your own row?" Helena found herself dizzy with rage at the crude statement. How could her sister have ever thought it a sound idea that she should marry this man? "Isn't that rather heartless?"

"Heartless?" Rand was surprised at the outrage that made Ros's voice quaver. He would have expected her to be amused at the thought, if she remarked upon it at all. "Of course it is, Ros. Do you think I could have survived this long in life if I had a heart? You did warn the girl not to expect love or devotion, or any—"

"She knows." The answer came quickly and flatly.

Was that the sticking point, then? "She is not the sort to believe in love and fairy tales, is she?"

Ros was uncharacteristically hesitant. "Under the circumstances—"

"She does not want her lover to return and marry her, does she?" The thought horrified him. He did not want to tie himself to a woman who pined after another man.

"No!" The answer was vehement enough that he did not doubt she spoke the truth.

"Good." He watched Ros, puzzled at the unusually indecisive expression on her face.

"Why? What if she did? Surely you expect her to take lovers, with this unconventional arrangement you desire. Why not the man who she foolishly gave herself to?"

"I don't know. The thought seems . . . A woman who loves another man, who hopes for a match and is cruelly disappointed, does not make a good wife."

"I did not think you wanted a good wife."

"I suppose you are right." Rand put his head in his hands. "I don't want a wife at all. I thought I had found the perfect woman for me in you, Ros. Why did you have to decide against the match?"

She looked away, her blue eyes focusing on the fire as she did not answer immediately, and her fingers plucked idly at her sleeves, until she said abruptly, "Perhaps I am in love with another."

His impulse to laugh aloud died as he saw that she was not smiling. Rand raised his head and contemplated her carefully. "Love? You? I cannot imagine you saying the word without a curl to your lip."

"In lust, then," she answered impatiently, turning the brilliant blue of her eyes upon him. She drew her knees together and sat as primly as a woman, as she added, "Do you not imagine I could lust after a man?"

A suspicion popped into his head. He gave her a lazy, seductive grin. One that usually made the lady of the moment melt to his will. "Was I not lover enough for you, then?"

She licked her lips and said with only a hint of stammer, "Perhaps I want more adventure."

"More adventure than we have found in our nights together?" He rose, amused to see her cross her arms tightly as he approached. "I am hurt. Perhaps I should remind you of what you will lose."

"How?" Her voice was a whisper. Her eyes wide as she watched him. He was so close, he could see how her throat worked as she swallowed dryly.

He reached out his hand, not surprised when

she eased backward until her head rested against the back of the chair. ''A taste of the past, Ros.''

He placed his fingertips against the soft skin of her throat, so that he could feel the pulse beating wildly there. He knew that she wanted to pull away. He knew just as well that she would not. Gently, slowly, he drew his fingers up her neck to trace the line of her jaw. He grasped her chin without warning and bent down until their faces nearly touched.

She shrank away from him, and then forced herself to remain still. He took hold of her arms and pulled her to stand before him, slowly, reluctantly, inexorably. He brought his lips to hers and kissed her gently. Still, she did not pull away. ''Open your mouth for me,'' he ordered. He had thought he would stop the game then, whether she obeyed or not.

But when her lips parted under his, he found himself compelled to kiss her. To brand her mouth with his. His kiss was not soft, and when she would have pulled away, he reached for her hips and held her to him, trapping her arms so that she could not push him away. A primitive rush of triumph filled him when she softened to him. He brought his lips to her ear then, and whispered gently, like a true lover, ''Ros would have slapped me as soon as I reached for her throat, Helena.''

The softness of a moment before disappeared as she pushed away. He let her. He did not want his body to betray his own response to her. She was not an uninformed virgin; she had had a lover and knew the feel of a man's ardor. It would not do to have her know how much he desired her. Not if they were to have the kind of marriage he needed.

Hectic color still flooding her cheeks, she asked, "You and Ros are not lovers?"

Resuming his casual position in the chair opposite her he waved her to do the same. "Our arrangement was much more practical. Surely she told you?"

Helena did not resume her seat, but stood staring down at him with fierce anger. "She agreed to bear you a child; was I to think you would manage that without touching each other?"

His reply was without heat, though he knew it would sting. "It seems I can do so with you; why not with your sister?"

She flushed in anger as she dropped into the chair with a defeated air. He felt a faint breath of shame for his petty attack as she replied acidly, "Ros is not nearly as foolish as I am."

"It would have been ungentlemanly of me to try to get a child upon her before the marriage—after all, being the reprobate I am, I might not have made it to the altar alive, and then where would she be?"

She dropped her head into her hands, making a hissing noise that most likely meant she did not believe him. Rand tried to reassure her that he spoke honestly. "I do not obey all the codes of a gentleman, but that one seems most sensible to me. Ros does not deserve to be treated so shabbily just because I couldn't wait for the parson's trap to close upon us before I made love to her." Now that he thought of such a thing, he realized with a start that he had never even contemplated kissing Ros. The idea did not rouse him, like another kiss with Helena did.

"How decent of you," she answered with a touch of bitterness. He realized his mistake then. After all, hadn't her lover left her in the very predicament they discussed? And he, apparently, had not wanted marriage. "Still, I find myself unable to believe that you do not care about the paternity of your potential heir."

He did not know how to convince her. "When did you conceive?"

"I don't know that I have—"

He interrupted her denial. "When were you last with your lover?"

She blushed, but he waved away her discomfort. "Come, I am a man who has seen and heard much worse than an intemperate love affair." He had a dawning suspicion. "Were you with him only the once?"

She shook her head.

"Many times?" He wondered how she had found the time to sneak away from her family.

"No. I . . . Twice, my lord. If I had had Ros's will, I would have refused him the second time."

He found himself growing quite angry at this bully lover of hers. "How long since your last menses?"

She blushed. "My lord!" Rand decided that pointing out how ridiculous she appeared dressed as a man and blushing like a woman would not help him sort out matters between them.

"It is a simple enough question between us if we are to be man and wife. Pretend for a moment you are the man you are dressed as and we are simply chums discussing the weather."

She looked at him doubtfully. He realized he would have to see her home. She could convince no one who looked twice that she was a man.

"You can do it," he urged. "Nice deep voice. 'The rain is miserable today.' 'I long for some good shooting weather.' 'My courses are two weeks late.' "

His foolery gave her spine some steel. She said curtly, in a distinctly feminine voice, "Five weeks, my lord."

He hid his dismay at the length of time. "That is hardly a cause for concern. Your reason for the delay could be worry or ill health, could it not? Are you always regular?"

She raised an eyebrow at him, but said nothing.

He felt a need to defend his knowledge. "A man must know these things if he wants to make certain any bastards he chooses to support are truly his own and not some other man's seed."

She made a choked sound of dismay, but did not address his comment directly. "By the time of the wedding, if I am . . ." She could not bring herself to say the word.

"You will be as much as two months gone. I see. We will just say that the child was premature. It is done all the time; surely that does not shock you?"

As if she were instructing a backward child, she said slowly, "You will know it is not your blood." She paused for a moment, and then blurted miserably, "How can I trust that you will not denounce a male child?"

"Is my word not enough for you?" He found himself absurdly hurt at the skeptical glance that was her only response.

"Is that your only concern? That I will change my mind and send the child away because I am certain it is not mine?"

She nodded.

"Then why don't we remedy the matter now."

"Plow your row, you mean?" She shrank back

from him subtly, even though he had made no move toward her.

He had made the suggestion merely to ease her mind. And perhaps, he admitted to himself, to seal the bargain. Once he had made love to her there was much less chance she would change her mind. But her words jolted through him, sending an unbidden image of her naked hips working rhythmically against his.

He hoped his answer gave no hint as to the blinding surge of desire he fought. "If we make love tonight, there will be no way to tell whether the child—if there is one—is mine, or that of one of the footmen on the duke's estate."

# Chapter Three

Helena closed her eyes against the dizzying feel as her face drained of all blood and then heated to what she knew was a fiery blush. Had he truly just proposed . . ? He had. And was she going to agree?

She found, as she rose without conscious command, that she was. Only to seal a bargain, nothing more. To make any child she carried less likely to be called a bastard by her husband.

She did not look at him as she crossed over to where he reclined quite casually on his small sofa. She thought for a moment of sitting beside him and easing into the act with a few kisses. She had liked his kisses. His green eyes were too hard to read, though. She did not know what he thought of her. Of them together.

His right brow rose like a dark wing when she walked behind the sofa and gripped the carved back for support. She looked away from him, down to her hands, and was surprised to see that her knuckles showed white. Not wanting to see his face in case his expression became suddenly readable, she closed her eyes. She did not want to face his contempt.

He did not move; she knew by the silence and fought the temptation to open her eyes and see what held him still. Tersely, she said, "Get on with it, then, my lord. I have to be home soon."

His deep voice startled a shiver out of her when he asked, "Wouldn't you be more comfortable in my bed?"

She shook her head and refused to look at him. "Here will be fine. The sooner we are done, the sooner my mind will be at rest."

The sofa shifted under her hands as he rose. She caught the scent of him, but did not hear his approach. He moved as silently as a cat. For a long moment he did not touch her. The tension drew tighter and tighter inside her, but she refused to open her eyes. Refused to do more to encourage him than she already had done.

At last he moved close behind her and bent to press a gentle, tentative kiss against her neck. He was not like William, she thought as she suppressed a sob of frustration when he did nothing more than stand there behind her, their bodies almost, but not quite, touching. She had expected him to move surely, swiftly, to seal the bargain between them. What was he waiting for?

On the verge of losing her nerve, Helena remembered what had seemed to release the primitive male in William. Holding her breath, she pushed her bottom against him, wiggling as much as she dared.

His arms came around her, tightened. He held

her hips to his and answered her movements with his own. She wanted to sob with relief. Now it would be done quickly.

And then, as quickly as he had responded, he became still. His arms continued to hold her tight against him, but quietly, without passion. "Who was he?" he asked softly in her ear.

"Who?" She knew what he wanted. She also knew she would never tell him.

"Your lover. The man who showed you this." He ground his hips against her roughly and then stopped. "Your stallion. Who was he?" He was furious. But why? She had not lied to him.

She closed her eyes, seeing her last hope for respectability fleeing. "I will not tell you. Not even if you will not marry me without knowing his name."

His arms loosened around her, so that she could breathe freely again. She braced herself for his rejection, but he said only, "You are a loyal little fool, aren't you? Just like your sister." He rested his chin lightly on her shoulder and held her loosely within the circle of his arms, saying no more.

Had he changed his mind? "Do you find the idea of my lover more distressing than you had thought?"

"No." The tension drained from him and his grip loosened. "Keep your secrets, Helena. I do not need to know them. I have enough of my own."

Still, he did not continue with his lovemaking. The feel of him behind her, the rise and fall of his chest as he breathed, was unnerving. She steeled herself to whisper stiffly, "Is it too difficult with me wearing men's trousers instead of skirts?"

His laughter was a soft exhalation that tickled her ear. His hands caressed her hips restlessly for a moment. "No, it would be easily enough managed, I assure you." Without warning, he moved away from her and returned to the sofa.

She opened her eyes and stared down at him. "What are you doing?" His expression gave away nothing of his feelings.

He smiled at her. His famously wicked grin. "Nothing." She did notice his earlobes were pinker than she thought they had been earlier. Whether it was a clue to his feelings she could not say.

"But—"

"I've changed my mind, Helena."

Disappointment jolted through her. He didn't want to marry her. He was refusing Rosaline's suggestion out of hand, now that he had met her.

"I see no reason to muddy matters before we marry." His words took a moment to become clear to her as he continued on in a rational tone. "A wife should be able to take a husband's word about certain things. And I give you mine that I will not treat any child of yours, now or in the future, as a bastard."

*In the future.* He spoke so casually of a future together. Husband. Wife. She frowned. "Do you imply that I would be unfaithful?"

"If you take a dozen lovers it will be no matter to me. I give my word upon that matter as well."

She could not help a shudder of distaste at the thought. "I do not want a dozen lovers."

"That will be your choice."

"So, then, you are agreed that I shall take Rosaline's place at the wedding?" She wanted it clear. "If you need more time to decide—"

He shook his head sharply. "I need no more time. You are perfect for what I need."

"Even though—"

He sighed. "I do not want to hurt your delicate sensibilities, Miss Fenster. Let me be blunt. I am overjoyed that you are not a virgin. I have never had a virgin; it has always been a matter of pride with me, if you must know. Experienced women only. Certainly, I had been prepared to make an exception for a wife, but I am relieved that I shall not have to do so."

Perhaps his honest words should have reassured her. No doubt he thought they would. No doubt Ros would have found them soothing enough were she sitting here with him. "How can I trust you?"

"I will not lie to you, Helena. No doubt sometimes you will wish I did. I have no intention of giving up my vices for marriage. But it is of no consequence to me who fathers the brat that will provide me the freedom from my grandfather's tyranny that I desire."

"But . . ."

He shifted restlessly, turning away to stir the fire so that she could not see his face. "Those are my terms. Make no mistake. I need a wife, but I will not have one who does not understand what I offer. You—and any child you bear—will have my title, my name, and my protection, such as it is. But do not expect my company, my love, or my reform."

He turned back to her, his expression as revealing as if he were a stone. "Do you accept those terms?"

She wanted to refuse. Her instincts screamed that she was making a mistake she would live to regret. Not because he would humiliate her or call her child a bastard. No. She was certain he had told the truth in that.

What made her heart heavy was the ease with

which he could speak of bastards and lovers. The ease with which he accepted her as a substitute for Ros. And most of all, the way her heart still beat fast at the thought of marrying the wicked earl, even though she knew he would break her heart if she were ever fool enough to give it to him.

After a few moments mastering her temper, she dropped her gaze to the carpet and said quietly, "I accept those terms, my lord."

"Excellent." Rand found himself slowly releasing his breath. Now, if only he could keep his skittish second best bride from running away, all would be well.

"I will see you home, now."

"I can see myself home, my lord." Her expression suggested that he had offered to throw her to the floor and ravage her.

"I would rather not risk it, if you please." He closed his eyes and sighed at the thought of surviving the next two weeks.


Rand had hardly returned from seeing the very unmasculine Helena home when he found himself again with a visitor. This time he made certain the "gentleman" was Ros before he welcomed her. "I thought you might be home bracing your sister."

"What did you say to her?" Ros did not waste time with pleasantries. "She looks as though she has just agreed to marry the devil himself."

"Hasn't she?"

Ros stared at him. "I won't have her hurt."

"Then you should not have convinced her to marry a man who will not care who fathers her children."

"Oh." She poured herself a generous helping

of his brandy and sprawled easily across from him. "She will come to appreciate having her freedom. So, you are both agreed?"

"Yes. I'll apply for the license tomorrow. I suppose I should speak to the duke, as well."

"No." Ros shook her head.

"We must—"

"Let them enjoy themselves thinking that the family has pulled off a less-than-scandalous match for once. Time enough to tell them after the marriage."

"Surely—" He did not like deceiving the duke.

"Do you want to risk them forbidding it?"

He subsided. She was right. The duke was one of the most upright figures in the whole of England. His wife was fond of fairy tales. Either one could prevent the marriage—or convince Helena to rethink her bargain. "Will your sister change her mind?"

"A dozen times until her wedding day, no doubt."

"Will I be jilted again?"

As usual, Ros did not go out of her way to offer reassurance. "She is as desperate as you. Will you change your mind at the last minute?"

"No." Ros's eyes trained on him sharply at his quick answer. He wondered if she guessed at his reaction to her sister. He thought of the unsettling strength of his desire for Helena as she stood, tense and stiff behind the sofa, grinding herself against him with all the seductive skill of a skittish virgin.

Her neck had smelled sweet and warm, like a hot cross bun fresh from the oven. He had not known how to begin with her. Not until she pushed her bottom against him and he understood with a flash of desire that was quickly wiped away by a firestorm of fury.

"Two weeks and you will both have what you want, then," Ros said, rising easily to her feet. He watched, trying to see her without the familiarity of the last two years. To his mind she looked the part of a man, even upon close scrutiny. Not just the sideburns, but the walk, the way she looked as if she commanded the room.

Not at all like Helena in the same getup. Watching Helena, he had had the urge to divest her of the foolish men's clothing she wore and demonstrate how a man made proper love to a woman. Only the sense that he must be cautious with her after her experience had made him return to the sofa, careful to keep his expression neutral despite his natural anger.

"Who was her lover?"

Ros shook her head at him as she slipped out the door. "That is a question you must ask Helena."

"She won't tell me," he said to the empty room. Lover. He snorted. She had not had a lover; she had been the victim of a libertine of the worst order. Her lover no doubt had considered himself a stallion mounting a mare. He wondered if there were tales being told about her somewhere. He had heard none as of yet. And once she was his wife . . .

He sat up with an uneasy exclamation that brought Griggson in with a concerned, "Yes, my lord?"

"Nothing," he said, dismissing the man. Nothing except that he had already started thinking about Helena as someone to protect and defend. A wife. He needed one, there was no doubt. He would simply have to avoid becoming too involved in her life.

Helena had watched Ros take care of herself all her life. She would just have to learn how to follow her sister's example. How difficult could it be? He was giving her what most married women wanted, after all. She had agreed to his bargain. Now he just had to make certain he kept to it as well.

The dressing room was filled with steam and excited voices. Helena lay immersed in hot scented bathwater and watched her sisters maneuver about in the small room, each one eager to offer a piece of advice—even Kate who knew little of men or marriage.

Miranda, the eldest of them all, a regal duchess who looked nothing like one, with her hair flying wildly about her head and her silk dressing gown buttoned crookedly, sat on the edge of the tub. "Rosaline, you always professed that you would stay unmarried. And now here you are, the morning of your wedding day."

Helena responded as she knew Ros would have. "The earl will let me have my head. How many men will I find who'll do that? I had to snap him up quickly."

"You do not love him?"

"I respect him." Helena knew that Ros would have jeered at love, but she could not bring herself to do so, even playacting as Ros.

"That is enough, I suppose. You have always been clearheaded enough—and of all people, you are the one marrying properly—courtship, engagement, a proper three-month lapse before the ceremony. After all our scandals, Simon has said he hoped the tide has turned and we'll have no more hasty, havey-cavey marriages in the family.''

Miranda looked so sincere. What would she say when she found out what had been done? What would the duke say when he found out he had another havey-cavey marriage to deal with? The deception of what they were doing was all too clear, even in the misty air of the bathroom. For a moment Helena felt as if she might cry.

Fortunately, Ros stepped in to say briskly, ''I need a moment alone with my twin, please.''

Everyone left to attend to dressing themselves, and they were alone together. The last time. Helena sank into the water until it touched her chin. ''I can't believe no one noticed that we switched places.''

Ros glared down at her. ''They won't as long as you don't do something silly, like weep.''

Helena had changed her mind about the switch several times over the last two weeks. Each time, Ros had reminded her that with each day her menses had not arrived, she was more and more surely carrying a child. Every morning she had awakened hoping to find there was no need to go through with her bargain. Now here she was, an hour away from marrying the earl, with her family addressing her by her sister's name. ''I didn't realize how difficult it was going to be—if only everyone would stop fussing so.''

Ros wiggled her fingers idly in the bathwater. ''You make a more patient me, I must admit. I'd have thrown them all out an hour ago so I could enjoy a hot bath in private.''

Helena caught her hand and squeezed. ''Ros, don't you realize that we are saying good-bye to them? I will be off to live the life of a countess, not too far away. But you—you will be in another country across the sea."

"America." Ros's eyes shone with excitement. "You can't imagine how difficult I find it to pretend to be peaceful, Helena, when I know I'll be aboard ship by the end of the day."

"Will you miss no one?"

Ros flushed guiltily as she answered hastily, "You, of course. But you will be busy making your mark as countess. You will hardly notice I am gone."

Helena did not argue; she knew her sister too well for that. "Thank you for delaying your departure until after the ceremony. I don't believe I could go through with it otherwise. Do you think no one will notice the switch before the ceremony? Not even Miranda?"

Practical and unsentimental as always, Ros squeezed Helena's hand quickly before releasing it to rise from the edge of the tub. "If we deny it, what can they do?"

"You have so much more courage than I, Ros."

"Nonsense. You've just gotten lazy, with me around to fight your battles. When I'm gone—"

Helena gave a quick shake of her head. "Don't talk about it, please. Let me just get through this horrible day."

"You'll have to say good-bye to me soon."

"Not now."

"Very well." Ros handed her a drying cloth with a click of her tongue. "Now get out, before you turn into a prune. That's the one thing I envy— you get a nice hot bath. Even the servants are treating you as if you were made of cut glass today."

"I feel as if I am. As if I could shatter at any moment."

"Don't get the vapors now. In a few hours you'll

be in the position most young women desire above all—wife to a titled man who will leave you to your own devices in the coming years."

"You do not listen to the chatter of the young hopefuls, if you believe that. They all wish for a handsome man to sweep them off their feet and declare undying love."

"True. I suppose I listen more to the conversations of the women who've been married a year or two."

"I had not thought to marry like this."

Ros looked pensive, as if she was not sure she should speak her mind. It was a most unusual state for her. Helena dreaded to hear her words, as her sister asked hesitantly, "Do you suppose you might love him, Helena? I would not want you to marry him if you wished he might ever return your love. It would be better to jilt him, then. For both of you."

Helena laughed sharply at the absurd statement, especially coming from Ros. "Love the man you have been set to marry? I would never have been so wicked."

"Wicked?" Ros smiled. "Rand is my best friend. I would wish him love, though I know it is the last thing he believes he needs." She shuddered theatrically. "I realize more every day how disastrous a marriage between us would have been."

Helena asked dryly, "Why, when you are both in agreement about the lack of necessity for love?"

"Perhaps because of it. Don't you think a marriage works better if at least one of the parties believes in love?" She shook her head as if shaking off an unwelcome insect. "I somehow thought you might love him, though. The way you always looked at him when you thought no one was watching you.

The way you stored away every detail of conversation about him. The way you said his name, sometimes, when you denounced his behavior."

Helena clicked her tongue as if Ros's suggestion were ridiculous. She would not admit to a foolish infatuation with a dangerous man. "He and I have made a bargain, just as you and he did, Ros."

Ros looked at her oddly for a moment as she wrapped her body with the drying cloth. "Good. Then you will not be tempted to back out."

Tempted? Of course she was. But—"I cannot. Surely you have not forgotten why I agreed in the first place."

Ros glanced at the towel Helena held. "I think you no longer need worry of that, at least."

Helena glance down to see the spattering of pinkish stains. A rush of relief weakened her knees as she realized what they heralded. Her menses. She would not have William's child.

# Chapter Four

Ros did not look completely pleased as she helped Helena dress. "I hope this doesn't mean you will jilt the man with all the guests watching."

Helena thought of facing him at the altar. "I don't know if I can go through with this switch. Not now."

"You promised," Ros reminded her relentlessly. "He is counting upon you."

"I only agreed to give my child a father. Now there is to be no child; we will both be better served if I halt things here and now."

Ros did not argue, although Helena knew she wanted to. "Well, then, you must tell him yourself, or let him face being jilted at the altar."

Face him? She could not. "You would have done so."

"I would never have left him to stand before the guests and face the humiliating recognition that his bride would not show herself. And I'm surprised you would."

True. "You tell him."

Ros bundled her into her dressing gown and tied the sash at her waist. "I will not. You are the one jilting him this time."

Helena made one last argument, weak as she knew it was. "The world thinks he is marrying you."

"You and he know differently, though."

She thought of the earl's unhappiness at her news. It could not be helped. "I don't have time to get into your man's getup—"

"Go like that." Ros pushed her toward the door. "I'll explain to the others," she whispered. "But hurry, or you'll be caught in his room and the duke will make you marry him anyway."


Rand had almost convinced himself that the wedding switch would succeed without a hitch when he heard the soft knock at the door to his room. As Griggson had gone down for some blacking for his boots, he answered the door himself.

Helena. He was certain, which surprised him. But there was a softness in her Ros had never shown. He did not allow her into the room, perhaps in a mistaken belief that she would not deliver her news standing in the hall where anyone could overhear.

Her hands twisted in the material of her primly tied dressing gown as she stood staring at him, waiting for him to move and let her into the room. He raised his eyebrows at her in question, but said nothing.

To his dismay, his ploy was met with sheer panic by his bride-to-be. The color drained from her face as she glanced down one side of the hall and the other. She turned back to face him, her hands stilling. Softly, quickly, but alas all too clearly, she said, "I am afraid I have decided that I cannot marry you."

Before she had finished her sentence, he had jerked her into his room and closed the door. He stood uncomfortably close, so that she pressed her back to the door to avoid touching him. Good. He wasn't going to make this easy for her. "This sounds familiar. Are you running off to America with Ros?"

"Of course not." She was miserable with guilt; he could tell by the way she looked everywhere but into his eyes.

"Your lover has returned to beg your forgiveness and your hand?" He was astonished to realize that he found the idea distasteful. What should her poor taste in lovers have to do with him?

"No!" She did look at him then, a flash of humiliated blue before she closed her eyes. "I need no longer marry."

"You need no longer ..." Comprehension dawned, and he moved away from her a hairbreadth as he absorbed the information. "Well, I still need a bride, and we made a bargain. Surely you will not break it for this reason—you knew the possibility existed when you agreed to take your sister's place."

"I was not thinking clearly then. I'm certain you would not wish an unwilling bride, my lord." The fear that tightened her lips until they were white indicated that she was not quite as certain as she sounded.

Damn. "Are you absolutely certain you are not with child, then?" He reached out to stroke her flat stomach as he asked, needing the confirmation of his own senses. Her muscles quivered under his palm.

"Yes," she ground out as if she were admitting that she had the French disease. She grasped his hand in both of hers and held him away from her. "I am sorry that I could not give you more notice, but I only became certain this morning."

He needed to put her off balance so that he could think. He must find a reason for her to say the vows with him today. "Too bad. I had hoped you were already breeding."

She was growing stronger as he watched. She pushed away from the door a bit, dropped his hand, and chided him, "You do not mean that."

"But I do," he argued, desperate but not willing to show it. "If you had been with child, I would have been assured of both a wife and a speedily delivered heir."

"Who was not your own child!"

"What would that matter? To the world the child would have been mine. I would have treated it so."

"Most men would not be so sanguine."

Had his indifference to the parentage of his children somehow made her wary of the match? "Is that why you will not marry me now?" He raised his hand gently to her cheek and made her look him in the eyes. "Because I am not most men." He waited a moment before lowering his face close to hers to add, "Shouldn't that make me more desirable rather than less?"

She stared at him, her breathing shallow and rapid. The pulse at her throat beat frantically. She closed her eyes to shut out the view. "You are a reprobate." Her words were sharp, but he was too familiar with the ways of women to miss the sudden way her head tilted upward. She expected him to kiss her.

He didn't kiss her. Perhaps because he wanted to do so very badly. Instead he moved so that his mouth nearly touched her ear to whisper, "Many women find that attractive." He prayed that Helena did. That she would be seduced by her evident attraction to him. For he could think of no good reason why she should marry him. And several excellent ones why she should not.

"I do not find you attractive." But she did not push him away, he noticed.

"No?"

"Certainly not!" Her outraged denial sent a rush of warm breath against his neck. This time she tried to push him away and he moved back from her a half step. Not enough for her to escape. Just enough so that he could think more clearly about how to change her mind.

"You are not an innocent." To hold her indiscretion over her head seemed distasteful to him. But the time for the ceremony was approaching rapidly.

"I never tried to deceive you." He could see her trembling with the thought that he might threaten to expose her secret. But the threat seemed to make her stronger rather than weaker, and she met his eyes squarely.

He could see his defeat in her gaze. She would win if he could not show her the advantages to marrying him. "Do you think you will find a better man to marry you?"

"I will not marry. I am resolved to remain a spinster, as Ros has."

*A spinster? Helena?* He could not contain a grin,

sure that he knew better than she did in this. "You will not."

"I will," she replied stubbornly.

"No, you are not like your sister. She has found herself able to resist the lure of taking a lover, no matter that she drinks, gambles, swears, and runs among the worst rakes in London in disguise. She is too afraid of the bonds of love. You are not."

"What do you know?"

He pressed her body, gently, relentlessly, between his own and the door. "I know that your pupils grow larger when I press you close like this. I know that your breath quickens if I touch you—like this." He untied the sash of her dressing gown and slipped his hands around to cup her buttocks.

She made an inarticulate cry, whether to encourage him or discourage him he was not certain. Knowing that he must make his case more persuasively than he had ever done in his life, Rand redoubled his efforts to seduce this woman who had agreed to marry him and now wanted to break the bargain.

He touched his lips to hers briefly. "I can feel your heart beating fast." Again. "Marry me." Again. "You took a lover, Helena; you are not made of stone, as Ros is."

A lover. Helena turned her head away so that the earl's next kiss fell on her shoulder. She had thought herself daring, independent, full of courage. Fool. "Then I will find a way to harden myself. I do not want to marry. I do not want to feel what I let myself feel with—I will not." His words reminded her harshly of how easily she could be deceived by the intoxicating feel of a man's desire for her.

"You have opened Pandora's box; how do you

think you will close it now?" His fingers tightened on her hips, smoothing the silk of her shift against her. "I do not want to boast, but many women have declared me the best lover they have ever known."

Many women. The words cut through the fog of want that threatened to steal her breath and her sense. "Words to warm a wife's heart, my lord."

"Perhaps not her heart, then. But other regions." His fingers slid down to cup her bottom again and press her to him. "This is the way a man and woman should join, Helena. Face-to-face. Your lover didn't teach you that. I wager there are other things he neglected to teach you as well. I, however, promise to teach you one new thing a day—until you beg me to stop."

She shook her head at her own folly. At his. "There is nothing I need learn from you."

"No?" He backed away, and she thought she had convinced him at last. Until he knelt swiftly before her and lifted one of her legs so that her foot rested in his lap. He did nothing but smile at her shocked protest, as he traced around her ankle with only the tips of his fingers. "Has a man ever touched you here? Not your lover, I think."

She tried to pull her foot from his hands, but he laughed and tickled the sensitive arch until she stopped resisting, afraid the sound of their struggle would bring a servant to investigate. His gaze held hers captive as he kissed each of her toes, her ankle, and played his fingers against her skin as if she were an instrument of which he was master. He trailed his fingers up over her calf, playing a tune at the back of her knee that made both her knees buckle. He rose and caught her against him in one swift movement.

She thought he might kiss her, but he did not. Instead he held her tight against his body and lifted her slightly, as his fingers continued to stroke higher now, to the sensitive inner flesh of her thigh.

She began to resist him again, as she realized what territory his fingers reached for. "No. I cannot. I-I told you. I am certain that I will not have a child."

He released her, and suddenly she was standing facing him, her shift back in place, just as if he had never touched her. Except that her legs offered only uncertain support. She leaned against the door as he smiled and offered a slight bow. "I understand. There is only one way for a woman to be certain she is not carrying a child. We will have to save some games for when you are no longer indisposed."

Helena turned her face to the door. How could she convince him she would not marry him when she let him do such things to her?

"Don't be shy. A husband and wife should be able to speak of these matters. I will not be angry at having to delay consummating our marriage."

She mumbled her words into the solid wood of the door, afraid to turn to see the face that made all her resolve melt away. "I told you. I cannot marry you."

"Of course you can. You must."

Helena laughed weakly. The man was impossible to convince. Perhaps she should ask Ros—But no. There was someone who could stop this wedding, no matter what the earl wanted. With that knowledge, she had the strength to turn and confront the assured gleam in the green-eyed gaze fastened sharply on her.

"You can hardly force me down the aisle in this."

She indicated her shift and dressing gown with a gesture. "And if you did, I should still refuse to marry you. I'm sorry, my lord, but you must find yourself another bride."

"I have found the bride I want." He said it softly, almost sweetly. Helena might have been convinced he meant it—might have let her heart lead her astray—if she had not noticed the way his hands clenched into fists at his side as he spoke.

"We shall see what the duke has to say about that." To her surprise, he made no protest when she opened the door and fled back to her room, where her sisters waited to help her into her wedding gown.

Miranda was the first to catch sight of her. "There you are. I thought you were going to run away from your own wedding." Her sister's smile disappeared as she gazed more closely at Helena. "What is the matter?"

As if she knew what Helena was going to say and wanted to prevent it, Ros said, "Every bride looks like that just before she marries. Come, we need to get you into your dress and do your hair. There's no time to waste."

Miranda looked at Ros oddly, and then glanced back to Helena.

Before her courage fled, Helena said, "I don't want to marry. I have changed my mind."

Miranda frowned. "You intend to jilt the earl? Why?" As if she had just noticed Helena's half-dressed state, she blanched as her gaze took in the untied sash of the dressing gown. "What has he done?"

Miserably, thinking her sister would be horrified to know what the earl had just done—and would consider it a perfect reason to go ahead with the marriage—Helena said only, "I just know that I have made a mistake."

"Rosaline . . ."

Helena could bear the deception no longer. "I am not Rosaline."

Confused, but determined to get to the bottom of things, Miranda turned to Kate and Betsey. "Girls—go fetch the duke. Tell him I need him urgently. And then you may sing for our guests. I think the ceremony may be delayed somewhat."

The two did not argue, evidently seeing the seriousness of the situation in Miranda's set smile. Dressed in their finest gowns, they scurried away to find the duke like the true hoydens they were.

Ros, an unreadable expression on her face, brought the wedding gown over to Helena and gestured. "Better get into this, unless you want to entertain the duke as casually as you did the earl."

"Hel—Rosaline!" Miranda scolded her sister unhappily, even as she helped fit Helena into the dress.

"Perhaps you should wear it," Helena muttered as her sisters tugged and fastened and fitted in haste.

"I'm not meant to wear a wedding dress," Rosaline demurred. Her fingers toyed with a button on the bodice for a moment. "Although the sword buttons that Raster Booth made for me don't suit you as well as they would have me, I admit."

Helena eyed her darkly. "Perhaps they suit me better than you think."

To her annoyance, her irate words spurred a grin from her incorrigible sister. A grin that quickly disappeared when the duke strode into the room, scowling.

Explanations seemed to muddle the matter even

more for a moment, but finally, both Simon and Miranda understood what had happened. Neither looked happy.

"You will not marry him?" the duke asked Rosaline—the real Rosaline—at last.

She shook her head firmly. "I gave him to Helena. She agreed."

Miranda sighed. "You cannot give your sister your fiancé, Rosaline. He is not a possession."

Like a wife, Helena thought, grateful that the duke would see the marriage did not take place. "Will you tell him so for me, Simon? And tell him I'm sorry."

"You've made the man a laughingstock, the pair of you." Simon glowered at them. "Don't be surprised when he refuses your apologies—and mine."

Miranda said sharply, "He should have had the sense to refuse Ros's suggestion, Simon. Or, at the very least, come to you about it before now."

Simon nodded. "Don't think I won't tell him so, the young fool." He left the room muttering and shaking his head.

Unfortunately, he had not been long gone before Kate and Betsey came into the room, still solemn faced. "Helena. The duke wants to see you in his study."

"In his study?" Helena glanced at Miranda. "Will he send us to Anderlin in disgrace, do you think?"

"Let us go and see," Miranda said briskly, but with no reassurances. She gestured to Ros to come along, but added to Kate and Betsey, "Go and sing another song or two for the guests."

Ready to be banished from London, Helena was unprepared to see the earl standing next to the duke, holding a glass of brandy. She would have halted at the doorway, but Miranda and Ros behind her impelled her inside against her will.

"Have you nothing to say to me?" Rand asked, his brows quirked up in question.

Helena stood frozen in disbelief. Did he still think to change her mind somehow?

Miranda, with a puzzled glance at her husband, said, "I'm sorry, my lord, but it seems that the marriage will not take place."

"I understand." His smile held no hint of offense or anger. Indeed, he seemed all solicitude. His attitude seemed wrong to Helena, who could not understand his calm demeanor. Until he said to the duchess, "You see, Your Grace, when she came to my room earlier, Helena was so relieved to find she was not in a certain indelicate circumstance that she gave me no chance to assure her I still wished the marriage."

The room grew quiet. Helena thought she would die, right then and there.

Miranda's gaze settled upon her in distress. "Helena—"

Ros was no help at all. In fact, she had gone to stand beside Rand as if she supported his infamy.

Rand nodded to her traitorous twin, and continued spouting his poppycock to Miranda. "You understand, of course, that we meant no disrespect to Rosaline. It seems that I proposed to the wrong twin and we were all resolved to right the matter. I suspect Helena is simply feeling a bit guilty at stealing her sister's intended."

Outrage gave her a voice at last. "How dare you accuse me of feeling guilty—"

Rand crossed the room as she spoke and took her hands. Gazing into her eyes as if he were a lovestruck swain, he said, "Come, my love, do not tell me you would not have married me if you were to have the child as we first feared?''

"I—" She intended to tell the truth. Until she realized how it would sound to her sister and brother-in-law. She could not confess she had had another lover. No—a single lover. Somehow he had confused her into thinking that they had been lovers when all he had done was touch her ankle. Her . . . Oh, he was a devil.

She turned to her sisters, to the duke, looking for support. But there was none to be found. Helena was shocked to realize that the earl had turned the entire room to his will with a few clever half truths and that wicked charm that seemed to come to him as naturally as breathing.

# Chapter Five

Rand wasn't certain whether he had won or lost as he stood gazing solemnly down at the woman he was vowing to protect, honor, and cherish. She was gazing back at him in a way that many watching might describe as adoring. But he felt certain she did not see him.

Up close, he could see a panicked blankness to her gaze that suggested she looked into the future rather than at the present, at her groom standing before her. Her lips were slightly parted and her breath shallow and quick. She did not seem pleased with whatever future she was seeing for herself.

Had he misjudged? He had at first thought Helena would make an even more acceptable bride than Ros. She was more tractable. Ros would have shouted to the world that he was not her lover, rather than allow herself to be coerced into marriage. Helena merely tightened her lips into a thin line and unprotestingly allowed herself to be led like a lamb to the slaughter.

Slaughter. Not so amusing when he remembered the life he led. The life he was determined to lead. Ros would have joined him, dressed as a man, or amused herself with gusto as she traveled the world. He had thought it the perfect solution for them both, but he understood Ros's belated skittishness. Her nature did not lend itself to motherhood.

Helena was another matter altogether. He could picture her with a babe in her arms. She would know how to soothe tears and coax smiles. Surely she understood that he would not interfere with the child, or with her running of his household, once he had one. Wasn't that enough for a sensible woman?

Although, the only sensible woman he had ever met was Ros, and she was more like a man than a woman. The same could not be said for her sister, even though Helena swore she did not believe in love. He liked that Helena responded so easily to him. He would enjoy bedding her. But he must guard against letting her fall in love with him at all costs.

And he must guard against having her hurt . . . as much as he was able. She obviously put more stock in her reputation than Ros ever had. She might be hurt by the gossip that swirled around him. She might care what people thought of him— and of her because she was his wife.

Wife. The very word caused his belly to knot. He had done it. He had married and soon he would have a child, and with it control of his life would be back in his hands. Unable to contain his elation, he grinned at Helena as she quietly repeated her vows.

Her eyes widened, and she hesitated a moment as she uttered the word "obey." But she recovered smoothly enough to finish the vows that would bind her to him. She even gave him a tentative smile in return.

He shouldn't show his joy, not here, with his grandfather watching. That he knew. But he could not contain it. Most of his contemporaries considered marriage the end of their freedom, understandably enough. But to him, thanks to his agreement with Helena, and his life becoming his own again, it was not the end of freedom, but the beginning.

As the minister proclaimed them wed, Rand took Helena's hands. She looked at him in confusion, but did not pull away. No doubt she was afraid to cause a scene when every eye in the chapel was turned upon them. He wondered how long she would take to learn that very fear made her vulnerable to him? And how would she react to the knowledge?

He knew he shouldn't, but still he waited impatiently for the last words of the minister to conclude matters definitively and then swept her up into his arms for a full-mouthed kiss, which made their guests gasp with surprise—and murmur with envy, no doubt. They were already in the mood for scandal, as the duke had announced the change in brides before the ceremony began.

He kissed her until she stopped resisting and returned his kiss in full and then he laughed in her ear when she made a faint sound of distress as she looked out at the sea of faces watching them. Let another black mark rest on his reputation; what did it matter? He had a bride and soon would have an heir and control of his own destiny at last.

He pulled her to him and put an arm around her as he escorted her away from the chapel and into the open carriage that would carry them the few streets back to the duke's home and the magnificent feast that awaited them there.

She barely touched his hand when he helped her into the carriage, and sat stiffly apart from him. "Sorry?" he asked, when the horses were underway. "I thought I saw a distinct rabbit in the grip of a fox expression upon your face for a moment. Was it the word 'obey'? For you needn't, you know. That was our bargain, after all."

Was she sorry? Helena sorted through the various emotions that roiled inside her. Worry for the future. A dreamlike sense of her life rushing past too fast for her to grasp hold of. Desire and fear to take what he offered and make her future her own. Seeing that he waited for an answer, she looked away. "Too late for regrets, my lord."

"Sensible attitude," he said with annoying heartiness. "Even if you don't entirely mean it at this moment, I have no doubt you'll come to see that this was for the best. Your lover may have shown you that love was fickle—"

She would have protested, but he put a finger to her lips as he said, "I'm glad he did. Because now I may show you that autonomy and independence are the best gift a husband can give his wife."

She looked at him without masking her skepticism. "Or a wife her husband, my lord?"

"Indeed." He sat back, turning his face up so that sunshine caressed the strong beautiful lines of nose and jaw as the carriage horses trotted in a leisurely manner. "Indeed."

Husband. Helena itched to sketch him as he was then. The jumble of her feelings—ire, dismay, admiration, even fear—would give a strength and boldness to her strokes that would capture him perfectly. Elemental male at one with his universe.

She sighed. A sketch of him she could admire. The man himself, as husband, was another matter altogether. "I am not Ros, you know."

"I am glad of it. You are much more kissable." He gave no warning at all before he turned his face away from the sun, leaned in toward her, and kissed her soundly on the lips. His body molded against hers, the arm he had rested behind her head becoming a tight band holding her to him, preventing escape as his kiss deepened.

Helena stiffened, acutely aware they were in an open carriage on a public street. "You are no better than—than *he* was, to use me so," she replied, turning her head so that his lips moved down to press against the corner of her jaw. She pushed against his chest without leverage, her arms trapped between them.

"Your lover, you mean?" he whispered against her jaw. "The one who wouldn't marry you?"

"That's not fair—I did not want to marry you. You made me."

"You could have told your sister and the duke the truth. Wouldn't they have tracked down your faithless cad for you—and tossed me out on my ear for lying?" His words were spoken in a soothing tone, but had the opposite effect on Helena. "Why didn't you, Helena?"

"I should have. I meant to." But she had not wanted them to know—

"I understand. Shameful secrets. I know all about them. You were right, you know. The fewer who know, the better for you in the end."

Not sure she spoke truthfully, Helena muttered,

"I wish I had told the truth, rather than allowing you to force me into this farce of a marriage."

"You will thank me for it later." His teeth nipped at her ear playfully, as if she were merely scolding him for stealing a biscuit instead of a wife. "You are too afraid to see you have made a good bargain."

"A good bargain?" she scoffed. "A husband who treats me like a trollop in public." She shoved him away, but he simply pressed closer. "Stop. People will talk." She tried to squirm away from him but there was little room on the seat for her to escape.

He pulled back, a momentary reprieve so that she could see the deep green of his eyes and be struck anew at the crystalline clarity that belied the disreputable life he led. "People will talk because they envy me."

"Only a man could say such a thing. Women know better. We will be laughingstocks. I will not be able to show myself in public for the shame."

His lips turned up and a half-moon dimple appeared in his left cheek. "But that is the simple beauty of being married to me, Helena. You can reap the fruits of disreputable behavior and everyone will blame me." He kissed her again, deeply.

"I would rather behave correctly," she answered, when his lips had roamed purposefully away from her mouth and he nipped the lobe of her ear again, sending a warm bolt of lightning through her.

"What fun is that?" he teased.

"I don't think marriage is supposed to be fun, my lord. Even a bargain marriage such as ours. I would prefer that no one label me scandalous."

He pulled back to gaze at her again and after a moment touched her bottom lip with his index finger, tracing it restlessly from corner to corner, his touch as light as a feather. "Would you?"

Her throat was dry, so she swallowed before she answered, with a rather weak "Yes."

"Then you would not like to be kissed again?"

"No."

He laughed softly. "Liar. You like my kisses as much as I like bestowing them."

He spoke as if he believed his kisses were tiny gifts to her. The arrogant—She would have replied, but at that moment the carriage jolted to a halt at their destination. She contented herself with a sniff and presented him her back once he had handed her down.

He swept her pique aside, however, with a warm, familiar hand at her back as they hurried up the broad stairs with the servants wishing them well at each step. Was there no shame in the man at all?

She stood next to him without touching as they welcomed the guests and received their well wishes for a happy, fruitful marriage. Very shortly, however, she found she was pressing herself against him as if to protect herself from the very hearty wishes that she should soon find herself a busy mother.

The congratulations sent his way were not only hearty, but pointed as well. For a moment she wondered if she had still been innocent, whether she would have understood half of what was said. Would that have been preferable to this constant feeling of fiery embarrassment that everyone knew what would happen between them once they were alone?

To her horror, in the midst of the litany of well wishes and handshakes, an all-too-familiar hand grasped hers. An all-too-familiar voice said, "My congratulations upon your most unexpected marriage, my lady." William. He bent low to press a kiss to her hand.

She said faintly, "I thought you in France, Baron." She wished the words back immediately when he straightened without releasing her hand.

"I could not miss seeing you again." He smiled, the brown eyes she had thought so warm only a few weeks ago now looked predatory to her. "Although I had expected you would not be the bride. Yet."

Helena did not know how to answer. His implication that he had wished to marry her was patently false. Yet she could not call him on it without embarrassing herself, her family—and Rand. Although the earl might relish the scandal.

Her heart dropped to her knees when Rand's arm came around her shoulders and his warm, deep voice said congenially, "Much can happen when one is away, Baron. I hope your trip was pleasant."

William's warm smile turned brittle as he released Helena's hand to take Rand's. "Disappointing, my lord. But I am certain you will not find your bride the same."

Helena felt Rand tense. Had he understood the insult? Please let him not realize that William was the one. She could not bear it.

Rand pressed a quick kiss to the top of her head and gave her a squeeze before releasing her. "After all I went through to get her, Baron, I cannot imagine that I could find her anything but a treasure."

Though Rand had again twisted the truth until it became a most pleasant lie, Helena allowed herself to smile up at him as adoringly as if he had married her for love. "My lord, not many men would have the courage to admit such sentiment aloud.'' To her great pleasure, William looked discomfited as he moved away from them.

Rand bent, his voice low and warm in her ear, "I'll kill him for you, if you like.''

Helena's heart jolted in her chest. For a moment she could not breathe. He suspected. But she would not confirm it. She forced herself to behave as if William were nothing more than an inconsiderate acquaintance. Pretending she did not understand the reason behind his offer, Helena replied in an equally low voice, "Why ever for? He cannot help his lack of manners, poor man.''

Rand had been certain the man was her lover. His offer to kill the baron had not been entirely in jest. He had hoped Helena's reaction would have confirmed his suspicions more clearly, however. To his surprise, he found his bride was more than capable of enigmatic answers when he least wanted one.

His grandfather, the marquess, had been seated near them at dinner. Rand supposed a family as close and loving as Helena's would have no reason to know that some families were better off seated far apart.

The wine had scarcely been poured when the old man turned to Helena and launched the first sally of his campaign. "Welcome to the family, m'dear. I hope you are not fainthearted, for I fear it will take a miracle worker to tame my grandson.''

"I am not fainthearted in the least,'' Helena replied with a shy smile guaranteed to please the old man.

He showed his pleasure with a wide smile that

had lost none of its power as he aged. "Good. Good. I should have been more stern with him, you understand. I know that. But as he is the last of the line, a remembrance of my own dear son and his late wife—"

Rand picked up his wineglass and downed the contents when Helena was touched to the point that she gave a sympathetic pat to his grandfather's trembling hand. "I do understand. We will do our best to make you proud."

"I've always done the best to win the games I played, Grandfather." Rand shifted beside her, wishing to remove her from the old man's grip, but unsure how, since she seemed to have become a supporter. "Didn't you teach me that one must risk much to gain much?"

The old man scowled. "I was not speaking of gambling, as you well know." Rand noticed the wrinkles around his eyes and on his forehead were more deeply grooved than last time they had sparred over his idle habits.

Helena kicked him under the table. A wifely kick that would leave no mark. The gesture was unexpected, reminding him that she was not the only one of them who would have to adjust to this new state of marriage. He had a wife. A wife who was displeased with his behavior. He supposed he should not be surprised. He could not expect someone with such a sense of proper behavior to behave as badly to his grandfather as he did. Her quick glance of reproof told him as much.

The marquess sighed gustily as Helena reassured him she would tame his grandson. Rand wondered if she believed her own words, as his grandfather said approvingly, "Been a long time since we had a woman amongst us. Will be a welcome addition to my bachelor abode.''

Rand signaled to the footman for a refill of his wineglass, smiling as he always did when the old man spoke of him, just as if he did not care what was said. He hoped his bride wasn't fool enough to think he intended to be tamed.

"Thank you, my lord. I am looking forward to learning about my new home.'' Helena glanced at him curiously, her brow lifting when she saw the footman approach and refill his glass. He grinned and winked at her as if he were not uncomfortable to be seen overimbibing in his grandfather's presence.

"Parsleigh?'' Rand interjected as casually as he could manage. "I thought a tour, first.'' He overrode his grandfather's impending interruption. "My bride has never traveled. I know Rome would please her. Perhaps Venice as well.''

The old man frowned, the sharp green eyes that were his legacy to Rand searching for the truth behind Rand's wish to travel. "Nonsense. You'll have time for that after you've filled the nursery. Then you can run off and leave the nanny to care for the children, just as your parents did. With an heir and a spare, won't matter if you two get swept off your skis, as they did.''

Rand set his wineglass down carefully, afraid he might snap the stem. His father had indeed died in an accident. But his mother had not. He wondered whether he should test the old man's patience by revealing one of the family secrets here. His mother's madness.

Before he could say a word, however, Helena interposed, "I'm not the adventuring type, my lord. I will welcome settling into my new home without delay.''

Rand examined her expression closely, wondering if she sided with his grandfather simply because she was still angry with him for forcing the marriage despite her objections.

Her blue eyes were guileless. Which meant nothing, he knew. Rand nodded, knowing that both his grandfather and Helena watched him closely.

There was no point in letting either of them see that he was bothered by the disruption in his careful plans. "As you wish, Helena.''

Ros might have cozened the old man around, but Helena was no doubt innocent to the undercurrent of control the old man embodied. No doubt she would be willingly fetching and carrying and coddling him. No doubt he would show her only the most charming side of him, too. Unless she forced the conqueror side of him to surface. But she would not, he consoled himself, with another glass of wine. Ros might have. Helena would not.

For a moment he contemplated unhappily what the change in bride and travel meant. His plans with Ros had called for an extended trip abroad and resettlement in London. Now it seemed he could stay in London, but that would leave Helena alone with his grandfather. He had just vowed to protect this woman. How could he leave her to the old man's wiles?

But how could he convince her Parsleigh was not as congenial a place to live as it might seem? His grandfather continued to charm his bride through the sweet course. Rand welcomed the signal for the ladies to retire and leave the gentlemen to their cigars and port. He wanted Helena away from the old man. How the devil was he to manage it?

# Chapter Six

After the gentlemen had rejoined the ladies, and a toast been made to the new couple, wishing them a safe journey to Parsleigh, Rand saw his opportunity. He spied the duke and duchess approaching and turned to his grandfather with an excuse that might serve to free them. "My bride might be more comfortable here, with her family. At least for a time."

The marquess, as usual, brushed aside his suggestion as if he were an errant child. "Nonsense. We are her family now; she should be with us."

Rand smiled as if he did not care one way or the other. But he waited until the duchess was within hearing to reply. "If she remained with her sister, she would be in London still. I would be able to see her more often."

"Stay with us?" The duchess appeared distracted for a moment, and Rand feared she had something else on her mind and would not agree. However, as he watched, her gaze cleared of distraction and focused on what he had just suggested. "Of course." The duchess quickly supported him, although he noticed the duke was quietly observing the interactions of all parties and did not nod at his wife's invitation. "Helena is certainly welcome to make her home here for now. As are you, Rand."

The last thing he wanted was to be in a household with so many servants to observe his actions, never mind the duke and duchess who had already proven themselves quite observant. "I think a man with my habits is better off in a bachelor abode."

His grandfather frowned in disapproval. "You mean to keep your rooms?"

He met his grandfather's gaze steadily. "I do."

The duchess appeared as unhappy as his grandfather, and cast a glance at Helena, who was stiff beside him, showing no emotion whatsoever. She also, he noticed curiously, sent a glance to her husband, which caused the duke to melt away from the group in some haste. Rand dismissed his curiosity and turned his attention back to his own battle.

Genially—did the old man ever issue his commands less than genially?—his grandfather said, "Well, then, I want your bride with me. She won't grow so lonely for her husband when he is off." He frowned. "That way, I can keep an eye on him, help you bring him to heel," he said to Helena in reassurance.

Ah yes, Rand remembered. The old man eschewed geniality only when he had to pay his grandson's debts, or see to his obligations.

Rand weighed the risk of objecting openly to the idea of immuring Helena at Parsleigh. He did not want the old man to know how much he wished to keep his bride away from him. He did not want the old man to smell a weakness upon him. "Perhaps the dower house could be made ready for us, then?"

Quickly, before the old man could make a pronouncement he would feel duty bound to adhere to, Rand added with a wink he knew would give the old man indigestion, "So that I can chase my bride around the rooms in quest of an heir without disturbing the peace of the manor house and its master."

His grandfather pondered his answer so long, Rand thought he would refuse. Fortunately, he did not. Instead he beamed with delight, as if the idea had been his own. "I'll send a message home this very minute. You can move in at once."

"You are too kind, my lord." Helena smiled at the old man, already showing signs of being smitten with his grandfather's charm. The glance she gave Rand froze his toes off. He supposed she found him somewhat less charming than she did his grandfather. He pushed aside his disappointment. In that, she was no different than most other people he knew.

Rand sighed. "Wait until you have children, my love; then you will see how he dotes upon you."

His grandfather eyed him shrewdly at the casual "my love" that had slipped from his lips, and Rand's heart chilled. He had forgotten to be on guard. Helena's defection into the old man's camp had rattled him. He hoped he had not put her in danger. But no, there would be no danger for her until his grandfather had the heir he wanted. And there would be no danger at all if Rand proved he did not care for his bride as more than a broodmare for his heirs.

The tension in Helena had drawn very fine. He

could see her glance at her sister and the duke as if to judge what they made of her new husband. She would have to learn to think less of other people's judgment if she were to be happy.

He took her hand and lifted it to his mouth for a kiss. "Now that we have settled the matter of where we shall live, I must take my leave, dear wife."

"Your leave?" Her hand trembled in his, before she thought to snatch it away.

He smiled in false apology. "The cards are calling me."

"You are going to gamble?" Helena's voice was calm, but her face revealed her shocked dismay.

Rand longed to comfort her. "As my wife, you will have to accept that my cards are my mistress, and a well-loved one at that." With a peck on the cheek, Rand left the room—and his bride—behind.

Helena watched in shock as her new husband walked away from her. For a moment she forgot there was anyone else in the room. And then the full public humiliation of his actions came clear as the marquess said gruffly, "I am sorry, my dear. I had hoped marriage would curb his gambling ways."

The marquess's expression was sympathetic. But something in his tone made Helena wonder if he truly had believed marriage could change his grandson. She was suddenly very grateful that she had entered this marriage with no illusions of love.

"We have an understanding," Helena assured him. "I will not curb his gambling and he will not ask me to give up my art."

"You are an artist?" Though the marquess's smile did not disappear, his lips compressed until they were pale. Helena did not know the man well, but she had no doubt what that expression signaled. Definite disapproval. She wished Rand had not disappeared. Perhaps he could convince his grandfather her drawing was not something to concern the marquess.

Miranda stepped in quickly. "Helena has always been able to capture in her drawings that indefinable something in a person. She is quite talented."

"An artist?" The marquess studied Helena for a few moments. "Perhaps that is why Rand chose you over your sister at the last minute. He has always had a weakness for women in the arts."

"I believe he chose me because my sister wished to break the engagement," Helena confessed. "I was the next best bride for him."

"Ah. I'm glad to hear he didn't cozen you by claiming to love you beyond pearls."

"Most certainly not!" Helena protested, and then realized how her words must sound to the gentle old man and her already worried sister. She hastened to add, "I am certain we will come to have affection for each other, in time."

There was no offense in the shrewd eyes of the old man assessing her. "You'd be better to save your affections for your children." The marquess shook his head. "I hope you're not a silly chit who believes in all that love claptrap. I've never known the boy to love anything or anyone beyond himself."

"I'm certain they will find a satisfactory arrangement." Miranda frowned at the marquess, putting an arm around Helena's shoulder tightly. "Now, if you will excuse us, my lord. At the moment I need my sister's advice on a family matter."

Helena did not understand her sister's urgency,

as she pulled her toward the empty library. No, it was not empty, she saw. Simon stood by the fire in the regal stance of lord of the manor. Beside him was Ros, one hip resting against the back of a chair. Both were looking directly at Helena as she entered the room.

Miranda closed the door gently behind them, and Helena felt as if she had been trapped with wild creatures who looked tame enough but hid a penchant for mayhem. Miranda moved to stand beside her husband. She, too, said nothing, just stood looking at her as if she expected a confession of some sort. "What is the matter?"

"Ros wants to go to America."

Helena examined a small stain upon her bodice as she answered as nonchalantly as possible, "Ros has always wanted to go adventuring. America strikes her as a grand adventure, this week."

"No. It is more than idle talk this time." Miranda shook her head and glanced at Ros, who lifted her eyebrows in a gesture of defiant resistance. Miranda gazed at Helena pleadingly. "You must help talk sense into her. Simon caught her trying to run away."

How many times had they played out this scenario? Ros and Helena against Miranda and Simon—or back at Anderlin, against Valentine, their elder brother. This was one thing she would not miss when Ros was gone. When she began her life as Rand's countess. "She is going to America." Helena could have used the lilt at the end to make her sentence a question. But she did not.

Miranda pressed her lips together a moment before saying, "You knew?"

"Yes." Helena nodded, fighting back shame. Ros

felt no shame; why did she? "That is why she asked me to marry Rand in her place."

"How could you—" Confusion clouded Miranda's features. "I thought you and Rand—"

Helena did not want to discuss the details of the fiction that Rand had created of a couple who had been indiscreet before their wedding ceremony. Close scrutiny would tell her sister that things were not as they seemed. Quickly, she interposed, "Who has ever stopped Ros from doing what she wished?"

Miranda might have pursued the matter, but Ros stepped in and said firmly, "I'm going to America, and if arguing with you causes me to miss my ship, I will merely find another."

"Ros—"

Miranda's distress must have softened Ros, for she gave up open defiance for an appeal to Miranda's understanding of her sister's true nature. "Miranda, I am not made for this society. Do you deny it?"

"No."

"How can you ask me to stay?"

"Then you must go to Juliet." Simon stepped in. "You are too young to go to a strange country on your own." Helena held her breath, hoping her twin would be swayed to the idea. Ros would be safe with Juliet and R. J.

Ros seemed startled at how quickly she had persuaded them to her side. But she was not so easily swayed to give up her idea of solo adventure. "Boston is too proper, if R. J. is anything to judge the city by."

Miranda stared at Ros for a full minute before answering firmly, "The dowager says that the Carolinians are not so proper. I will write you a letter and she will take you in."

Ros shook her head impatiently, bowing to the sense of it at last. "Then write it quickly." Helena suppressed a sigh of relief, fearing it would make her sister change her mind once more.

"The safety of people who love you is not so terrible, Ros," she said softly, aware that she would be leaving her family behind when she left with Rand for Parsleigh.

"It can be, if the people who love you will not let you follow your dreams," Ros answered sharply.

"You are going to America," Helena replied. "No one is preventing you. And I wouldn't, even if I could. Even though I wish you would be here for me."

"You will be fine." Ros hesitated, and then in a gesture uncharacteristic of her taciturn nature she pulled Helena into a tight hug. "If you need anything, write me and I will come immediately."

"You will be in America."

"If I were on the highest mountain in China, I would come like the wind. I promise."

Helena returned her sister's embrace fiercely. "I know. It will be good for me to be apart from you, I suppose. I will learn to fend for myself." She stepped away and turned her back for a moment to wipe away the tears she knew would only exasperate her twin. "I don't suppose I should count on my husband for such things. Do you know he has gone gambling—on his wedding night!"

Ros gripped her shoulder and turned her until their gazes met. "He is a better man than many think, Helena. Do not hesitate to trust him in grave matters, even if you find he disappoints you in the everyday."

"Trust needs to be built," Helena said doubtfully. "If he cannot be trusted in small things, how could I ever believe in him when matters become grave?"

Rosaline did not seem to have an answer to that. At last she sighed and said, "You trust me, do you not?"

"Yes." Helena gave a mock glare. "Even though you pawned off your bridegroom on me, in a bargain I shall likely regret."

"No," Rosaline disagreed. "I don't believe you will regret it—any more than any woman must regret putting herself under a man's thumb."

"Ros—" Helena did not know what to say in the face of her sister's unwavering belief that marriage was not for her.

"Trust me. You can be happy. I know it. You are made differently than I am, no matter that we look alike." The blue of her eyes burned when she added, "Trust Rand because I tell you that you can." There was such conviction in her that Helena was almost convinced. If only Ros hadn't added, "But only when matters are at their gravest."

Helena did not find her sister's words reassuring, but she did not want to quibble when they had so little time left before they were separated by a distance so great she could not really comprehend it. About trusting her husband, she would have to see—assuming that he ever returned from his gambling to collect his wife.

Dawn was breaking when he came to their room. Helena stirred when the door latch snicked into place. Rand stood still, hoping she would return to a deeper slumber. He would prefer she not know the hour he returned. Too soon for the maid. Much too late for a bridegroom who wished to get an heir in an expedient manner. The old man would know, however. His grandfather's spies would work as well in the duke's household as they did elsewhere in London, Rand was certain.

When there were no further sounds of movement from the bed, he dared move away from the door, toward his dressing room.

She sat up. "Good evening, my lord. Or should I say good morning."

The reality of a bride in his bed became startlingly clear for Rand. He must come up with an excuse. No, no excuse, he decided abruptly. Simply an apology. "Helena. I apologize if I disturbed you."

She waited for a moment, as if she thought he might follow his rather short apology with an excuse. And then she said, with all the grace of a long-suffering wife, "Did you forget that we set out for Parsleigh today? Your grandfather says it is a hard three days' travel. You will not like to begin it without sleep."

"Then I will not do so." He leaned wearily against the bedpost, staring into the shadows where she sat watching him. Where had she learned that manner, when she had yet to be a wife for a full day?

"We must start out early to get full use of the day," she argued.

In his eagerness for the advantage of a wife in his bed, he had forgotten the disadvantage. She must be placated before he could rest. "Only if we insist on taxing ourselves."

"Surely we do not want to be on the road longer than we need be."

He had not moved from the foot of the bed as they spoke. The shadows in the room made him feel as if he might be talking to a ghost his imagination had conjured up. But she was no ghost; she was his wife. He wondered if she felt the same uneasy fluttering in her stomach at that fact as he did. "There is no true hurry. We will travel slowly. There are inns aplenty along the road. We will find a good one to shelter us each night." A wicked thought chased away the weariness for a moment, as he reflected that he was not married to a ghost, but a flesh-and-blood woman. "And, as I promised, a new lesson each day."

She stirred restlessly at that statement. Did she remember too well the feel of his hands gliding over her ankle, her leg? What would she do if he joined her in bed and—

She interrupted his thoughts with a very curt, "I need no lessons from you, my lord."

"I must say you have mastered the skills of harpy wife well," he replied. "But I wish a wife who responds to my kisses with more pleasure and less shame."

"I am indisposed," she said hastily, as if she believed he would leap on her then and there. The thought was surprisingly tempting. "I supposed that was why you saw no reason to retire early."

"I have not forgotten, Helena." He had, however, considered showing her there were still pleasures to be found in the marriage bed. But it had suited his purpose better not to come to bed before dawn. "Just as I have not forgotten the promise I made to you earlier. I always keep my promises."

She said quickly, "I had heard otherwise."

He pretended her words had no impact on him. No matter that he heard the fear behind them, and knew that she would hear worse things about him in the future. "Liars all. I simply make very few promises." Turning away, he carelessly discarded his waistcoat.

She moved, as if she would leave the bed, and then hesitated. Crawling back safely under the covers, she asked, "Should I ring for your valet?"

He shook his head sharply and then groaned at the resulting pain. "No. Leave Griggson to his bed. Poor man does hate to travel so; he could use a few hours more rest. I can manage—" He broke off. He could manage by himself. In fact, he had done so many times before. But he need not do so today. "This would make an excellent lesson for the day; would it not?" he said, anticipating one of the advantages of a wife in one's bed.

"What?" Helena slid down further into the bedclothes. "Watching you undress?"

"No." He hesitated. Perhaps that would be a more sensible lesson for an exhausted man with a reluctant bride in his bed to manage. But hadn't he proven definitively today that he was not a sensible man? "No," he repeated more firmly, sending Helena deeper into the bedclothes. "I don't mean watching your husband undress, although that is a lesson for the future, my imaginative wife."

He pushed away from the bedpost against which he had been leaning. "The lesson for today is learning to undress your husband."

"You must be joking." Her voice did not convey conviction and he smiled, thinking she was beginning to know him already.

"Not at all."

"But I have had my lesson for today," she objected. "And we weren't even properly wed at the time." As if she might shame him into giving up on his notion. Never.

He crossed the room and parted the curtains a

few inches. The early light fell upon her face and she buried herself in the covers with a faint squeal. Though she was no longer watching him, he bowed deeply toward the bed. "Behold, it is the dawn of a new day, Wife."

# Chapter Seven

Was he mad? Helena peeked out from under the covers at her husband. The early dawn light threw odd shadows across the room. Across his face. But she could swear that his eyes were gleaming at her as if he were a jungle predator. A tiger. Or a lion.

"It is too early for such games," she said crossly as he rose from his bow and grinned boldly at her. She sat up in the bed, cradling her knees in her arms. He could not be serious.

But he was. He held out his arms. "Come. Undress your husband, wife."

She did not move. "You are drunk."

"I assure you I am not." He stood waiting, staring at her in a most unsettling manner.

"I will call Griggson for you." Helena moved to pull the bell rope, and squealed as she was lifted bodily from the bed with no warning. His breath was scented with brandy. So much for his not being drunk.

"I can choose another lesson, then, if you like?" His mouth was inches from her ear as he whispered, "Would you like to know what it feels like when a man suckles your breasts? Or do you already know?"

Instinctively, she drew her arms across her chest. "I do not."

"Do not wish to know, or do not know?"

Helena struggled to escape him, but he only laughed as he set her on her feet and placed his hands at her hips. "Well, Wife? Decide. I am tired and want my bed."

Helena reached for the shirt that was half unfastened and jerked at it angrily.

His hands came over hers. "Not like that, unless your husband has taken a mistress and you wish to punish him."

"What if he is a drunken fool?"

"You can hardly punish him for such a minor transgression, surely?"

He guided her to gently unfasten his shirt and then again he took her hands and brought them to his shoulders. "Now, a loving wife would allow her hands to skim her husband's shoulders as she pushed the shirt from him gently."

"Would she?" Even her fingertips, touching as lightly as she could manage, detected the powerful muscles in his shoulders. Muscles that coiled and flexed in his arms as her fingers skimmed quickly down their length. Helena felt as if her fingertips were being scalded. Were all men so warm? She could not recall from her brief encounters with William.

"Definitely." He caught her hands as she

reached for the fastening of his trousers and brought them back up to his shoulders. "A gentle caress. That's it. And then, her hands would trail down his chest." His grip was not painful; his thumbs did not hurt her as he pressed her fingers open, one by one, and trailed her hands down his chest, almost as if they did not belong to her at all.

Helena was fascinated to feel the taut contours of his muscled breastbone and ribs. The fine hair that covered his chest. The warm steady pulse of his blood beneath his skin. His heart beating steady and rapid beneath his rib cage. She did not know when he let go of her hand and she began exploring on her own, unwilling to draw back from an exploration of the male anatomy she had wished to make for a very long time.

He drew in a startled breath when one index finger dipped into his navel and she could not help stopping there a moment. "Have I tickled you, my lord?"

Tickled was not what he would call the sensation, Rand thought. Torture was more like it. Still, it was a sweet enough torment, even if he knew he must cut it short tonight in light of her indisposition. "If I said yes, would you stop?"

"Of course not." There was a shadow of laughter in her voice as she answered, "Not even if you begged and pleaded on your knees, tears in your eyes." Her finger teased his navel more surely as she spoke.

She had warmed to the game, he realized. Now that she was in control. The weariness of a misspent night fell away from him. "What if I were to throw myself on your mercy?"

A distinct flavor of well-savored revenge in her answer. "Who says I have any mercy?"

"I say you do," he avowed. "You can be sure I would not be standing before you if I were a poor judge of women. Especially women who dispense mercy freely."

Her finger stopped its teasing motion for a moment, and he feared his careless words had broken the spell between them. He had forgotten that a mistress might not mind the reminder that she had won him from others. A wife—his wife—apparently did.

He found himself oddly uncertain how to recapture the ease between them, and might have ended things there, for the night. But then she redoubled her efforts and her voice showed only a shadow of hesitation as she replied, "Those women were not your wife. They were not tasked with curing your reprobate ways. A wife should be merciful sparingly. Or so I have heard."

"Maybe you will make a good wife yet." Did he want a good wife? He had not thought so until she spoke the words. For a moment, to see her smile, he wanted to swear he would not drink, would not gamble, would not—but that was impossible, and the sooner she learned that lesson, the better for both of them. "I can promise you that mercy or no, I will not be tamed by any woman, not even a wife. I like my life as it is."

That comment broke the spell. Her finger jabbed him once and then she turned her back on him.

Perhaps he should have let her have her sulk. Mischief made him say imperiously, "You are not finished."

Her answer was flat and final. "I am."

He refused to accept defeat. He wanted his playful Helena back. "I do not sleep in my trousers. Or my boots."

Annoyed, she impatiently unfastened his trousers and would have shoved them down to the floor, if he had not again stopped her by taking her hands in his.

He said as patiently as if he were instructing a child, "First, the boots."

Helena gave him her best glare to show that she did not appreciate being treated as his doxy. "I have never taken a man's boots off before." Perhaps, she hoped, he would relent and finish the task himself.

He sat in a chair and held out his left leg as if her pique were of no consequence to him. "Your lover was not terribly demanding. I'm amazed he knew enough to manage the thing successfully between you. Perhaps you are still a virgin and don't even know it."

She felt herself flush hotly at the insult and wished he could not see how his words affected her. "I assure you, I am not."

He shrugged. "Then give me his name so I might offer him some pointers on how to treat a woman properly."

Helena did not reply, although his words reminded her sharply that she was not able to take the high ground with him as much as she wished. She had come to him with a blotched reputation. Nevertheless, she did not wish to be treated as if she were his servant. Take off his boots! She had taken off her sister's boots many times, but she would not give him the satisfaction of saying so. Whatever he wanted from her, he would have to ask for.

She stood mutely, making her expression as

deliberately blank as she could manage with the fury that flowed through her veins.

After a moment, he sighed. "Turn around."

She did so, expecting him to then ask for her to grasp his foot. Instead, she felt a nudging between her knees and gasped as she realized that he was insinuating his leg between hers, lifting the lawn of her nightdress high up her legs with the toe of his boot.

She opened her mouth to protest that Ros had never done such a thing when she realized she would give herself away. So she stood quietly, as if she could not feel the supple leather sliding back and forth against the inside of her bare thighs.

His voice was a soft purr. "Pull."

She moved back to clamp his leg at the knee with her own knees. Perhaps her hold was tighter than he expected, but he made no protest as she pulled at the heel of his boot. The snug fit gave some resistance. She suppressed her gasp when he placed his other foot firmly on her bottom and pushed against her as she tugged at the stubborn boot once more. She could have wept when it came free in her hands and his stocking-clad foot slithered back through her knees.

Before she could catch her breath, his other boot was sliding between her knees. "The other one, please."

This one proved even more stubborn than its twin. And Helena found her breath becoming more rapid and shallow as he placed his foot on her bottom again. Clad in only a stocking, his foot seemed to exude a warm, masculine strength as he pushed against her. When the boot came free she moved her legs apart and stepped away so that he could not tease her thighs with his foot once more. Even between a husband and wife that could not be proper. Could it?

He stood, grinning as wickedly as any boy caught stealing sweet buns from the kitchen. She would have turned and fled for the bed, but he held out his arms and said, "Now the trousers."

She saw no point in protesting; she just wanted to be done with this. Hastily she reached out to the already unfastened trousers and pushed clumsily at them.

She should have known he would not let her off so easily. He enjoyed her torment too much. "No. Again, like the shoulders, only this time you caress the hips."

She was shocked to realize he wore nothing underneath the trousers. But it gave her an idea of how to end matters between them quickly. "And do I caress farther down, to your thighs?" she challenged, realizing that he was fully aroused.

She was not too naive to know that was an uncomfortable state for a man who was not going to be able to make love to his wife.

"No." He laughed breathly. "Over the buttocks, like this." His hands guided hers over the hard, tight curve, and the movement pushed his pelvis against her belly.

Still holding her to him, her hands to his nether regions, he stepped out of his trousers. For a moment she was almost free, and then he held her against him, tightly, and bent his head to capture her mouth. His hands swooped up her arms to capture her shoulders when she made to pull away. Helpless, she stopped struggling and allowed herself to adjust to the feel of a naked man pressed against her. Kissing her. After a few moments, she began to realize there was pleasure to be had in this kind of embrace.

She almost wished that he would lift her and carry her to the bed, as a hero in a romantic novel might do. But then she realized that was impossible. Surely he had not forgotten? He had been so casual in the use of the term menses. She did not want to have to say it aloud. She turned her head away, murmuring objections that were only half-hearted. His kisses, his touch felt too good.

"I find myself wishing you were going to have a child," he murmured heatedly in her ear. Despite his words, he did not pull away from her. For a moment she thought he would not stop. She closed her eyes and told herself sternly not to scream. She was his wife, after all. How silly to be afraid of the inevitable.

But after a moment the harshness of his breath evened and he released her with a soft kiss on the top of her head. "That wasn't so awful, was it, my dear?"

"Not at all," she lied.

He laughed softly. "I suspect you are relieved that your indisposition saved you from more of my attention."

"Not at all," she lied again. "I want a child as badly as you do. It is the one thing about this bargain we both agree upon."

"Come to bed," he said, smothering a yawn. "I am feeling guilty for disturbing your sleep."

"In a moment." The thought of climbing into bed beside her new husband sent a sensation through her she had only felt once before—when William had first touched her as a lover. There was both pleasure and a twisting of unease in the feeling. The unease was compounded by Helena's suspicion that the earl was incapable of feeling guilt. Without looking at him, she bent and gathered his discarded clothing into her arms. "Griggson will have our heads if we do not hang this properly."

She drew out the chore, smoothing unseen wrinkles from the fabric as she listened to him climb into the bed and make himself comfortable.

At last she turned. "There, not even Griggson could complain—" She broke off. Her husband was unmistakably asleep, his lips parted, his shoulder rising in an even rhythm.

Asleep. After . . . With a sigh she donned her dressing gown and settled on her chaise with a book. She was not getting into bed with him. She intended to heed the warning about letting sleeping lions rest. Or was it dogs? No matter.

Her husband, despite his many flaws, was no dog. He was a lion. She only hoped he did not see her as a lamb.

The trip to Parsleigh could have been accomplished in three long days of riding, as his grandfather planned to do. Rand decided that they would stay a day longer so that they might see Ros off, now that her trip to America had been both discovered and sanctioned by her family.

He welcomed the delay, in truth. He had no intention of traveling at a breakneck pace. Hard travel would only get them to Parsleigh earlier, and he had little desire to see much more of his home than he had already been forced to endure.

While he did not normally enjoy staying at inns during his travels, preferring instead to sojourn with friends on the way, he found himself looking forward to doing so with Helena. The journey might be the only time the two of them would be truly alone. He even schemed to send the servants ahead of them, so that he would have to share his wife with no one on the journey.

Helena had not objected to being without a maid, because she was used to sharing with her sisters and did not even have her own maid. His grandfather would select one of his own servants for her at Parsleigh. But until then, Rand looked forward to doing the service for her. She had already proven she could stand as his valet quite satisfactorily.

Months traveling Paris, Venice, Rome—even to Egypt, should she have wished—would have pleased him more. But these days on the road to Parsleigh would have to serve. He did not expect to be bored. He had the daily lesson in lovemaking he had promised her, as well. Amusement and satisfaction to delight any man.

He need not hurry the journey for anyone, especially himself. Perhaps they would have a repair or two that might necessitate staying an extra day in a particularly fine inn. Anything to delay the return to his grandfather's control was welcome.

Helena did not directly oppose the idea of traveling more slowly. Her objections were phrased more diplomatically. "Will your grandfather not worry?"

"Not at all. I told him we would no doubt see him within two weeks," Rand reassured her. "I explained that you must see your sister off to America."

Apparently, that was not what she wished to hear, for she continued to question him about his plans even as they stood upon the dock to wish Rosaline farewell. "Still, if we travel at this pace—"

He was pleased when Ros saw fit to rebuke her sister. "Helena, you have spent the entirety of your life between Anderlin, London, and Simon's country manse. Surely you are adventurous enough to enjoy discovering new territory?"

Helena narrowed her eyes at Ros. "I suppose I should consider that I am going nowhere at all, if I compare my journey to your own."

"Nonsense," Ros replied with a cheeky smile. "You are venturing into a territory I fear to tread—matrimony."

Rand once again felt a slight lift of disbelief as he looked at the sisters. They were both dressed as fine ladies, and if he had not spent the past two years carousing with Ros, he might never have guessed she was anything but a gently bred lady.

He knew that was due to the duchess's influence. And he heartily suspected that Ros's male disguise was safely tucked into her trunks somewhere deep in the hold of the ship. He wondered what the Americans would make of Mr. Roscue Anderlin. Belatedly, he realized that his one true friend was virtually abandoning him. "I'll miss you, Ros."

"You'll have Helena to remind you of me." No one would accuse Ros of excess sentiment, Rand reflected ruefully.

"Be safe," he said, folding her into a tight embrace until she made a sound of protest.

"Take care of my sister," she countered. If he had not known her so well, he almost would have sworn he saw a tear in her eye.

"Are you certain that you won't stay?" Helena made one last plea.

Ros shook her head and gave both of them stiff hugs. "I'll write. And I'd best get letters from you two, or I'll worry that I made a mistake turning you over to each other.''

"I'll write every day," Helena quickly promised.

Ros shook her head. "Every week is more than enough. Every month and I'll know you're busy and happy." She held up a tiny sketch of the family that Helena had framed for her in a gold brooch. "Send me pictures, Helena. I'll know by them that you're doing well, and everyone else is, too."

"Will you ever come back?"

Ros did not answer, as the ship's whistle sounded then. But Rand could see the answer in her eyes. Perhaps, for a visit. But Ros's heart was far from England, and most likely always would be.

He put his arm around Helena and they leaned against each other for support as they watched Ros walk with jaunty steps up the swaying ramp to the ship and away from them, perhaps forever. It was an odd feeling to be part of a pair.

He saw the duchess lean against the duke, and sigh. Just as Helena leaned against him. He watched the woman he had planned to be his wife walk away, leaving him with the woman who had agreed to marry him and then wanted to back out of the deal. He felt the vulnerability of her slender shoulder and wondered if he would regret the hasty switch he had agreed to.

He turned to the duke and duchess and smiled brightly, as if he were not plagued with misgivings. "Well, it is our turn to be off, I suppose."

There were more hugs, a few tears, and then the carriage carrying Rand and Helena toward Parsleigh jolted off.

Helena fell against him as the carriage jolted forward, losing her view of her family out the window as her fashionable hat tilted over her eyes. He reached to help right her and her silly hat, but she made an anguished sound low in her throat, brushed away his hands, and bent to grab her sketchbook from her basket.

Without a word of apology for her behavior, his wife quickly found a clean page and searched out a sharp pencil from the basket. Frantically, as if afraid that she might forget one small detail, she began to sketch, ignoring him as if he no longer existed.

Ros had told him Helena could draw. He had even seen a few framed sketches that must have been hers. But nothing could have prepared him for the sight of her strong, sure strokes creating magic before his very eyes. With one more glance at his wife hunched in concentration, Rand settled back to watch the scene she was creating unfold.

# Chapter Eight

"Your talent astonishes me."

Helena looked up, shocked out of the trancelike state that she often entered when sketching. Rand had positioned himself so that he could see over her shoulder, down to the sketch of her family on the dock. The position seemed oddly familiar—Ros had often done the same thing—and uncomfortably intimate.

Belatedly she realized that she had ignored him for what must have been quite some time. She flipped the sketchbook shut. "I'm sorry. I did not mean to be rude. I wanted to capture the vision while it was still strong—"

"Don't apologize, Helena." He put a finger to her lips to silence her when she would have apologized again. "I am grateful for the opportunity to see you at work."

One glance into his eyes told her he was not lying. She felt a warm pleasure rush through her at his compliment. "Such as it is," she said quickly, so that he would not think her immodest. Another warmth spread through her when her lips brushed his finger as they moved.

He smiled, his eyes growing darker, his finger tapping lightly on her bottom lip as he chided, "Don't belittle your talent."

"I'm not. But I must keep my art in perspective, if I am to have a happy life." Helena recited the cautioning lecture she had received from disapproving elders her whole life: "A lady's drawing talent is of little use in this world, except for marking her own intimate memories."

"Intimate, indeed." Rand's finger left her lips to trace over Ros's sketched image. "I can't imagine anything standing between you and your muse when it comes upon you. Do you do everything you love with such passion?" His gaze was frankly speculative and Helena wished she was not already nestled into the corner of the carriage as closely as possible. "Do you realize we will soon be stopping for fresh horses?"

Already? To her it seemed they had scarcely begun the journey. Helena examined her sketch. The detail was exacting, but she could not believe she had spent hours—she broke off the thought to examine his expression. His left brow lifted in question, but there was no sign of annoyance. "I . . . I will learn to put such things aside, my lord."

"Could you be happy without your drawing?" His gaze was searching. He wanted the truth.

Without meaning to, Helena answered honestly. "No." She held her breath, certain that he would be angry with her blunt answer.

He seemed more pleased than annoyed, when he smiled broadly and gave her shoulder an approving squeeze. "Then you do not have to live without it, Helena."

"A wife—"

"Don't say a wife must put her husband's wishes first." He shook his head. "Perhaps if you had married some other man. But not with me as your husband. Have you ever wished to go to Paris to study with the masters upon the Seine?"

That was a wish too private to share, even with a husband who appeared to approve of her unfeminine obsession with drawing. "I could not."

"Why not?"

She was astonished he needed to ask. "I am not good enough; I am a woman. . . ."

He halted her excuses with a look of reproof. "Would Ros have let that stand in her way if she had your talent?" His finger tapped against the sketch of Ros. Her sister stood fearless upon the bow of the ship, shoulders back, legs wide, a smile of anticipation lighting her face in an almost unearthly fashion.

But even Ros had to pay a price for choosing adventure. "Ros does not desire a home and family, my lord. A woman cannot have both happily, unless she is extraordinary."

What would happen to her sister if she ever wanted her freedom and a family? Whatever it was would almost certainly guarantee unhappiness. Society frowned on women who put their own needs above those of their husband and children. Thankfully, she could not envision Ros ever wanting to settle down. No doubt her sister would be more careful than Helena had been about any lovers she took, as well. After all, Ros did not have Helena's romantic, sentimental streak.

"Nonsense. You can have whatever you wish."

He paused. "For example, have you ever sketched a nude?"

"Many times." She had a plaster miniature of the famed David done by Michaelangelo. She knew the lines of it by heart.

"Have you now?" He inched a little closer, although Helena would have thought that impossible but a moment before. "Again you astonish me."

"The lines of the human form are classic. There is no shame in sketching them," Helena answered a little briskly, misliking the gleam in her husband's eye.

"Still, for a sheltered miss to have a nude model—was it your lover, by chance?"

"Of course not!"

"Ros?" He sounded puzzled.

Did he know her sister that little? "Ros would not like to be captured in so vulnerable a state."

"Who, then, did you paint without clothing?"

"David, of course."

"David . . . ?

She sighed. Did he know nothing of art? She should have guessed it the way he seemed to think her own masterful. "The statue of David. Done by the artist Michaelangelo? Have you never heard of it? It is quite famous."

"A statue?" He seemed disappointed, but not angrily so. Instead, a grin had crept wide upon his mouth, showing his dimple again. "So you have never had a living, breathing nude human form for you to sketch?"

"Of course not." She had wished to. But William had proved shy—or rather she had interpreted his reluctance as reticence. No doubt he had been afraid that something so tangible as a nude sketch of him might get him trapped into a marriage he evidently did not want. "It would not be proper."

He shook his head at her as if to reprove a recalcitrant child. "You are married to me, now. I would not object."

She struggled to strangle the scandalized gasp that emerged from her as she realized what he suggested. "I could not," she objected. Even as she did so, Helena thought of his body as she had explored it last night. She knew, with shame, that if she had been one whit weaker, she would already have sketched him from the memory of last night.

"Could not? Or will not?"

How did he know so well what tempted her to stray outside propriety? "Imagine what talk it would cause if anyone found out."

"What? That you had seen me without a stitch? I believe most everyone has guessed that you will have done so by now." He grinned. "We are married, Helena. I want an heir. Generally, clothing only gets in the way."

"Nonsense." She realized he was deliberately trying to scandalize her and sniffed with as much disdain as she could muster while he pressed against her so very tightly. "That is why nightdresses are thin, and lift easily."

He did not reply, merely threw his head back and laughed as if she had told a ribald joke. After a moment he stopped his laughter, with effort, and asked, "If no one were ever to know, would you wish to sketch a live nude?"

Again, Helena answered honestly. "Yes. But—"

He touched her lips again, just briefly, to stop her words. "Very well; then I command it."

"You command it?"

"I am your husband." His look was imperious,

and she knew suddenly that he could be a very good earl, if only he would give up his profligate ways.

He commanded her to sketch his nude form? So much for his promise to let her do as she pleased. But, as he said, he was her husband. "When it suits you, I suppose," she grumbled aloud.

"It suits me now." He grinned and tapped her sketchbook. "You have no choice, Wife. Your husband desires that you capture him in the nude."

She blushed at the image his words raised. "My lord . . ."

"Am I not well made enough to grace your sketchbook?"

She thought of the shape of him beneath her fingers. As she had seen him in the early morning light. "You are well made," she conceded reluctantly.

"Then how can you refuse my offer and still consider yourself an artist?" He had such an air of a naughty child that she wanted to laugh at the image of Rand that popped unbidden to her mind: lying nude upon a white bearskin rug in a painting that would hang grandly over the parlor fireplace for all visitors to view. She might even have given in to the impulse to laugh, if she was not afraid that he meant it.

"A model needs to stay very still, for a long period of time, my lord. You would become bored."

"I think you are searching for any feeble excuse to avoid putting your talents to the test."

"I am not—"

"Tonight. I will be your model."

Rand had a physique to make David envious; she knew that well enough by now. To sketch him would be any artist's joy. Helena wanted to agree, but she was afraid. What if he did not like the drawing? "The light will be gone by the time we stop, take our supper, and retire."

He struck an absurd pose, his head thrust back and his hand in his vest. "I have always fancied a shadowy night view of myself in all my glory— before I run to fat and dissipation."

It was difficult to imagine Rand with silver hair and a huge barrel belly. "I—"

He leaned in to plant a kiss on her lips and then pulled back with a mischievous smile. "Consider it tonight's lesson."

Helena's will dissolved in one rush of breath. "Very well." She wanted it. How could she object? She would rip up the sketches when he wasn't looking—toss them in the fire if need be, so that no one but she saw them.

He flipped open her sketchbook and examined her work. "Do you only make ink drawings?"

"I have worked in oils, but not often. They are difficult to manage." Not to mention that she had not wanted to ask either her brother or the duke to bear the expense and inconvenience of outfitting a studio for her painting.

"Good. Then you shall do a series of sketches of me as we travel, and I shall choose my favorite and commission you to create it in oils to hang in our home."

Helena swallowed. A nude. In oils. "Perhaps you should wait to see if you find it flattering."

He looked down upon a sketch she had done of a London pickpocket. The sketch wasn't very detailed; she had seen the lad for only a moment before the duke's carriage clattered on its way. But the lean look of a hungry, wounded animal was clearly captured. The amusement leached from his features unexpectedly, and he said with a touch of bitterness, "Hang flattery, my love. Paint me as I am."

She sighed. "Only as I see you, Rand. That is all that I can promise." She tore the sketchbook from his hands, suddenly aware of how many of her secrets it held. She wished he wouldn't use that casual endearment. The way his tongue curled around the syllables made her believe that he meant them, though his eyes told her otherwise.

She had not been lying when she told him that he would be bored trying to keep as still as the statue she had practiced her skills upon. Five nights of this torture made him wonder if he had truly lost his mind. Perhaps it would not have been so bad if he could have ended the night making love to her.

A disadvantage of a wife, he supposed he should count it. If not for the monthly flux, he could be resting in this very bed with his wife next to him. He could be free to move, to kiss, to touch. . . . Would she let him kiss her knees? He had wanted to since the morning she had come to his room to jilt him. But he had been more than careful of her propriety. He had done little more than kiss her good night before turning over to his fitful sleep.

His mistresses had never bothered him about such things, although looking back he supposed that those nights when they sent notes regarding "illness"—or even the nights where he found himself ministered to quite satisfactorily with only mouth and tongue and hands with no requirement for him to participate in the matter at all—those no doubt had something to do with the mysterious workings of a woman's body. But now he had a wife. Despite her lover, she was not worldly about these matters. He needed to learn patience. These things didn't last long . . . did they?

Until then, he would simply continue to imagine the ways he would please her. The ways she, he hoped, would learn, in order to please him. Then, perhaps, they would find other ways to disport themselves when she was "indisposed."

He suspected his proper little wife would be shocked to know how he was amusing himself as he reclined in tumbled splendor upon the White Boar Inn's grandest four-poster bed. Perhaps tonight he could show her some small portion of what he had imagined in these hours lying under her gaze. Yes, surely tonight he could follow up his time as a human statue by showing her the pleasures of making love.

Had she had any of the same thoughts? She had, after all, been examining his form more closely than any of his former lovers—all without touching him with anything but her gaze. That faraway gaze that made him wonder where she went when she drew. Her head was bent over her sketchbook just now. But she knew if he moved, and made a little sound in her throat to remind him to remain still.

He speculated for a time on whether she would blush, where, and how deeply, if he were to ask her bluntly if her flow had ceased. Of course she would, he finally decided. All over. A bright deep pink. She was still unnerved by his presence. By the wedding she had not managed to escape.

When they had been led to the room by a maid, she had tried to pretend she was too tired to work.

Just as she had every night they traveled. He smiled, remembering the first night he had insisted she sketch him. How she had stared at him with wide eyes, clutching her sketchbook in her hand and darting looks about the room as if wondering where her escape might be.

He had forestalled her delay by peeling off his waistcoat and asking, "Where should I pose?"

"In the chair?" She had pointed to a rather uncomfortable-looking easy chair perched by the fire. No doubt hoping that he would agree and she could once again suggest postponing the session.

He had thrown himself onto the four-poster, arms wide. "How about the bed?"

The scandalized look in her eye suggested she was about to make an objection to his boots on the bed linens, when she blushed, subsided, and said in a small voice, "Very well."

He had propped his arms beneath his head and stared at her.

For a moment she had looked as if she might object, but then she settled herself in the chair she had first meant for him, and found a clean sheet of paper to draw upon. And she laid pen to paper.

She would have drawn him as he was; he was certain of it. But that had not suited his plans. So he had risen from the bed and come to stand over her. She held the pen inches from the paper and regarded him with curiosity. "Yes?"

"I am supposed to be nude," he had reminded her. Not that he thought she had forgotten.

Her excuse was the most feeble possible. "I thought you had changed your mind."

*You hoped I had changed my mind,* he thought, but did not say aloud. "I was waiting for you to undress me, as you did last night." She had done so that night without further protest. And every night since, as well.

She had blushed to her neckline, and no doubt beyond, each night. Each time she did he had the urge to peel away her bodice and see for himself just exactly how far down her flush carried.

Prudence dictated that he save such a delightful experiment for a time when she had grown used to him—at least, a little more used to him. Could that time be tonight?

He shifted, uncomfortably aroused at the thought of making love to his wife. Tonight. He glanced at her. Had she noticed his arousal? She had posed him so that one bent leg obscured her view of that part of him. Still, she was an artist and noticed little details. Not that he was little. Surely she had to have noticed. He shifted again.

Helena made her inarticulate sound that meant he should not move and, without looking up, tucked a stray wisp of her hair behind her ear.

Suddenly feeling no more important than her tiny replica of David, he allowed his annoyance to show in his tone. "I have an itch."

Her voice sounded rusty, as if it came reluctantly from some great well. "Don't move." Still she did not look up.

The trouble with modeling nude was that he had no boot or pocket watch to throw at her to break the spell her work put upon her. "Come and scratch for me, then."

"Mmm." Her pencil scratched at a rapid rate. She paused, frowning at the page.

"I need you to scratch my itch," he said, as loudly as he could without bringing the landlord and a dozen concerned maids to the room.

At last, she looked up. The spell had been broken. But the woman herself was left highly annoyed with him. "Can't you do it yourself?"

"I can't reach," he lied. He thought of a way to find out if he would be making love to his wife tonight or not, now that he had her full attention. "And since you are indisposed and I am forced to suffer the pangs of unrequited love—" Her glance spent only a moment at his groin, but it was enough to tell him that she was not oblivious to the meaning of his words. Good. Perhaps she would suffer some guilt. He continued as if he had not noticed where her glance had gone. "It seems only fair that you do me that small service."

She blushed, but to his chagrin he could not tell from her expression if she was still indisposed or not. He would have to ask her outright.

She closed her sketchbook, which released him from his own spell of immobility and he sat forward, watching as she stowed her tools carefully in her basket. He was not allowed to see the sketch she was making. Sketches, actually. She had used more than one paper in the days she had been drawing him. And she had posed him differently, as well.

She came forward, stretching her back and arms as if she had done something more strenuous than run a pen over paper. He did not remark upon her movement, though; he was too busy watching the rise of her breasts as she stretched. "Where do I scratch?" she asked, her gaze carefully going no farther afield than his face.

# Chapter Nine

He did not answer her question at once, though she knew what he wanted. She had become intimately, if distantly, acquainted with his body over the past five nights. The curved scar on his abdomen, the jagged one on the back of his left thigh. The crescent shape of his dimple when he wanted to coax her to stop for the evening because he was, as she had predicted, wearied to boredom by the need to be still.

The rise and fall of the part of him that indicated he was becoming increasingly frustrated by her indisposition. Catching herself, Helena redirected her gaze to his face.

As if to hide that part of him from her scrutiny—not that she would dare scrutinize it while she stood so close to him—he turned over and presented his back, rotating his right shoulder. "The itch is there, below my shoulder."

She rubbed her fingernails and fingertips along

the taut muscles of his back. She rubbed thoroughly and vigorously, but he did not relax under the fury of her ministrations.

"Are you still indisposed?" At last he asked the question she did not want to answer.

Not yet. She did not know him well enough. His body perhaps, but not his heart or his mind. She moved away from him a step and stopped working on his back. "Yes."

Instantly, she wished she had not spoken. The lie came from utter cowardice. Afraid if he turned to look at her he would see her dishonesty, she focused her gaze on his back. To her horror, where her fingernails had raked his back there were fiery-red marks.

He did not turn to look at her, though for a moment she thought he meant to, the way his shoulders tensed. "Damn." He butted his head into the pillow and collapsed onto the bed, his face buried under the crook of his carelessly flung arm.

Guilt swamped over her. Was the postponement more than inconvenient? Was it physically painful for him? "I'm sorry," she offered, tentatively touching the skin still inflamed from her handiwork. "Is there anything I can do?"

He turned over to face her. "Yes."

"What?" she asked carefully, afraid to move. Her hand had rested safely in the middle of his back before he turned. Now her fingers were much too close to the drafted object plaguing them both—albeit in very different ways.

He glanced quickly from her hand to her face. There was no movement of the muscles under her palm. He did not so much as draw breath. Neither did she.

Unexpectedly, the tension that vibrated from

him shifted, loosened somehow, and he grinned. As he did so, he lay back, resting his head loosely on his clasped hands, stretching himself before her like a preening cat. "I expect you've noticed I've had some difficulty being patient."

She nodded, a brief bob of her head, dreading what must surely follow. His skin, under her hand, seemed to be growing fever-warm.

"I have been patient, haven't I?"

Helena managed another brief bob and began withdrawing her hand, slowly.

In one swift motion he captured her hand in one of his. The tension thrummed through him full force once more. "And patience should be rewarded, shouldn't it?" Both his dark eyebrows rose above green eyes that strove for innocence but fell far short.

A saying from her governess popped out of Helena's mouth with more speed than planning. "Patience is its own reward."

He laughed, holding her palm against the flat of his stomach so that she felt the vibration deep inside herself. "Helena, look at me."

She did. The naked want in his expression turned her knees to useless joints, unable to hold her upright. She leaned against the bed for support. He wanted to make love to her. And he saw no need to make even a token attempt to hide his desire from her. To him the need was no more than his need to eat, to sleep. Natural. Inevitable.

"Not at my face, Helena. Elsewhere."

Would he believe she didn't know what he meant? No. She closed her eyes, turned her head, and opened her eyes slowly, reluctantly.

His fingers tightened on hers as he asked softly, "What do you see?"

How to answer that? He saw it as well as she; he was not blind. She answered cautiously. "I see a certain . . . elongation."

"Elongation." He paused, his thumb stroking the inside of her wrist. "I have never heard it called such before. I like it. Elongation. Is that what your lover called it?"

She tried to pull her hand away, but he held fast. Angrily, she caught his gaze and held it. "I haven't the faintest idea what my lover called his . . . elongation. Perhaps he had no need to name it."

"No? He never told you his desire for you made him stiff? Hard? Erect?"

"He did not."

"No. Well, he sorely neglected your education then. Did he by any chance teach you any names for that part of a man that . . . elongates?"

"Poker." William hadn't used the term. She'd overheard two of the kitchen maids talking, once, but they'd stopped as soon as they saw her. They'd gone back to their tasks with red-faced giggles, and her anatomy lesson had ended as quickly as it had begun. William had only ever said he wanted her. He needed her. She had not even understood what it was he wanted or needed until it was done.

"Poker." Rand made a face. "I don't care for that one myself. Too stiff." He grinned, and she flushed with heat, first at his crude joke, and then again, more violently, because she had understood it all too well, thanks to his efforts to educate her. "Not to be confused with erect. As your husband, I feel you should know some of the more common names."

"I hardly think—"

He interrupted her. "Some choose to call it cock,

organ, member, rod, staff, even names like peter and willie.''

*Willie.* She shuddered, and glanced at him to see if he'd noticed. He had. To distract him, she asked, ''What do you call yours, my lord?'' The question was hardly out of her mouth before she wished it back.

His grin widened and his eyes gleamed. ''Lord of pleasure, of course.''

The absurdity struck her. She glanced at his . . . member. . . . Yes, that was a good term. ''That? Lord of pleasure?'' She laughed. To her surprise, his . . . member . . . shrank perceptibly before her eyes.

Abruptly, he sat up, his hold on her hand tightening, almost as if he was protecting his . . . lord of pleasure . . . from her. He looked as though she had struck him.

Involuntarily, not understanding what she had done, Helena said, ''I'm sorry. I did not mean to offend you—or your lord of pleasure.'' She struggled to suppress a giggle as she repeated the absurd name.

He exhaled a harsh breath of laughter, and shook his head. ''Call a man's cock anything—except little,'' he said. ''But *never* laugh at it again, unless you're ready for a new lover.''

''Surely no man is that vain that he cannot see the humor . . ?''

''That vain and more.'' His green eyes were twinkling, but she sensed a serious note in his reply, as he reclined against the pillows once again. ''Helena, a woman who understands the extent to which a man's cock controls him can make him do anything.''

''Lust is so powerful, then?'' Perhaps that was

why her sister's husbands were so willing to please their wives? But no, time had amply proven there was more than lust joining them; there was love. As there had not been between William and her. As there was not between her and Rand.

She examined her husband, trying to see beyond the handsome exterior to the heart that beat somewhere inside him. "Lust can toss common sense out the window, I suppose." She shook her head, sadly, understanding what he had left unsaid. "Only for a brief time, though."

He tightened his hold on her hand and pulled her toward him relentlessly, until her face was perilously close to his. "A brief, sweet time. As I hope to show you, Helena." A swift glance confirmed for her that his member had elongated once again.

She closed her eyes, waiting for him to . . . what? Kiss her? Throw her to the bed and thrust himself into her? What did a husband do when he wished to make love to his wife? She waited for him to do something to force her hand.

But he did not. Nor did he ask of her what she had expected. His voice low and deep, he said, "Let me undress you tonight, Helena. As you have undressed me."

"But—" Her objections all seemed foolish, even to her. After all, she had undressed him the last six nights and nothing untoward had happened besides pleasant kisses. He would not hurt her; she was almost sure of it.

A soothing note in his voice, as if he sensed her fear, he bargained with her. "I will leave your shift on."

A shift hardly seemed enough protection from the heat and want vibrating from his needy body. "I don't—"

He sat up and swung his legs off the bed, pulling her toward him again so that she stood between his knees. Her hand gripped his muscled thigh for balance for a scant second before she pulled away and instinctively stuck her hand behind her back. He only smiled a lazy smile and shook his head. "I let you take my clothes off. Fair's fair."

"You *let* me?" As if he had given her a gift, the conceited man. He hadn't even given her a choice.

"Are you saying you didn't enjoy disrobing me and studying the human form?" His eyes shone with amusement even as they dared her to lie.

He couldn't know how much she had come to look forward to the clearing of the dinner dishes and the beginning of their sessions, could he? Had she been that obvious? She had been careful to protest she was too tired each night so that he would not know how she loved to look at him lying nude on the bed. How she loved to sketch him. She flushed. Surely he couldn't realize—

As if he understood the thoughts churning within her, he pressed his point. "Fair's fair, my love. Let me act your maid."

He could be relentless when he wanted something; she knew that well enough by now. "You'll only take my clothes off? Nothing more?" She searched his face for signs of a trick.

"Your virtue is safe with me, my lady." His voice was smooth and deep with sincerity. But other parts of him indicated she might not be wise to put all her faith in his words. After all, they both knew she had lost her virtue some time ago.

"Very well." How could she object? She knew what he wished to do to her, and having her clothes taken off couldn't be worse than that.

He rose from the bed, brushing against her as

he did so. She stepped back so hastily that she would have fallen if he did not catch at her shoulders. "Careful," he murmured.

"I think it must be too late for that," she replied, almost but not quite under her breath.

She stood stiffly as he unfastened her bodice and slid it from her shoulders. He bent to press a kiss to each shoulder and she shifted restlessly beneath his hands. "You smell like a treat," he murmured.

"I smell like orange and cinnamon," she answered, shrugging away his kisses. "That is the scent of the soap I use."

"A sweet treat." As if compelled by her scent, he rubbed his rough cheek along her back, from shoulder to shoulder.

Her skirt and petticoats were a simple affair to remove. She would have stepped out of all of them at once, but he stopped her from helping. "No, let me."

First he bent to remove the overskirt, lifting each ankle as if she could not do so alone. His hand was gentle and warm as it lingered for a moment longer than necessary. Involuntarily, heat flooded through her as she recalled the day she had gone to his room to jilt him and ended up . . . Was this a weakness in her? If so, she should no doubt be grateful she had a husband to keep her from outright disgrace.

He rose to stand before her, slowly, his hands skimming along her calves, her thighs, her hips, and took the measure of her waist with his hands. Unfastened another petticoat. Skimmed it down her hips, her thighs, lifted her feet one by one to free the froth of material.

She grabbed his hands as he stood to repeat the process with the next petticoat. "I have three of

these; must you take all night?'' She prayed he
would not notice that she had forced the words
through a dry throat.

"What else is there to do?'' he asked, kissing the
tops of her breasts where they showed above her
corset, as if he had just noticed them. She pushed
him away.

After the petticoats, he unlaced the corset, slowly
releasing her breasts from their confines so that
they lay firm and defined beneath the thin lawn
of her shift.

Standing behind her, where she felt most vulnerable to him, he dropped the corset to the floor and
pulled her against him. She thought she should
protest when he rubbed his palms over the curve
of her hips, her waist, and then up over her breasts.
Her ears pounded with the rising of her blood,
and she felt dizzy as he continued his caresses, all
the time holding her against him, breathing heavily
into her ear. She should tell him to stop. But she
did not.

His hands lingered at her breasts, shaping and
smoothing, stroking with a gentle pressure on her
nipples. William had liked touching her breasts,
too. But Rand's gentle hands made William's
almost painful kneading seem like mauling to her
mind. How had she ever . . ? She could not think
of that now. Not with Rand's warm lips kissing her
neck, her shoulder, her ear—anything he could
reach with his mouth.

The desire to return his caresses grew wildly
inside her. But something held her back. Fear? She
had nothing to be afraid of. He was her husband
now. Even as he touched her she realized that she
had accepted him, though she could not say when
it happened. Perhaps when he lay obediently still

for her as she sketched. Or when he said she had talent. Maybe she had even been fool enough to accept him when he courteously saw her home, the night she had gone to his rooms dressed as a man.

Her conscience nagged at her. She knew he wanted to go further than a few kisses tonight. She could feel the tension thrumming through him everywhere he touched her. Could feel the press of his erection in the small of her back. But coward that she was, she did nothing to give him what was, in all truth, his due. He had been patient, more patient than she would have been willing to wager on.

After a measureless time, he sighed in her ear once, and then again. Languidly, he lifted her into his arms and carried her to the bed. She went willingly enough and snuggled next to him as he followed her onto the well-stuffed mattress. With a sigh she rested her head against his shoulder.

"You are driving me mad," he muttered under his breath as he drew her close. As he spoke, she turned so that his mouth was near and he kissed her. He meant only a light kiss, to bid her good night, as he had done each night they traveled.

But tonight, after the sensual assault she had suffered, the touch of his lips flared through her once, then again, like streaks of lightning, and suddenly all her fear burned away. Desire was the only emotion left. Desire for her husband, for the wicked earl. For Rand. She deepened the kiss, daring to touch a teasing tongue to his lips.

He groaned and broke the kiss, pushing her away. "That is enough patience for tonight." He rolled away from her with another small groan and tossed the covers over her.

Helena followed him, her arms going around his neck to prevent him from leaving her. "Don't." Her protest was a faint murmur, but her mouth found his neck. His ear.

To her satisfaction, his arms came around her and his mouth closed in upon her ear. After one kiss he offered what she knew well enough was all that kept him from making love to her. "You are indisposed."

"I am not," she murmured against his lips. "I lied." His mouth fell open under hers and she touched her tongue to his.

Rand wasted a moment in utter astonishment. Although, he supposed, having Helena's tongue teasing his, even if he did not respond, could not be considered a waste. *She had lied.*

He wanted to kiss her. He did kiss her, deeply, with the need that had been building within him for days. Thankfully, she did not protest at the ferocity of his passion. He could no more have released her than she could have sprouted wings and a tail and tried to fly from him. "Why?" he whispered, though he did not care. It was enough to know that he need not stop at the gates tonight.

She offered no excuses, only the truth he had already known. "I was afraid."

"Don't be. I won't hurt you."

Her fingers traced the scar low on his belly and her mouth nuzzled his neck. He knew her need had overcome her fear when she moaned softly, and said, "I don't care if you do."

His patience at an end, Rand nudged a place for himself between her knees and ignored her frantic hands as he teased each breast in turn with his fingers, his lips, his tongue. When her hands stopped their fluttering protest and settled on his shoulders in encouragement, he rubbed the head of his shaft against her, teasing, sliding, almost but not quite entering.

Not until she moved her hips under him restlessly did he allow himself the pleasure of pressing into her slowly, deeply. Buried inside her at last, he took her mouth and kissed her deeply.

Her hands stroked from his back to his thighs; her hips rose under his. He allowed her to set the rhythm of their movements as he pulled slowly away and then pushed back in, teasing a gasp from her. He lifted his head up to gaze into her eyes, satisfied to see an unfocused haze of building passion. "What are you doing to me?" she murmured.

As he watched her, her hands traveled upward, over his shoulders, skimming his neck and jaw. Her fingers traced his lips and she pulled his head forward and kissed him with an abandonment he willingly returned tenfold.

She turned her head aside, gasping for breath. "Now I see why they call you the wicked earl," she said, and her hands tightened on his neck, demanding wordlessly that he kiss her again. Without warning, she increased the tempo of her movements, bucking her hips against him.

Caught by surprise, he lost control and found himself plunging against her in a frantic rhythm, his breath harsh in his throat. He felt his climax begin, knew it was coming too soon for her, but he was past the point where he could halt the sweeping pleasure of his own release. All he could do was hang on for the ride until he lay gasping for breath into the pillow under her head.

For a moment Rand lay stunned and disbelieving. He had never lost control of himself before. "I'm sorry, my love," he whispered when he could speak again. "Sometimes patience is not its own reward."

Aware that he made a heavy weight, he rolled away from her, feeling the onset of the drugging sleep that always followed sex for him. Fighting the lethargy, he pulled her into the shelter of his arms just as she said, "Don't be sorry, my lord. You didn't hurt me at all."

His last thought before sleep overtook him was that he should perhaps thank her lover, whoever he was, for being a singularly clumsy clod.

# Chapter Ten

Helena lay in the circle of his arms, comforted by the steady rise and fall of his chest as he slept. So. It was done. The experience had been nothing at all like it had been with William, which should not have surprised her.

The earl was a renowned rake. William, the cad, was a mere shadow lover compared to Rand Mallon, who seemed to live for his next amusement, be it at cards, on the back of a fast horse, or in bed. There was no good reason for her be unsettled by the fact that she had almost forgotten herself in his arms.

Almost, but not quite. Still, the fear that had made her hesitant was gone, finally. She didn't even remember now what she had been so afraid of. Perhaps it had not been the intimacy of their bodies, but of their hearts. That was the danger in marrying a rake, she knew. Apparently even a rake who had made plain that he wished no part of love.

How effortless it would be to confuse the uncomplicated physical intimacy he had shared with her with something deeper and more lasting. Such as love. She knew she would fall in love with him too easily. She was half in love with him already, and had been since his reckless, laughing courtship of Rosaline had begun. If she were to be honest, William had been a distraction from her forbidden attraction to her sister's future husband. She had given him her heart so easily, perhaps in hopes he would keep it safe from the earl.

Fortunately—this time—only her body, not her heart, had been stirred by the pleasant feel of him moving against her, kissing her, the pulsing flow of his seed when he reached his release. But for how long would that hold true? For how long could she guard her heart against a man who had the devil's own ability to tempt her?

She wasn't certain why he had apologized at the last. He had done what was necessary to get his heir, and more. He had taken care not to hurt her, to please her. Indeed, she had found the act unsettlingly enjoyable, which prompted the hope she was soon expecting a child. For every sensible bone inside her warned that too much time spent with him like this would leave her vulnerable to giving away her heart foolishly again.

She watched the even rise and fall of his chest. How easily he slept. Did that mean he had done this so many times, with so many other women that it no longer affected him deeply, as it had her? Was she a fool to wish he would wake and make love to her again?

Restless, her thoughts churning, she rose from the bed and threw on her dressing gown. To give her heart to William, who had at least proclaimed his love for her—false though it was—had been an understandable mistake.

She took up her sketchbook, fiddled with the shape of Rand's bent knee and then switched to a clean page. She glanced up at her husband—sleeping deeply, his eyes closed, his dark lashes fanning his cheek, and began to sketch. To give her heart to Rand, who had made it clear he would never see her as more than a convenient amusement as well as a handy way to obtain his heirs—that would be disaster.

The dawn light woke him and a pleasant rush of memory caused him to turn over to embrace Helena. Her side of the bed was empty. He sat up, panicking for a moment that his lovemaking had sent her back to her family in tears. She had been afraid enough to lie, after all. And he had been as clumsy as a boy at the last.

He was halfway to the door when he saw her. She was curled in the chair by the fire, her sketchbook open on her lap. Her arm hung down limply by her side. Her dressing gown gaped open just enough to reveal the swell of a breast. Asleep.

He approached cautiously, hesitant to wake her. Would there be tears? Had she been afraid to stay in the bed with him, for fear he might wake up wishing for another bout with her? Was she disappointed in him? He wasn't entirely sure he wanted the answer to those questions.

As he approached, he saw what she had been sketching as he lay in an exhausted slumber. Him. She had only managed to capture his face and shoulders in any detail. His body was suggested by a few strokes of the pen. But his face. Did she truly see him like that? She had called him the wicked earl last night, but she had drawn him here with an almost innocent grace. He leaned in to examine the work more closely, inadvertently brushing against her shoulder.

She woke with a leap, clutching her sketchbook to her breast as if she feared someone would wrest it from her arms. She relaxed when she saw him. "Rand."

He settled himself in the chair opposite hers. "If you find the chair so comfortable you wish to spend the night in it, you have only to tell me, Helena, and I will have the landlord send it on ahead of us to Parsleigh."

She rubbed her neck and massaged her arm alternately. "No, thank you, my lord. I wanted to capture something—" She gestured to the sketchbook, but closed it before he could examine her drawing of him any further. "I must have fallen asleep."

She stowed the sketchbook and pen in her basket and stood to stretch her cramped muscles, oblivious to the view she gave him of her breasts straining against the thin silk of her dressing gown. She turned to smile at him, and the welcome in her eyes took his breath away. "I much prefer the bed, Rand. I will be glad enough to leave these chairs behind."

Apparently, then, last night had been more successful than he'd believed. He moved behind her and massaged her shoulders and neck until she leaned in abandon against him, murmuring her approval. He rubbed his unshaven cheek against her sleep-cramped shoulder.

Recognizing a golden opportunity when it was presented to him, Rand slid his hands down the silk, warm from her body. The swell of her hip gave way to the curve of waist, which led to a swell of breast. She offered no complaint, so he unfastened the tie that held her dressing gown closed and slipped his hands inside. To his astonishment, she turned to him, putting her face up to be kissed.

He obliged her willingly, gratified but wary of the change. After a moment he took her face in his hands and looked into the deep blue eyes focused on him. "I have a different wife today, it seems. I know for certain that Ros is on her way to America. Were there perhaps three identical sisters and you are the third?"

"Would you wish for that?" Beneath the openness was still caution, he saw. He could hurt her with the wrong words. So he said nothing, simply kissed her again and carried her to the bed. This morning there would be no excuse to deny her the full measure of satisfaction she deserved.

He began by kissing her toes, watching her eyes change from self-conscious enjoyment to wanton arousal as he moved his attentions upward, slowly. He used all the means at his disposal—fingers, tongue, teeth, lips, breath—to inflame her, determined to see her climax come before his own this time.

When she was ready for him, he teased himself inside her, almost languidly, pleased with the way her hips moved restlessly beneath his. He would have been willing to wager she was on the edge of her own climax, ready to go over with a little more tender attention from his fingers and lips. Attention he was more than happy to give her.

But then she tensed beneath him, not from pleasure but from fear. "The maid," she whispered hoarsely against his shoulders. She would have pushed him away from her in a panic of modesty, but he held her close with one arm while he reached swiftly to pull the covers over them. The rocking motion of his movement drove him deeper inside her until he wanted to groan aloud.

He stilled her gasped protest with a hard kiss and a warning. "Lie quiet. The girl will assume we are simply sleeping."

Lying motionless, locked together, under the covers, they listened to the maid sweep the grate, lay new coals, and light them. Every task seemed to take a thousand years to Rand, who only wanted to finish what he had started. Helena gripped him tightly with both her hands and her thighs, as if she feared he would rear up and begin to plunge into her like a reckless stallion, despite the shock such an action would give the unwitting maid.

Rand gritted his teeth, trying not to move, knowing he had a relative innocent in his bed. The interruption might have been the opportunity for a heightened encounter, if Helena were less new to the experience of lovemaking. But she was not. The maid worked slowly to set out the cold breakfast they had ordered yesterday. He could feel his bride's fevered arousal cool as, no doubt, her embarrassment grew.

Damn. He would not have her disappointed this time. To fan the embers to heat once again, he rocked his hips against her in tiny motions, sliding ever so slightly away and back again. Not enough motion to catch the maid's eye, but enough, he hoped, to remind his wife that they had business yet to finish.

Her breath caught and her hands clutched his hips as if she would stop him, which only served to press him even deeper. He laughed soundlessly in her ear. Closed his eyes against the desire to ignore the maid's presence. Against the burgeoning desire to drive himself into his wife until she understood what it was to make love to the fullest.

He moved his fingers, slowly, determined to find the nubbin that would restore her cooling ardor. As he reached the sensitive bud and rubbed gently, she clenched around him, in surprise or protest he could not tell. He risked a low whisper. "Don't move."

But his warning came too late. She clenched around him once more, more forcefully this time. No matter what had compelled her movement, his control shattered and his own climax flooded over him in an inexorable rush. The effort to remain silent and still against the force of his desire to move nearly killed him. But he managed. Barely.

He collapsed slackly onto Helena, unable to support his own weight. As the sound of the blood rushing in his ears receded, he heard the door shut behind the maid. He groaned. Cursed girl. Why couldn't she have been a few minutes quicker?

Helena heard the sound of the door shutting out the maid and let out a rush of breath she hadn't realized she'd been holding. "How could you?" She released her sadly ineffectual grip on Rand's hips and pushed his heavy body away from her.

"I am sorry, Helena." He didn't look nearly as repentant as he should have been, lying there sated and drowsy-eyed. "I wanted you to find your pleasure before me." He shrugged laconically, his dimple flashing. "But . . . you moved just so . . ."

"My pleasure?" She was furious with him. So furious that she could barely control her temper. How dare he fall asleep as if he had done nothing wrong. "Is that all you can think of when that maid is no doubt telling the entire inn what we . . . you . . . were just doing. What of my humiliation?"

He came alert, at last. "You're only angry because I brought you so close to release before the maid interrupted us." He reached for her. "Let me see to your needs and you'll find yourself in a much better mood."

She twisted away from his grasp and landed lightly on the floor. "My only need is to be fully dressed before she returns to bring us hot tea."

He made no move to follow her, to her relief. He merely coaxed in his drattedly seductive voice, "Come back to bed, Helena. When I show you what that slug of a girl interrupted, you will no doubt demand the landlord fire her."

"She interrupted nothing, you lummox. Or have you forgotten? If so, may I assure you that you were not in the least inhibited by her presence."

"You cannot hold my climax against me, Helena. I did not will it." His grin crinkled the skin around his eyes. "Indeed, I promise you, I fought against it valiantly."

"She was in the room." The thought still sent a numbing wave of dread through Helena. What if one of them had made a noise and the maid decided to investigate. She shuddered.

"I'm certain she thought us soundly sleeping." He smiled, as if he remembered his sin quite without shame. "We hardly moved, you had such a hold on my hips, Madam Propriety. You cannot shift all the blame to me when it was your own sweet muscles tightening that sent me over the edge."

"You touched me!" And that touch had sent a shock of sensation coursing through her that clenched every muscle in her body tight. "With the maid in the room, you touched me—" Helena had no words for what he had done. "She could have seen."

"Seen what?" The little repentance he had shown earlier disappeared. Most likely it had not been in the least bit sincere. "Our covers lifting and rising? No doubt she has seen patrons coupling without the benefit of cover in her service here." He sat up and swung his legs over the edge of the bed, apparently accepting that he would not get her back into the bed this morning. He grumbled, "Not everyone has your ability to cool so quickly."

Stung, she replied acidly, "Or yours to boil over with a stranger in the room." Did he speak from experience when he said the maid had likely walked in on people unashamedly coupling in the past?

"I have never done so before," he admitted, quashing the little seed of suspicion that had begun to take root. "And it is certainly nothing I intend to boast about."

She went cold. "You wouldn't dare tell anyone—would you?" She would never tell a soul, not even Ros.

"It would make an amusing story. . . ."

"Rand! You cannot mean that. I would never be able to show my face in public again."

"I am only teasing, Helena. Your secrets are safe with me." His green eyes narrowed and focused on her, and she saw that beneath his amusement was a touch of embarrassment at what he had done. "I don't know why I—" He paused to look at her accusingly. "Perhaps if my wife had not kept me at bay for nearly a week with a lie."

So it was her fault he could not control himself?

Helena snapped, "Two days." And then, when he grinned at her again, wished she hadn't admitted that particular fact to him.

"See? The whole episode is entirely your doing. I am innocent of everything except wanting to see you reach your own climax." There was a look in his eye that warned her he had not yet entirely given up on that ridiculous notion.

"You have no need to see to my climax, my lord. I have lived perfectly well without one all these years, I can do so for many more."

"Spoken like a woman who does not know what she is giving up." His eyes had begun to warm again. "I suppose this is another area of which your lover saw fit to keep you ignorant. Climax. Orgasm. The moment when pleasure takes you over the edge of reason into a new world of sensation."

"Is that how you convince women to come to your bed without benefit of marriage?" she scoffed. "Telling them a fairy story about this new world of sensation? Please. I am your wife. You do not need to coax me to your bed. It is my duty—except, in the future, when there is another person in the room."

His mouth opened for a moment in surprise. "Helena, do you think I am lying to you? As an excuse for . . ." He shook his head. "I am not."

Perhaps if she had not lied . . . Helena had the feeling that if she argued with him much longer, she would find herself back in bed beside him. She sighed. The maid had likely thought them sleeping, and if she had seen anything it would have been only, as he said, the covers moving.

She held up her hands in surrender. "Very well, Rand. You are not lying. There is a world of sensation for me to discover. Everything that has happened is my fault. The maid knows nothing of what you were about. Now, please may I get dressed?"

He stared at her silently, as if he might refuse her request.

She added impatiently, "I'm sorry I lied about my indisposition for two days. I was silly to be afraid. After all, that is the reason we married—to have a child."

"True." The heat in his eyes banked at her reminder, to her relief. He rose without another word and began to dress. "We are fortunate, then, that even an inconvenient maid cannot prevent me from going to stud."

Helena ignored his pique, afraid that they would begin an argument about climaxes and orgasms again. What kind of foolish women did he associate with, who would believe such claptrap? Even William had known better than to suggest such an unlikely possibility to her. She struggled into her shift and stared helplessly at her corset. She would have to call the maid. The same maid who—"I don't know how I'll face the girl this morning, when she helps me dress."

He answered curtly, as he tucked in his shirttails and fastened his trousers. "Then don't call her."

Helena looked at the corset, which laced in the back. "I cannot manage by myself."

His green eyes gazed at her for a moment, as if he didn't understand her dilemma. And then, in a transformation so swift she could not mark it, he grinned, his good humor apparently fully restored. "I undressed you last night. Let me dress you this morning."

"You?" She was doubtful. He was more likely to undress her with all his talk of going over the edge.

He bowed low. "Me, my Lady Propriety."

Only the thought of facing the maid knowing what they had done made her agree. "As you wish."

She thought for certain she would need to call the maid, but he proved to be skillful at dressing a woman. Though he provided service beyond that of maid and venturing into the territory of lover, he was willing enough to accept her firm rejection of his renewed offer to take her to bed and show her what she had missed.

She had a strong suspicion, however, that he was not done with the subject. No doubt it would show itself as one of the lessons he plied her with each day. She thought of how he had taught her to use her tongue when they kissed. As pleasurable as that had been, she had not been in the least afraid of going over the edge of reason. Truly, she thought he spoke arrant nonsense. So why was there a spreading warmth low in her belly when she thought about what he had said?

As they breakfasted, he asked, "Would you care to ride today, rather than travel in the carriage? The journey by horseback would be about four hours."

She hesitated.

"Can you ride?" There was more uncertainty in his voice than she liked to hear. He had no doubt been thinking of Ros, who was an excellent horse-woman.

"I can," she reassured him. "Not as well as Ros, but then, I ride sidesaddle and she does not."

"The day promises to be fair. If you do wish to ride, I will have the horses prepared."

She nodded. "Yes. Do. After so many days' jour-ney, I look forward to an escape from the confines of the carriage.'' On horseback she would not be forced to sit closely beside him for hours, either.

Rand, too, was grateful to escape the rigors of carriage travel. Though his carriage was well sprung and well upholstered, the roads in this part of the country were deeply rutted.

To his relief, Helena proved to be as excellent a horsewoman as she was an artist. They made good time and pleasant conversation as they rode, when they were able. Although he found himself hard-pressed to pay attention to what she spoke of as they approached Parsleigh.

He took her by a path that avoided a view of the main house and came out before the dower house. He stopped his horse when the small house came into sight.

"Is that our home?'' Helena asked.

"The house in which I was born,'' he said carefully, not wanting his bitterness to show.

"My own house to manage.'' Helena could not hide her pleasure at the thought. "Would you mind terribly if I stopped to draw it.'' She looked apologetic, as if she were imposing upon his goodwill. "I'd like to capture it now, at first sight, if you don't mind.''

"I don't mind at all.'' He wouldn't mind if he never stepped inside that house again. But that was something he would not share with his bride. She had a happy family; she would not understand.

# Chapter Eleven

Rand dismounted, glad for the excuse to delay his return home awhile longer. He lifted Helena down from her saddle and helped her find her sketchbook and pen. He spread a blanket for them to sit upon and bowed low to indicate she should make herself comfortable.

Like a child, she sat with her legs crossed, and looked up into his eyes with a smile. "Thank you for indulging me."

"What is a husband for, if not to indulge a wife?" He stretched himself out next to her, enjoying the sun and the breeze on his face. Wishing they could stay like this forever, on the knoll.

Within a moment, his bride was entranced by her own private vision as she tried to capture the essence of her new home on paper. Rand leaned up on one arm, so that he could see both Helena's serious, faraway expression and the sketch forming on the page before her.

He thought how pleasant making love in the grass would be, but when he leaned over to kiss her knee, she slapped him away with an inarticulate protest. He wasn't completely certain she even knew she slapped at her amorous husband and not an insistent insect.

An hour passed before she took a deep breath and put her pen down. He watched as her eyes slowly began to take note of things around her. At last, she remembered he was there and smiled down upon him.

"Did you succeed?" he asked, in no hurry to rise.

She dangled the sketchbook in front of him, to his surprise. "What do you think?"

"I think I could watch you caught in the throes of your muse all day." Soon, he hoped, but did not say, he would see that look on her face when she thought of lovemaking. He sat up and pulled her into his lap for a kiss.

"Someone might see." She came into his arms with a laughing protest, dropping the sketchbook and pen. There was more wary indulgence in her than abandoned passion.

"No one is watching us," he answered, giving up his notion that he might convince her to make love there in the grass. Over her shoulder, Rand looked at the modest dower house as she had viewed it through her innocent eyes. True, the stone facade was plain and weatherworn, but there was a femininity about the place he had not noticed before. No doubt the curved shutters and the matching dormers were responsible for the softening of the boxy stone design. He wondered if some female ancestor had influenced the design of the house when it was built two centuries ago.

Somehow, her sketch had captured the flutter of the lace curtains caught by a breeze at the windows. Her work gave an overall impression of a quiet motherly welcome. Rand felt the familiar bitterness curl inside him and choked it down. His grandfather had indeed had the dower house made ready for them. A most attractive prison, but a prison nonetheless.

Not for much longer, he vowed. Soon, Helena would give him the means to escape. He would never look back.

They walked their horses down to the wide stone entrance. As if to prove he lied, to prove they had been watched, the servants filed out onto the steps to greet them when they were halfway down the knoll.

There were only two staff members to greet them: Mrs. Robson, the housekeeper, and Dibby, the scullery maid. Apparently that was all the staff his grandfather presumed them to need.

"His lordship will expect you to take all your meals up at the main house," Mrs. Robson explained. "No sense having two cooks for just the three of you. But I can fix you some tea, and something light if you wish, milady."

Helena glanced at Rand, and he smiled at her encouragingly. It was her household, now, small as it was. As graciously as any countess he had ever met, she turned to the housekeeper and replied, "That would be splendid, Mrs. Robson. Could you set it out in about an hour? My husband and I will retire to freshen up, first." If he had not seen her hands trembling ever so slightly, he might never have known the effort it cost her to sound the mistress of her own home.

The housekeeper curtsied. "Very good. Would

you like me to show you around after your tea, milady?''

Helena raised a brow in his direction. ''Does that suit you, my lord?''

To have Helena told the history of his life as she viewed the rooms in which he spent his childhood? No. It did not suit him. But he smiled genially, as he nodded to the housekeeper. ''No need to put yourself to the trouble, Mrs. Robson. I'll show my wife what she needs to know.''

''As you wish, my lord.'' Mrs. Robson's hooded eyes showed nothing of whether she was surprised or offended. His grandfather might have chosen her for housekeeper of the dower house for that particular ability. But he had no doubt she had received his message clearly.

The housekeeper curtsied again, and added, ''Griggson arrived day before yesterday, milord. The marquess sent a lady's maid, milady. They await you in your rooms with a hot bath.''

''It will be good to wash the dust of the road off me,'' Helena said, moving slightly toward the stairs and then halting. Evidently she realized that, mistress of this house or not, she did not know where her rooms were.

''I agree, a bath is just the thing.'' He came up beside her, as if he thought her hesitation was to allow him to follow. ''Let me show you to your room.'' He held out his arm, and she took it with a grateful look.

Mrs. Robson called up behind him, ''I have prepared your parents' rooms for you and the new countess, milord.''

''Your diligence should be rewarded, Mrs. Robson.'' Rand tried to ignore the ghosts of his childhood as he walked up the stairs, Helena at his side.

The past could not hurt him; all dangers lay in the present.

Helena stopped at the top of the stairs to give him a perceptive glance. "You do not like it here."

He shrugged. "I left when my parents died. I suppose I have childishly bad memories of the place."

"Well, if we are to live here, you must let me replace those bad memories with good ones."

"Memories cannot be replaced like curtains, Helena." When she looked distressed, he said lightly, "Though I am not averse to making good memories—say of me washing your back in the bath?"

Helena was not to be put off so easily, though. "You should not be unhappy. This is to be our home."

"Your home," he reminded her. "Mine will remain in London, as it has been since I left school."

Her astonishment was palpable, as she stared at him, her blue eyes reflecting dismay. He could see the open warfare carrying on inside her. The wife who wished a less difficult marriage against the honorable woman who had agreed to his marriage terms willingly—more or less.

"My lady." He opened the door to his mother's old room and bowed low, to indicate Helena should enter. The room was as it had been in his childhood. Nothing had changed—not the dark rose wallpaper, the pearl pink curtains, or the subtle scent of dried rose petals that wafted from the room. Nothing had changed, except that the maid waiting anxiously by the door for the countess to enter had probably not been born when his mother lived here.

Helena hesitated, still caught in her private war. But her gaze cleared and she obediently entered the room. The maid curtsied a little clumsily as Helena stepped through the door, glancing at him as though wondering whether to shut the door or not.

He did not follow. He was not yet ready for the wealth of bittersweet memories entering the room would evoke. Perhaps he could convince Helena to change the decor. Surely his grandfather would agree. Redecorating was the kind of thing a wife was expected to do, after all.

His father's room was unchanged as well, except for the presence of Griggson, who had set out clean clothes and shaving gear. "Welcome home, milord."

The dark oak his father had favored in both the bedroom and the study felt oppressive and stifling. Rand loosened his collar. "This is not our home, man," he said sharply. "Never forget that."

"Yes, sir." Griggson had been with him long enough not to question, but his stiff posture was reproof enough. Excellent. First he offended his wife with the truth, now his valet.

Rand sighed. "Help me out of these clothes, Griggson, and into that bath. After I wash a week of travel off me, no doubt I will be my usual charming self."

His valet, wisely, said nothing in reply.

Shaved and bathed, Rand sent Griggson below stairs to polish his boots and see to brushing down his clothing, dusty from the day's travel on horseback.

The man's absence made the room seem suffocating once again. Rand threw open the curtains, thankful that the day was sunny. He opened the window to allow the fresh breeze to mute the scent of leather and lemon oil from the room's recent cleaning.

He wanted to escape. But there was no escape. Not yet. He must bide his time. At least, he reflected, he had Helena to distract him. She had turned out to be a surprisingly pleasant diversion. Had she forgiven him yet for reminding her that he was only a makeshift husband? Might he still have the opportunity to chase away her maid and wash her back himself?

He tried the connecting door between his room and hers, wondering if he would find it locked. Fortunately, he did not. Unfortunately, neither did he find her in her bath. Instead, she sat at her dressing table while her maid went through her trunks. Her back was straight and slim and, from this distance, seemed formidably unbending.

Helena heard the connecting door open and debated whether to turn around and greet her husband or not. She did not know whether she was more upset over his blunt statement that he would live in London, or her own reaction to the idea. After all, as she had reminded herself several times already, he had been clear that their marriage was not to be a typical union.

"I favor the blue," the drafted man said, as if he did not know she was ignoring him deliberately. "The color matches that of your eyes."

Helena indicated one of the gowns that Marie had been holding up for her inspection. "Take the green one to be pressed, Marie. I will wear it this evening."

The maid bobbed a curtsy and shot a frightened glance toward Rand. She carried both gowns away in a death grip, as if afraid Rand might tear them from her and rip them into shreds. Helena shook her head. She was imagining things. No doubt the girl thought to save herself time by pressing the packing wrinkles from them both at once.

Helena decided to acknowledge him. She glanced into the mirror and met his eyes. "Apparently Marie does not think as well of you as most female servants, my lord."

She had expected a grin, perhaps a boast that he would have her in love with him and bringing him sweet rolls from the kitchen before the week was out. Instead, he glanced toward the door and said with an air of remorse, "No doubt she is afraid I will grow impatient with her lack of skill and send her back to the main house."

Surprised, Helena protested, "What would make her think such a thing? You are the most generous of men when it comes to such things. I would turn her off before you would."

He glanced at her and raised his brow nearly to his hairline. "You wouldn't turn her off if she ironed you bald." Still, he did not smile.

Wondering if he would reveal his reasons for his unexpected mood, Helena prodded, "This is a mystery I wish to solve. All the maids as we traveled looked at you as though you were a god."

He said disparagingly, "A god who dispensed coin, Helena. That is all."

"Perhaps." That would not explain the reaction of all the maids in Simon's home, who had followed him with their eyes, neglecting their duties shamefully. Marie's reaction was very unusual. Especially considering that this was his home. Surely the maid should know she had no reason to be frightened of him. "Do you suppose she fears she is in imminent danger of being seduced by the wicked earl?"

"That child?" With a hard glance at Helena, Rand's demeanor shifted again, until he was more as she had expected. "No doubt she has heard my reputation as a great lover. Would that my wife thought so highly of me."

How did he manage to bring all subjects back to this one point of his? "No wonder she twitches at the sight of you. I hardly know you, and I tremble at the thought."

He crossed the room to stand behind her, as if she had invited him to do so, and lifted her arm up to kiss her hand. "You lie. I feel not the faintest tremor." His smile was carefree. "Besides, you know all you need to know of me."

She removed her hand from his grasp. "And what is it that I know of you?"

He knelt before her so that they were eye to eye. "That I am generous enough to offer my wife complete freedom, that I am patient enough to wait two extra days to make love to my bride for her comfort, and that I am the best nude figure you have ever seen posed before you."

"I suppose the last would have nothing to do with the fact that you are the only nude figure who has posed before me?"

He shrugged. "Surely you will not deny that I speak the truth?"

She was sorely tempted to touch his smoothly shaven cheek. But she was still vexed with him. "And have you revealed all there is for me to know of you? Is that why you speak of London when we have just arrived at Parsleigh?"

"Helena—" His look was not unkind, but it held a warning.

She held up her hand. "I know. Our bargain." She examined the room. Her room. "I suppose everything is just so unfamiliar. All my life I have lived with my sisters about me. With Ros. And now—"

A sincere sympathy warmed his eyes. "You miss Ros, I suppose."

"Yes." More than he could imagine. More than she might have imagined. They had never been separated before. And now an ocean divided them.

"So do I," he admitted, as if the idea of missing someone was foreign to him. Somewhat shameful. "You are the only person at Parsleigh who knows her. When you leave . . ."

He stood. "Helena—" He pulled her into his arms a trifle roughly. "I cannot be your sister." He grimaced, tracing her ear with his forefinger. "Indeed, I do not wish to be your sister. However, I understand your need for your family. If you find that you wish to visit your family at any time, tell me."

"My home is here now." Though it was true enough, she said it more to convince herself. The desire to run back to London and throw herself into her sister's arms was overwhelming.

Again, he became serious when she thought he would make a joke. "Your home is wherever you choose it to be, Helena. And if you wish to be with your sisters—even Ros in America, once the child is born—you have only to tell me and I will see it done. Promise me."

"I promise." The child. He spoke with such certainty of the future. What if she, like Miranda, did not conceive? She pushed away the thought and remembered that the reason she need promise such a thing was because he did not want to call this place home. "If you are not in London, carousing."

He grimaced, took her by the shoulders and planted a kiss on the tip of her nose. "If I am in London, darling shrew, send a note to my rooms. Night or day."

She rested her hands on his arms lightly. "You sound as if you imagine I might need to flee in the night."

He laughed, but the muscles of his arms were tense under her fingers. "If you do, you will make a pretty picture in this dressing gown, white silk against the dark of night."

She was certain that he would kiss her. She had begun to recognize all too well that look in his eye that presaged a bout of lovemaking. Only Marie's discreet knock on the door kept him from it.

The maid came in, eyes widening when she saw them in an embrace. "Excuse me, milord. Mrs. Robson says your grandfather asks that you and your milady join him for a drink before the evening meal."

"Thank you, Marie." His charm was as evident as ever to Helena's eyes, but the maid did not respond.

She curtsied again and, staring at a spot on the floor as if it might bite her, said timidly, "If you wish to be prompt, I should begin to dress her ladyship now."

"Of course." As if he thought nothing of the maid's nervousness, Rand stepped back into his room, closing the door behind him.

The girl let out an unconscious sigh of relief and helped Helena out of her dressing gown. She kept a nervous eye on the door that led to Rand's room, though.

"Marie, the earl will not be angry with you for

doing your job. He is a charming man." Helena smiled. "You do not need to be afraid of him."

"Yes, milady," the girl said softly. But she did not seem reassured as she dressed Helena in the freshly pressed gown.

"Oh, milady. There were some clothes in your trunk packed by mistake, I believe. What should I do with them?"

"What clothes?" Helena hoped she had not packed some of Kate's gowns in her haste to pack. If so, her little sister would never forgive her.

Marie brought her a set of Ros's gentleman's dress. Atop sat her next best pair of boots. There was a sealed note peeking from one boot, addressed to her in Ros's hand.

The note, typical Ros, said only:

*My next best armor, for Rand's next best bride.*

Armor. Was that how Ros saw her gentleman's dress? As protection? Protection against . . . what? Being a woman? Helena took the neat bundle of clothes and said, "No, Marie. No mistake."

The girl stiffened in shock. "Surely you do not wear—"

She did not see the need to explain her sister to Marie, who would likely never meet her. "A costume," Helena said. "From a role I played in a family dramatic event."

The maid still seemed shocked. Helena could not but wonder what the girl would have made of Ros, if Rand had married her as he'd first intended. She glanced about the room. Ros had been right to refuse to marry Rand. She would not have been happy here. Even with their bargain. But did Rand recognize that? Or did he detect her wish for a real marriage and regret his impulsive agreement to the switch?

"I keep it for sentimental value." To remember Ros as she had been, and imagine her as the years passed. Rand's offer to send her to America suddenly seemed less foolish. With a sigh, Helena stored the clothing and boots carefully in the trunk at the foot of her bed. Just in case her sister might ever come to retrieve them.

Rand knocked lightly and came through the door before she could grant him entrance. Marie looked frozen to the floor. Helena did not know how to convince the maid that the earl was harmless—at least to servants. Rand gave the girl a sympathetic glance and gestured for her to go, which she did with alacrity.

"Are you ready to enter the lion's den?"

"I am fully armored," she answered, thinking of Ros and the suit of men's clothing in her trunk. Perhaps she should have donned that as protection from the ill feelings that were obvious between grandfather and grandson.

"Good. You'll need to be, or the old goat will eat you with the main dish."

She wished he would not be so disrespectful of his grandfather. But she decided wisdom should keep her tongue still, tonight at the least. When they stepped outdoors, a carriage was waiting. The marquess had sent the best for them, Helena reflected. She paused for Rand to help her up, but he said sharply, "Thank you, Halsey. We will walk."

He said, "You don't mind, do you? It is a beautiful evening." But as his arm was at her back, propelling her away from the startled coachman, she did not feel as if she had a true choice in the matter.

# Chapter Twelve

Another disadvantage to having a wife was that she wished to know her husband, at times much more than he wished to be known. Rand was acutely aware that Helena regarded him closely. So closely that she tripped on a stone in the path and would have fallen if he had not grabbed her up against him.

She was sweet; he loved the feel of her. He loved that he could hold her like this because she was his wife. But he wished she was not nearly so observant of his behavior.

He set her back on her feet. "You should watch the road, Helena, not me."

She merely raised a brow. "I had expected that to be the coachman's job."

Perhaps she was more angry than observant this time, he hoped. "I am tired of coaches after our travel. Do you mind the walk?"

"No." She started off on the path again without

waiting. She spoke without turning back toward him. "I would, in the future, prefer to have you wait for my answer before you make the decision for me."

"Very well." Would she believe him properly chastened if he followed three paces behind her? He caught up to her side and took her arm to halt her. Once she had stopped, and stood facing him, a small frown on her brow, he said, "If I promise you should be the mistress of your own fate, it is only fair that I wait for you to express your desire. I apologize."

"One would think we were going to our hanging rather than to dinner with your grandfather. Really, Rand. Perhaps your relationship with him would be better if you had a less mournful face when you thought of spending an evening with the poor man."

Poor man? "Perhaps you're right. I remember a good evening with him once. I was in a more cheerful frame of mind that night. Perhaps I should force myself to be so again. The trained monkey present that evening might help matters."

Dread was a cold knot in his stomach, even when she laughed in amusement. He was so close to ending his grandfather's games for good. But to succeed he needed to outwit the fox a little longer. Patience had never been his strength.

He trusted Helena to please the old man. She was everything a wife should be: pleasant, soft-spoken, kind . . . He made her sound a saint. If only the old man thought so. Maybe the next few weeks would not be unbearable.

As they approached the house, he felt the dread deepen and slowed his steps. Deliberately, when Helena glanced at him in concern once more, he made himself move at his normal pace. One consolation was that the food would be good. He only hoped they could plead exhaustion from their recent travel in order to escape the ordeal early.

Dinner was as trying as he'd expected.

His grandfather began with the drinks. Turning to Helena with a benevolent smile, he asked, "What shall you have, my dear? Sherry? I know Rand will have a brandy. A double. He appreciates fine brandy. Just not the obligation to drink it with discrimination."

"Sherry will be fine, my lord." Helena's expression indicated that she knew she would need the fortification of spirits if she wished to survive the evening.

She was nervous, he realized, watching her careful movements. Hearing the tremble of her voice. The tremor of her hand as she held her sherry.

"How was your travel?" The old man was watching her closely. "Not too exhausting, I hope."

"No. We traveled only six or seven hours a day."

"I prefer to do it all in a hard go, myself." He glanced between them. "Not so soft as the younger generation."

Helena flushed, obviously feeling rebuked.

"We chose to travel more easily, Grandfather." Rand had planned to be more discreet than usual, for the first few days of Helena's arrival. He hated throwing an innocent in the middle of their ongoing war.

But seeing his wife blush with shame over not traveling until exhaustion turned her gray and her bones ached from being jostled in the coach, he discarded that plan. "I needed my energy for the nights, Grandfather. After all, we want an heir as speedily as possible, do we not?"

He nodded to his wife, as if he had said nothing more than could be considered conversationally polite. He knew he danced a fine thread—if the old man understood the nature of the game he was playing, all was lost. But playing the game at all could mean hurting Helena, and Rand did not want to do so—at least, not more than he feared would become necessary.

"So, you did not want to ride hard, in the desire to get to work producing my great grandchildren, eh?" His grandfather trained his most penetrating gaze on Helena, apparently deciding she was the weaker of the pair.

Helena replied numbly, "That was our hope, my lord."

Rand laughed. "I wouldn't say we were afraid of hard riding—we just did not do all our hard riding in the carriage. Wouldn't you agree, my dear?"

"How could I argue with you, my lord?" Her eyes were focused on his chin as she replied.

Rand wished he could do battle without touching Helena. He hated to see her embarrassed. But that could not be helped. If his grandfather sensed that he wished to spare his bride, he would only make things more unpleasant for her in the end.

"So, you've finally taken a bride and started a serious campaign for children." The old man wore a genial smile, as if he were pleased. Rand supposed the smile was to fool Helena. It certainly did not fool him. "I hardly believed it would happen, myself. I thought you'd lose your nerve and jilt the girl at the altar."

"I must admit, the thought crossed my mind," he lied. "But I find I quite enjoy having a wife in my bed."

The old man watched Helena like a hawk, even

as he baited Rand, once again comfortably settled into their old pattern of verbal warfare. "Might have thought of that while you were out gambling till dawn on your wedding night."

Rand saw Helena's eyes spark with concern that he might reveal her indisposition. She knew him disconcertingly well, he reflected. What had Ros told her of the wicked earl? She had sworn to him that she had spilled none of his secrets to Helena. He hoped she had not lied.

He said, instead, "My bride was shy. I wanted to give her time to adjust to me—which she has done quite nicely." He winked at Helena, who choked back an astonished cry. "I wouldn't be surprised to have a son in nine months' time."

The marquess frowned in warning. "Perhaps you ought to be wise, boy—don't count your chickens too soon."

"I'm not counting chickens, Grandfather. I'm counting months."

His grandfather glanced at Helena, but addressed Rand. "I hear the duchess is barren."

"She and the duke have not yet been blessed with children," Helena interjected stiffly. "But my brother Valentine has three, and my sisters Hero and Juliet each have one." Loyal little thing, she was. He wanted to kiss her.

"Your sisters have only girls?" The marquess phrased it as a question, but Rand knew the old man had an intelligence network still, from the time he worked for the government as spymaster during the war with Napoleon.

Rand watched the old man examine Helena. He was all kindly solicitousness. No doubt he knew the names, ages, and foibles of each member of Helena's somewhat notorious family.

Helena bristled. "They each have a daughter. But they have been married only a short time."

Rand poured himself another brandy. "Nothing wrong with girls, Grandfather. They liven a place up with all their chatter, and they smell nice, too."

His grandfather seemed disappointed in his comment. "A boy is necessary—"

"Yes." A boy. A son and heir. No man should be without one. "And I *will* have a son."

"You cannot be certain," his grandfather said, green eyes narrowing. Rand braced himself, recognizing what was next. "Even all the bastard sons you've planted don't guarantee you'll have a legitimate one."

Helena started, but said nothing. Rand did not think his grandfather could even see her reaction, hidden as it was by his resourceful bride twitching her skirts away from the fire.

She could not be happy, he knew. But that was unavoidable. "Thank you for reminding me," Rand said, wondering if he would see another of the disadvantages to having a wife once she had him alone. "There is a new one. His mother should be petitioning you shortly."

Helena stared at him openly.

The old man glanced at her sympathetically, as if he had just realized that she was present. He would have made a splendid Falstaff upon the stage. "Sorry, my dear, to shock you." He waved his brandy glass in Rand's direction. "With no ladies usually present, we have grown used to speaking freely with each other."

To Rand he said, "Perhaps we should keep the details of such business away from your wife."

"Not at all," Rand shrugged. "Helena is a sophisticated woman. She is not put off by my peccadillos or she'd not have married me."

"Would you prefer we take this discussion out of your hearing, my dear? I would not want you to think less of your husband." His grandfather phrased the question in such a way that Rand thought Helena might ask them to defer the conversation.

But she said, rather stiffly, "Not at all, my lord. I would not think to criticize my husband's habits, and I could never think less of him."

Rand suppressed the wince that threatened at her words. If she could never think less of him, then he supposed he was quite low in her estimation right now.

The marquess's sharp gaze studied her for a moment. If there was one thing the old man couldn't stand, it was a weakling or a liar. Rand was glad Helena was neither. For the old man would certainly test her. With a harsh look at Rand, he demanded, "You've verified the child is yours?"

"Yes. I had a look at the brat not two weeks ago." Rand was very much afraid to look over and see if Helena had fainted yet. She had not. "Spitting image of the old man."

The marquess had a hint of admiration in his voice when he said, "Eight sons in as many years." There was no quarter in his gaze, however. "Yet a dozen bastards does not guarantee you'll get one true heir on your wife."

"True." Rand could think of only one way to end the conversation, for Helena's sake. "Would you care to make a wager?"

"What?" His grandfather and Helena both stared at him as if he'd run mad.

"A wager," he repeated. "If I have a son within

ten months of my marriage, you will gift me Saladin from your stables."

"You would wager on such a chancy thing?"

"I don't consider it chancy. I have produced nothing but sons so far, haven't I? And my bride is a willing girl with serviceable hips." He avoided looking directly at Helena as he made that comment.

"You are not jesting? You would wager on such a matter with me?" The old man's eyes lit with a love of the game.

Rand shrugged, and tossed down the last of his brandy. It was excellent brandy, just as his grandfather had said to Helena. "I made the wager to all of London a week ago. Why should I not make a similar one with you?"

Helena put her sherry glass down abruptly. But she said nothing.

Even his grandfather seemed flabbergasted by his pronouncement. "You wagered on your own wedding day that you'd have a son within ten months?"

Rand poured himself another brandy, certain that he'd need it tonight, when Helena got him alone. "I did." Perhaps he should head back to London tonight, give her a few weeks to let her temper cool? But then he might lose his bet.

"Fool." The old man's tone wasn't condemning. "I suppose I will be expected to cover those wagers when you lose?"

"Don't you always cover my losing wagers? Wouldn't want to ruin the family name."

"You have a wife now. I thought you'd put these games behind you," his grandfather lied with a straight face. "You are likely to lose this bet."

Rand was relentless. "If you believe so, you must be eager to take me up, then. What can you lose?"

"Saladin. He's a prime Arabian stud. You know his value well enough. But that is only if I lose the wager. What do you put up if you lose your wager?"

*More months under your thumb.* But that went without saying. "What would you consider the equal of Saladin?"

"A gift for your wife, perhaps?" The old man glanced at Helena as he declared, "No more women petitioning me to support your bastards for five years."

Five years? "Done." The price was steeper than Rand had expected. But no matter. He would win the wager. And Helena would not be subject to humiliating conversations about her ability to bear children for some time to come—his grandfather hated to lose a wager.

Folkstone, the butler, announced dinner just then, sparing Rand any need to act as though he were pleased with himself.

He took Helena's arm to lead her into the dining room, and though her gaze was cold, he felt a shudder pass through her. No doubt she was grateful for the call to dinner. Poor girl. She had no idea that drinks had been the warm-up before the true, oh so civilized, hostilities commenced.

Helena readied herself for bed with quiet fury. He had bet on the begetting and birth of their own child as if it were a game. Not only with his grandfather, but with all of London. On his wedding day.

For the first time, she believed he would not have been unhappy if she had been carrying William's child when she married him. To him a boy child was all that was important. Worse, he had told her so, honestly. She had been the fool who did not believe any man could be so indifferent.

She tried to calm herself as Marie helped her off with her gown and unfastened her corset so that she could breathe freely again. She had no real right to berate him, much as she wished to tell him exactly how despicable his behavior had been. However, she could not keep silent if she saw him tonight. She was simply too angry.

And he would come to her tonight. After all, he wanted to win his wager. She sat before her dressing table, and Marie began to work on taking down her hair. Three deep breaths to calm herself. He would come. He had yet to give her the promised daily lesson. In seven nights of marriage he had yet to forget. What would it be today? How to gamble with the lives of those one should cherish?

Marie, her maid, was little more than a child. But she was perceptive enough to know that her mistress was angry about something. Her hands trembled as she took down Helena's hair, pins dropping from her shaky fingers.

Matters did not improve when Rand strode into the room as if it were his own. Marie gasped and dropped the hairbrush she held. He said brusquely, "You may go, girl."

Marie went, hastily, eyes down. Before she was at the door, however, Rand called her back. "Wait."

Marie waited, though it was obvious that she was afraid of what he would say. But, as if he realized suddenly that the girl was terrified of him, he smiled and said softly, "Don't come to the room tomorrow until the countess rings for you."

Helena felt a flush of warmth spread through

her as she realized the implication of his words. "Yes, Marie," Helena added, hoping the girl did not notice anything amiss. "I will ring for you when I need you in the morning."

"Very well, milady," Marie said, bobbing quickly and leaving them alone.

Helena turned to glare at him. He had not even given her the courtesy of a knock. Of course not. He could not risk losing his wager because she refused him entry.

She noted that Griggson had done the honors of undressing his master, and Rand wore only a loosely tied silk dressing gown the same deep green as his eyes. As if he had not shredded her patience and goodwill at dinner, he said with utter nonchalance, "The hour is too late for me to act the model for you. Are you ready for your lesson?"

Helena was tempted to throw a slipper at him. "Which one is this? The lesson in treating my elders as if they are fools? Or using my progeny for wagering?"

He quirked a brow at her and leaned against the door frame of the connecting door as if no longer certain of his welcome. His reply was patience itself—a lesson for a backward child. "I didn't wager my child, Helena. I wagered my personal ability—on how quickly I could father a son."

Exasperation made her speak her mind freely. "You cannot wager on such a thing."

He shrugged. "Tell that to those who wager against me. Tell my grandfather. I didn't hear you chide him for putting up Saladin. He seemed to think wagering one stud against another a fair bet."

One stud against another. Aggravating man. He would not admit he was in the wrong even if he thought so himself. She sighed. "What if I am barren?"

He came forward as if that was all the invitation he needed. His hands were warm upon her neck as he massaged the tight muscles of her shoulders. "You are not."

How was it that he could speak with such authority she could almost believe him. "What if I have a girl?"

"Then Grandfather wins the wager." His gaze was heated as he stared at her reflection in the mirror of her dressing table. "And we must try again."

He bent to press a kiss to her neck. "What does it matter? Surely you will not mind if Grandfather wins and I have to fulfill my part of the bargain."

She choked out the words, determined not to chide him. What he did with other women was surely none of her business. "No more . . . illegitimate . . . children."

"Yes." He smiled bracingly, as if he saw the effort it cost her to be sophisticated about her marriage. "Although, it would chuff Grandfather to know I don't mind that part at all."

"No?" Did she truly want to hear this?

"Why should I?" He knelt down and put his head against her breast, right where her heart was beating distinctly. "I can spend the time making legitimate children with you."

He flicked at the tip of one nipple with his tongue and sent a shiver down her spine. "You must admit, I have yet to complain that making love to you is a chore I wish to avoid."

"No." She traced the curve of his ear with one finger. She knew she should be angry with him. But somehow, he made it impossible. "I begin to think you would keep me in bed all day if you presumed I would agree."

"Indeed." He slipped her dressing gown from her shoulders and let the silk pool about her waist. "When I thought of having a wife, I had not considered how pleasant it would be to retire to a woman already in her nightclothes."

He traced her collarbone with his mouth, warm little kisses that traveled through her in pleasant waves. "I need do no more than walk into your room. No flowers, no wooing, no worry that you will refuse me."

"I am grateful to know that I have made your life so convenient." She put her hand over his mouth, to stop his drugging kisses. "Although, if you truly meant what you said, and I am to have rule of my own life—"

"After the child." He grinned and kissed her palm. "Until then, you are mine to bed at will." He smoothed a stray strand of hair from her face. "Such a thought almost makes me wish that I do lose the bet."

# Chapter Thirteen

His wife was a beautiful woman, Rand realized as he gazed into her expressive face. Anger only served to make that fact more obvious. "Rand." She took his face between her hands and spoke as fiercely as she could. "You cannot wager on such things again."

Beautiful, and determined to reform him, despite their bargain. "Helena, I can bet on anything—whether it will rain on Monday, or the corn will be sweet at dinner." He smiled to soften his words, and she released her hold on his face. "It is my gift."

"Your gift? To wager on—" Her lips parted to reflect her incredulity. "Be serious, Rand. A child is a profound responsibility."

He took both her hands in his own and gazed full into her eyes. "Helena, I have spent my life avoiding the necessity to be serious or to shoulder responsibility. The whole idea seems impossibly bleak to me. Why do you suppose I will change now?"

Flustered by his direct strike, she stammered, "Because you have married, and you intend to begin a family." As if she realized the weakness in her argument in light of their bargain, she added, "All men must shoulder certain responsibilities when they take those steps."

He kissed her fingers, as he said, "But not all men have my brilliant forethought to marry a woman under the express agreement that she will have complete freedom, as will I. We are not going to be a family, Helena. We are going to have a child, and then go our separate ways." She tried to tug her hands away, but he pressed a kiss to each palm before releasing her. "I did not dream your acceptance of my terms, did I?"

"No." She glared at him. Sadly, she was not at all impressed with his forethought. No doubt she wished she had told her sister and the duke the truth—that she had accepted him only because she was afraid she carried her lover's child.

He stood up and kissed the top of her head. "Which means, dear wife, if I care to bet that you will bear me a son within ten months of our marriage, I will. If I choose to wager that my child will have the beautiful blue eyes of his mother, I will do so."

She did not soften at his compliment to her eyes, although the same beautiful gaze looked into her mirror sadly. "Do I not count?"

He closed his eyes against the urge to soften. To explain the game he played. "Why, would you like to put a wager down as well?"

Her answer was sharp. "I mean, does my humiliation at having a public bet made upon the swiftness of my impregnation make a difference to my husband?"

"Helena, what other people think about foolish things should not matter to you." The bet was in London. He wished she had not had to know about it. "It has nothing to do with you."

"No?" She turned to face him as if she needed to see his expression. "Well, then, I suppose I should be grateful that you have decided to leave me here while you frequent London. Otherwise, I should have to bear the stares and whispers of everyone who has heard of the scandalous wager."

"Society turns on such scandal," he said soothingly. "Wagers are made hundreds of times a day in London alone."

Her eyes narrowed and her lips thinned to a fine line until she said explosively, "Not on me!"

"You will be safe in London, should you wish to go there." He did not want to discourage her from leaving Parsleigh if she chose to go. Fear of gossip might keep her here, though. "No one will remark on the wager."

"No? If you are mistaken, I might find myself with those interested parties on either side wishing to measure my waist to see the rapidity with which it increases—or does not."

"I would fight any number of duels to protect the privacy of your waistline, my lady." Rand waved his hand as if to dismiss her argument altogether. But there was something in her distress that made him long for another way to get what he wanted. "I warned you not to try to reform me, Helena."

She prepared herself for another protest, and he stood up and held out his hand to her. "You will get nowhere with this fussing. Come and have your lesson. I am eager to begin."

She did not move, though her shoulders slumped forward in defeat as she glared up at him. Her eyes burned with the light of thwarted reform, and he did not feel safe from her assessing gaze.

He did not think she was done with the subject, but he relaxed slightly when she said only, "Tell me what I am to learn tonight, my lord."

"Tonight I wish to show you the pleasure in having your husband brush your hair until it gleams."

It was a simple enough pleasure, and, as he had hoped, it calmed her temper enough that she did not refuse to join him in his room. In his bed. She did not, however, warm up to him enough that he could bring her to climax.

And afterward, as he drifted into a satisfied sleep, she climbed out of his bed and went to her own. It was the first time he had fallen asleep alone since they married. He found he missed her more than he liked.

He managed to find excuses to put off an investigation of the dower house for nearly a week. He showed her the gardens, the stables, a fishing stream, rode out with her to the nearby village. He pointed out a dozen scenes worth capture by her talented eye. And always she watched him, as if she wondered why he could show her the world outside the house and not the few rooms within.

But at last he could put it off no longer. As they took a light breakfast in the parlor, she said, "I have asked Mrs. Robson to take me through every room in the house, since you find the chore too unpleasant to manage."

"The house is small enough." He sighed. "Have you not seen it all by now?"

She stared at him implacably. He knew her well enough to know she would not be put off any longer.

He thought of what Mrs. Robson could tell her, and sat back, glancing around the parlor, remembering. "My parents moved here after their marriage."

"Just as we have done," she remarked encouragingly.

He shuddered, hoping they were not doomed to the same fate as his father and mother. "They quickly added me to the family."

"Within ten months?" She smiled.

"Eight, actually." He thought of his parents for the first time as a young, eager, and passionate couple. It was truly disconcerting. "That is my mother." He pointed to the portrait above the mantel behind him. "And that is my father." He pointed to the portrait that hung over the matching fireplace at the other end of the room.

He didn't care for the discerning gaze trained on him. "What a tragedy that they died so young."

"Yes." A tragedy he did not want to revisit. But it was impossible to avoid it here. He had shared these quarters with his parents in his earliest years.

While Helena studied the portrait of his mother as if she might pull the secrets of his past from the image, he thought of the evenings Nanny Bea would bring him down fresh from his bath for a visit with his parents—when they were not traveling. He had tried to be the very best boy he could, so that his mother's eyes would shine with love and his father would pat his head proudly.

His mother would hug him, give him a peppermint, and he would go away happily to bed, the scent of verbena and lemon still with him. That had all ended when his parents had been killed and he and Nanny Bea had gone to the big house to live with his grandfather.

Rand rose, restless. He would give her a short tour and a heavily edited story of his childhood. Every room had memories he could not escape. Even the entry hall, with the chipped marble tile. He had done that himself in a childish fit of curiosity.

"However did you make such a gouge?" Helena murmured.

He could not help the grin that spread across his face. "With my mother's favorite diamond ring. In order to test my father's assertion that diamonds are precious because they are the hardest substance in the world."

"Whatever did she do to you?"

"She kissed me and said I was not to indulge my curiosity with her valuables again." Restless at the memory, he moved up the stairs, Helena trailing behind. "And then she showed me how the diamond would carve my initials in the mirror above her dressing table."

"Do you suppose your initials are still there?"

"I don't know."

Nothing would do but that they check. The delicate engraving, hidden by a bottle of scent, brought back a flood of memories he struggled to suppress as his finger pressed against the flourish that finished the R.

"R P M." Helena bent, to peer closely at the faint but distinct initials. "Randolph Philip Mallon." She traced the letters. "She must have loved you very much."

She said it as if to love him was a good thing. He could not bear to disabuse her of the notion. Tracing the delicate bones exposed by the arch of her neck, he said, "Enough of this room. Come into the master's bedroom and I will give you an intimate tour, beginning with the bed itself."

She shook her head and escaped out into the hallway. "We should save that room for last, my lord. I have a feeling that any time spent there will leave you wishing for a nap."

Recognizing that he would be better off indulging her, he followed with a laugh and briefly recited the purpose of each room as they climbed up all the way into the attics where he had ruled as a boy.

Feeling that his indulgence should be rewarded, Rand captured her in the dark and dust of the attic and, amid the discarded furnishings of decades past, drew her to him. "Now, I think it is time for us to return to a close and thorough inspection of the bedroom where the lord and master rests."

"As you wish," she said meekly.

Feeling jubilant that the reward for his patience was at last at hand, he led her swiftly down the stairs. But then, just as he thought he had eluded the worst of his fears, Helena asked, "Is there a nursery, or a place for children, if and when we have them?"

He said curtly, "Yes."

He would have continued to his room, his bed, his well-deserved reward. But she stood still, stubbornly and silently questioning his swift change of mood. He kissed her, hoping that she would forget her question.

She sighed. "The nursery first, my lord." So he took her down the small, easily overlooked hallway that he had hoped she would assume was a little-used closet, and into the three rooms in which he had spent his first five years.

He steeled himself for a view worsened by neglect and the passage of time. The blow was greater, he found, when he saw that time had not touched the room. Everything remained unchanged—no, worse—everything in the nursery, from the oak cradle to the birchwood horse and carriage had been refurbished, polished, and left like new.

The nursery was exactly as it had been the day he left this house. Rand struggled to maintain his calm as Helena moved freely about the rooms, exclaiming in delight over each new discovery. He would not have her know his distress. She would only ask why, and he could never tell her. Never.

She returned to him after what seemed like hours but could only have been minutes. She smiled up at him, oblivious to the blind panic that surged inside him. "Our children will be happy here."

"No doubt." He took her hand and moved toward the door. Toward escape. He hoped to get a child quickly. He could not spend much more time here.

Helena paused before they reached the doorway, ignoring Rand's impatient pull. Why had he hesitated to show her these rooms? They were perfect. She took one more look at the rooms her children, if she were fortunate, might one day romp in. The only change she planned was removing the heavy drapes that kept out the natural light. Raising her child in such a bright, airy, welcoming set of rooms would be wonderful.

If there was a child, she cautioned herself. Wagers and open speculation made her wary to assume that Rand's plans would go as sunnily as forecast. She smiled at him, and squeezed his hand as she rocked the oak cradle gently.

She was not insensitive to Rand's distress, but she could not understand the reason behind it. After all, having a child was the very reason they were married. A nursery was not a torture chamber.

And even if he were the kind of man to prefer his children bathed and brought down only for a kiss at night, an empty nursery should not make him weak in the knees. She wanted to share her own delight in planning for a coming child. Wanted to know that the child was more than a means to an end for him.

How awful for a child to be nothing more to its father than a pawn. "Perhaps I should finish my sketch of the dower house. We could hang it on one of these walls for our children."

To her surprise, he showed the first sign of delight she had seen in him all day. "Excellent idea. I will have Dibby run up to the main house and beg provisions for a picnic from the cook."

"Sometimes you surprise me," was all she could manage to say. The transformation in his demeanor was truly startling.

They spent a pleasant time on the knoll above the house. The cook had packed for them cheese and bread, cold chicken, olives, little iced cakes and a flask of wine—but no glasses.

"No matter," he said when he noticed the lack. "We can share." He took a drink from the flask, and tilted it up over her mouth so that she could drink as well. She had the definite sense that he meant to share more with her than wine.

He watched indulgently when she sketched. Every so often he would insist she take a new drink of wine, but he did not kiss her. She knew he was disappointed that she left his bed each night after they made love. But the safety of her heart required such a move. Just as she resisted his attempts to get her to climax. Even if it were possible for some women to do so, she did not think she was one of them.

Unfortunately, her resistance seemed only to encourage him further. Perhaps she should pretend, so that he would not be so disappointed each night? So that he would not continue to try to show her the passion he wanted her to feel?

She had no idea what pretending to this over-the-edge sensation would be like. Should she gasp? Shudder? Moan aloud? Those were all things Rand did when he climaxed. But he was a man. What on earth did a woman do during such times? Dare she ask him? She thought not.

And then she wondered where these giddy thoughts had come from. Was he purposefully giving her more than her share of wine in order to get her drunk? He would have to if he wished to convince her to make love here, in the open. Even then, she could not imagine agreeing to such a daring thing.

The windows of the house looked out onto their picnic ground. The thought of Mrs. Robson catching them . . .

But she did not get drunk. Just pleasantly, warmly, dizzy. Enough so that she could no longer trust her hands to draw as she commanded. "Shall we go in?" she asked, packing up her supplies and the remains of their picnic.

He did not move. "Wait."

She eyed him warily. His gaze was searching, and she had the impression he was assessing how much the wine had loosened her normal sense of propriety.

Apparently, he was not certain enough to simply begin kissing her. For he remained where he reclined on the blanket he had brought for their comfort as he said, "I think this is an excellent place for the lesson of the day."

Though his words carried no immediate threat of her amorous husband tearing off her clothes, she could not help reacting with a touch of panic. "Here? In the open? Where others can see?"

"There will be nothing to see, my little prude."

She bristled. "So what is the lesson to be?"

He emptied the last drops of wine from the flask onto his tongue and licked his lips as he watched her. He enjoyed her impatience; she was certain of it. "I want to show you how the tongue can be used to heighten love play."

Helena went hot. "Then you are intending us to make love here?"

She thought of one of her "lessons" as they traveled—how to use the tongue to kiss. What else would he use his wicked tongue for?

"No." He smiled as if he thought himself brilliant. "To anyone who might spy us—from a window, let us say—we will simply be two people having a conversation."

"A conversation?" Helena felt oddly disappointed. They would talk? They did that every day. How could that bring the kind of pleasure he meant?

"Yes."

She shrugged. "I suppose I cannot object. I have talked all my life. There's no reason to object to doing so now."

"Good." He leaned up on one arm and plucked

a tiny blue wildflower from the grass near his head. "Why don't we begin with the subject of a woman's climax? You say you do not believe a woman can achieve orgasm. Why not?"

Had he somehow known what she had been thinking earlier? He couldn't . . . "A woman is not built like a man."

"And men everywhere are grateful for that wonderful truth." He smiled. "So grateful that we have spent centuries discovering ways to give women as much pleasure as the female form gives a man."

"Then how does a woman . . ?" She had not imagined having the courage to ask that question when they lay in bed in total darkness. Helena marveled that she asked it with the sun shining upon her face and the home where her servants worked within sight.

He did not seem at all shocked by her question. "You know a man is driven by his cock."

"His lord of pleasure?" She smiled.

He laughed. "I know it seems a grand name for something that so far has not met your expectations—"

She did not want the conversation to end in another attempt for him to get her to feel what, to be blunt, frightened her. "I expect nothing, my lord. Except a child. We are talking in the hypothetical here."

"Very well. This hypothetical woman could gain her pleasure by any number of means. Sometimes just the friction of a man's organ as he pumps himself against her . . ."

"That is pleasant enough," Helena admitted. "But I cannot say that I have ever felt I might go over the edge—whatever edge that might be."

With one finger, he brushed the petals of the

tiny flower he held. "Perhaps you are one of the women who needs a man to stroke her."

"Where?" She didn't need to ask, though. There were so many places that tingled as if he had stroked them rather than simply spoken of the possibility.

"The breasts—" He twirled the little flower by its stem, like a child's toy. "A woman's nipples are much more sensitive than a man's." The flower dropped from his fingers. "And between the legs there is a little pearl of pleasure."

# Chapter Fourteen

"Pearl of pleasure?" The wine had relaxed her sufficiently that she laughed aloud, although a bit breathlessly, at the silly nickname. "Is that the feminine version of a lord of pleasure? If so, I am sure I was made without one."

He grinned. "I suspect you are mistaken. I remember too well how tightly you clenched when I stroked you that morning."

Her stomach tightened and went warm in reaction to a rush of memory. "The morning with the maid in the room? The morning when you continued your lovemaking as if you did not care that we had an audience?"

"Be fair. We had no audience for what I did. A simple brush of my fingers? Did it not please you, to be stroked in that place? If the maid had not been there, I know—"

"The maid was there." She closed her eyes, still able to feel the embarrassment of the moment.

"Believe me, Helena, if she had not been there . . ." He paused, glancing at her as if to judge whether his words would shock her too much to be spoken. "I could barely contain myself. I wanted to shout, I wanted to move, to thrust against you until your . . . pearl of pleasure . . . made you shout in response."

"I am grateful you did not, then." She understood how much concentration he must have exerted in order to ride through his orgasm without the usual thrusts and plunges such activity required.

"What did it feel like?" She imagined that it had been painful. Not that she was an expert. But in the past three weeks she had learned what a man did to find his pleasure with a woman. And lying quietly was not something the wicked earl did while he made love.

He threw himself flat on his back with a rushed breath of laughter. "You cannot imagine, my sweet Helena. You cannot know. I cannot describe it." His arms spread wide, his fingers combing through the grass with restless strokes. "Think of it as if you were to have the most pleasurable experience and yet be able to speak of it to no one."

So it had not been painful, after all. She watched her husband through a haze of desire. She wanted him to touch her. And yet at the same time she did not.

"I cannot imagine such a thing." Though he had come close to showing her, with his words alone. Why was it that these lessons of his, seemingly so simple, bound her to him tighter and tighter with a web of desire that stole her free will? Her common sense? She wanted to give him her heart, though she knew she would regret it if she did. She wanted to give him her body, to give herself permission to feel this orgasm he spoke of. But the very core of her warned her that to do so would jeopardize her soul.

"I want to show you how such ecstasy feels." Rand watched her as closely as she watched him, looking for her response to his words. But she had the advantage of him, she realized.

"I think you are more concerned with your own desires." He stretched flat on the ground. She could see his erection, though they were both fully clothed and not touching.

"There is doubled pleasure when both are able to reach the ultimate pleasure, Helena." Was that true? She had nothing to give away her own growing desire. She could rise and walk back home and he would never know whether she had been touched by his words.

"How many women have you brought to climax?" She wished she hadn't asked that question. She thought of his eight bastards. She was very glad he could not see how that unpleasant thought had dimmed her glow.

Whereas, with one glance, she knew now that he was close to the bursting point. "All but one." His eyes were dark with want. "And her gates, I hope, will soon fall under my onslaught."

She understood in a flush of heat that his want was caught up with the need to bring her this flood of sensation. With her refusal to allow herself to be seduced into such abandonment.

He had been right when he told her that a woman who understood a man's desires might rule him. And to think that she had done it all without touching him once.

Something deep within her responded to the

way he wanted her even when they had not touched or kissed. Only talked of a woman's pleasure. And how a man might give it. Nevertheless, she had no intention of experiencing such a thing in the near future. "And if you are disappointed in your hopes today?"

"There is always tomorrow." He grew restless, turned one way and another as if finding no place comfortable. Helena understood the reason for his discomfort and reveled in the knowledge. What would he do to end this conversation?

Finally, he jumped to his feet and held out his hand to help her up. "Let's walk. I have been sitting for too long."

She was not fooled by his innocent smile. She knew what he wanted. "Is it a walk you want, my lord? Or a ride?"

He laughed as he pulled her to her feet. But he did not take her into his arms. "Do you offer me a mount, then?"

Speechless at his bold words, dizzy from the sudden change in position, she could only laugh with him.

With a glance over his shoulder at the little house at the bottom of the hill, he tugged her toward the nearest stand of trees.

The time for talking was done, it seemed. She knew what he wanted. But she was not as sure of her own desires.

She followed him into a nearby copse. But panic began to claw at her throat. They were outside, where anyone could happen upon them. It was too reminiscent of—

"Stop." Her feet refused to move. She pulled back on his tugging hand. She could go no further. Rand stopped and turned. Despite the raging fever that shone bright in his eyes, he heard the panic in her voice, saw the fear in her expression. His disappointment was palpable.

"I'm sorry," she said quietly. "I can't do this."

"No? Why not? We have done this before." His look was intense. Burning her with desire. "Would you truly object to my touching your breast?"

"Rand—"

"I thought you found it pleasant." He took a step toward her. "Through your clothing, perhaps? There is nothing too disagreeable with that idea, is there?" His voice was cajoling, like a child asking for a sweet he knew he shouldn't have but wanted past all reason.

Helena could find no reason to refuse that request, though she took a step backward involuntarily. If she were dressed, no one could fault them. "I suppose not."

"And kissing you." He moved a step closer. His lips were parted. "My lips on yours." He smiled. "That is innocent enough, is it not?"

Innocent. He knew nothing of innocence. "If it is only a kiss." Again she moved a pace away from him.

Another stride brought him near. "And if I wanted to peel away your bodice to expose your breasts to my eyes, and my eyes alone, would that be a sin?"

She could not think. Could not move. He had backed her against a tree, breathless, without a touch. And now he meant to kiss her.

He bent forward, but then paused, gazing at her in a puzzled manner. "You're pale as milk. It's not as though we've not done this before, Helena. What is the matter?"

She glanced around at the serenity of the copse, trying to calm herself. "Someone might come."

He shook his head, freeing her breasts to his view. "No one comes here." She did not trust the assurance in his voice.

She should not agree; she knew that somewhere, faintly. But she wanted to so badly. . . . Just as she had with William. But Rand was her husband. "Perhaps"—she rubbed her hips against his. Through her skirts she could not feel his erection, but she knew her movement would incite him—"if you were quick."

He sighed against her breast, a cool breeze over the heated nipple his tongue had laved. "This is not meant to be quick, Helena. Not if you are to find release."

Urgency made her frantic. "I am not the one who needs release—you are."

He moved with her, slowing her rhythm to a sensual grind. He continued kissing her, continued caressing her breasts. At last he lifted her skirts and she thought he would soon be done. But no, he acted as though they were locked in their bedroom, safe from prying eyes. His fingers played along her thigh as though he meant to take hours with her.

"Hurry," she said at last, reaching for him.

Rand felt her fingers hurrying him along and pulled away from her. "Damnation, Wife. Even a stud is given enough time to do the thing properly."

She was pale and more panicked than impassioned, he noted. "I cannot help but . . ." She looked around at the quiet trees, as if they all had eyes. She was clearly losing the mood as quickly as she had when the maid interrupted them.

For a moment he conceded defeat. And then a

solution to the dilemma occurred to him. "Come with me."

He led her by the hand, rushing more than was wise with the twisted roots and fallen branches on the ground.

At last he stopped. "Here. Here, blasted woman. No one will see us here if we take the rest of our lives to enjoy our pleasures."

She glanced around as if afraid someone followed. "What is this place?"

He pushed aside some dense shrubbery, revealing a spacious, secluded area. It was shaded, but still received enough of the sun that he could see her when he needed to—when she at last understood what it was he wanted her to feel.

"My secret hideaway."

Cautiously, she crept in. "This is a bower." At last she relaxed, a smile of appreciation lighting her face. "However did you find it?"

He watched her eyes, worshiping his secret place as he had done when he found it. His impulse had not been a mistake. She saw what he did when she looked at the shelter—a safe haven from the world. "When I was a child I explored here often. This was a place I could come to where no one could hurt me."

The effects of wine and passion had dimmed enough for her to catch more of his meaning than he liked. She put her hand on his arm in a soothing gesture. "Did others often hurt you?"

He pulled her toward him and began to unfasten her gown. "No. That was just my childish way of viewing things, I suppose."

She twisted so that she could look at him full-on. "I won't hurt you."

He could hear the urgency with which she spoke.

As if she thought he needed reassurance of the fact. He took her face in his hands for a brief moment, meeting her gaze. "You couldn't hurt anyone, my love. You are the most gentle woman I've ever known."

He pushed her gown down to her waist and began to work on her corset laces with eager fingers. She lifted her hands to his chest and tried to push away, but could not because his arms were around her, locking her to him. A touch of panic tinged her movements. "What are you doing?"

He released her, and he saw the panic that had begun to rise in her eyes recede. "No one can see us here. We can do the thing properly. We are safe here."

"Safe?" Her gaze softened at the word. There was more indulgence than passion in her smile, but she stopped protesting and began to unfasten his shirt. "You are a single-minded man, my lord. No wonder you made your wager so fearlessly."

He wished the reckless bet to Hades. No doubt his boast that he would have a son in ten months' time was the main reason for her refusal to give herself fully to him. "It is not the wager I am thinking of, Helena."

"No. " She smiled and there was a knowledge in her smile. A radiance that spoke of understanding. "You are thinking of me and my pleasure. You are thinking that if you please me, you will please yourself even more."

His groin tightened at the way her lips curled up and her eyes lit. The depth of her understanding might have made him wary if he were in the mood to be cautious. But he was not. He spread their discarded clothing on the ground and pressed her back atop the makeshift bed. The fever of his passion returned as he held her against him, warm and soft. "Do you feel safe here? With me?"

His heartbeat dipped in alarm when she turned her face away from him. "I should not." And then she rubbed her cheek against his. "But I do."

He pressed a kiss to the smooth warm skin of her shoulder.

"There is no need for haste, then?"

"No."

"Good." He rolled over to lean on one arm above her. "Then let me look at you."

She lay back shyly, allowing him to enjoy the sight of her body dappled with light and shadow. Tracing the patterns on her skin with one finger, he said softly, "I wish I could paint you like this, Helena. I would use oils and hang my portrait of you above my bed."

"I would not let you," she answered with a smile, rising up to twine her arms around his neck and kiss him.

He pressed her back to the ground gently. "Will you let me use your body for my canvas, then?"

Her smile held a puzzled question. He leaned in to kiss the tip of her nose, but escaped before she could capture him for a full kiss. "You, my bride, are a creative, imaginative spirit. Today, however, you will learn what it is to be the work of art that I create with my brushes." He fluttered the tips of his fingers across her belly and bent to dip his tongue into the little depression there.

She would have bolted upright at the shock of sensation, but Rand was done preparing the canvas. Moving over her, he put one hand on each breast to hold her down gently. It was time to create a masterpiece. His thumbs deftly stroked her nipples as he moved his tongue down her belly and dove for a pearl beyond price.

She gasped and surged against him, partly in protest, partly in surprise. He had found his prize, though, and moved his tongue against her, slashing and swirling until she moved with him and her hands came down to twine in his hair. Encouraging him. Guiding him.

She was such a quiet woman he had not been certain he would know when she climaxed. But there was no mistaking when the convulsion toward orgasm began. The pulsations strengthened even as she cried out.

He lifted his head to glimpse her expression as she fully realized the culmination he had promised her. Her gaze burned into him, fierce and bright. Focused on some distant point, and yet aware of him. Aware that he had shown her the truth of desire and fulfillment, at last.

An answering surge of desire shuddered through him involuntarily, and he rose up to capture her mouth with his. With a moan, she melted to him, and he felt her tensions releasing under his hands. His shaft slid into her still-pulsing warmth, and he had time to press into her once, twice, before he let himself go with a hoarse cry of triumph.

The harsh sound of his ragged breathing didn't completely mask Helena's own struggle to catch her breath. When he kissed her face he tasted tears. He rested his head against her shoulder, felt the way their bodies melded full length together. He had done it. He had melted his ice queen, at last.

*Over the edge.* As the last waves of sensation loosened their grip upon her, and sanity returned, Helena gasped for breath. She could see her husband falling into the familiar deep sleep he seemed to need after lovemaking.

He smiled at her tenderly. "I knew I could thaw you, Helena. I knew there was a passionate woman under all that propriety. Now tell me a woman's climax is a myth." He laughed drowsily, pushing back the tendrils of hair that had loosened around her face. His fingers were gentle. His words, however, shattered her heart.

Thaw her? Is that how he saw what they had done? She rose from the ground, ignoring his sleepy murmurs of protest.

She stumbled about, retrieving her rumpled clothes, dressing herself haphazardly without his help. Her head knew her heart should not hurt so. He had never promised her more than he had given. He only wanted to prove a point with her. She was the one who had misunderstood.

She glanced at the bower that had seemed so safe and welcoming not so very long ago. A part of himself no one else had ever seen. When he brought her to his childhood sanctuary, she had thought . . . No, she hadn't thought. That was the problem. How could she have forgotten herself so?

"Come lie down with me," he murmured lazily. He lay on the ground, a beautiful, sated, male creature regarding her with heavy-lidded eyes that slowly closed as she watched.

His dark lashes fanned his cheek. One hand curled under his jaw. The sleep of an angel. She thought Adam could have looked no less magnificent after Eve had—drat the man. She had fallen. He had held out the apple and she had eaten. Did he even realize what he had done to her heart when he "thawed" her body?

There was a smile of satisfaction on his face. Self-satisfaction. She was tempted to kick him. She had understood what he was about—proving his prowess as a lover. But she had forgotten the cost to her if he succeeded.

He had been determined to make her forget. Determined to teach her what she did not want to know. "Did you have a wager on that, too?" she whispered, as the breeze stirred the leaves and the dappled light shifted, caressed the perfection of the form she knew so well. She wanted to sketch him. Even now.

He stirred at the sound of her voice and asked sleepily, "What, my love?"

*My love.* She wanted to cry. She wanted to scream. "Did you wager how many days it would take you to push me over the edge?" His only answer was the deep, even breathing of sleep.

She took up her sketchbook and pen. Her strokes were fierce and sure as she captured him in his secret bower. His sanctuary. But not hers.

A tear smudged a taut, graceful line of ink. His left arm. Helena brushed away the tear, but did not fix the blemish on her drawing. This sketch was meant to serve as a warning to her heart in the future.

When she finished, she sat for a moment in the peaceful bower and regarded her work. Satisfied, she packed her things neatly and left him where he slept.


Marie turned white when she saw her mistress, pins askew and corset unlaced. "Did he beat you, milady?" She clapped her hands over her mouth and her too-pale face abruptly reddened.

"Don't be silly, Marie," Helena said to calm the

child. "The earl would not beat me." No. He preferred to use pleasure to torture her.

"Of course, milady. Forgive me." The maid stood staring at the floor, clearly disbelieving, but in control of herself enough now to know she should not display her misgivings any more than she could help.

Helena sighed. "Draw my bath, please. I took a spill. That is all." A hard spill. "I will be fine when I am bathed and changed."

The maid moved toward the door. "Yes, milady. At once, milady." Marie's quick glance of sympathy told her she had not been entirely convincing.

# Chapter Fifteen

The sun rode low in the sky by the time Rand woke in the bower. The dinner hour. He leaped up with a curse and threw on his clothing without bothering to fasten anything properly. Better to shock the servants than be late for dinner.

Why had Helena left him here alone? Perhaps, he reflected, she had tried to wake him and found herself unable to rouse him? He grinned ruefully. No, he had been sleeping the sleep of the dead after she roused him so thoroughly earlier. He had forgotten how effective a love tool the tongue could be, even when it was only used to shape words. She had an unexpected gift for wielding her own, his prim little wife.

Griggson informed him stiffly that his wife had already left in the carriage. Rand attributed his valet's starchy manner to the state his master's clothes were in. But he had no time to placate the man. Helena was alone with the old man.

The carriage had left a good quarter hour ago, too. Damn. He would be late. He hurried to change and waved away the valet's attempt to shave him. "No time for that. Don't want to leave my wife alone with the marquess too long."

He arrived before dinner was served, barely. Both his wife and his grandfather were seated. When he came hurrying into the room, he was greeted with twin glares of equal frigidity. He wished he had been in time for a glass of brandy. He was certain he would need it before the evening was finished.

"Ah," the old man intoned, when he arrived breathless from his trot to the main house. "Decided to join us, have you? Don't trust me with your wife?"

As he settled into place and forced himself to appear unaware of their displeasure, he noticed that there was an atmosphere of suppressed tension in the room. At first he thought his grandfather had said something to put Helena on guard.

"I may not trust you, Grandfather, but I trust my wife." He smiled at Helena, hoping she would forgive him for leaving her in the lion's den unguarded. "Forgive me?"

Her look was colder than a dripping icicle. "You have no need of forgiveness from me, my lord. I have no expectations that you will join me for dinner if it does not please you to do so."

He supposed he could not blame her for being put out when he had fallen into deep sleep and left her to return to the dower house alone. Belatedly, he remembered that she could not lace her corset herself. So Marie, at the very least, knew what had gone on between them. And that meant the old man would soon know as well.

Damn. He would have to find some way to

appease her wounded pride. But not here, in front of his grandfather. He ignored the complaint that underlay her words and chose to respond only to the outward sentiment. "I am fortunate to have been blessed with so undemanding a wife."

She lifted a forkful of beef to her mouth, and he thought she would not answer him. But she paused, the fork held suspended as if she were struck by some profundity. "Fortune has little to do with it, I suspect."

The old man looked from one to the other, his eyes kindling with interest. Rand drained his glass of wine and signaled for more. His grandfather had caught the scent of tension between them and wished to know more.

Indeed, he did not bother with his own meal before he aimed his first question of the evening. "You have been here longer than usual, Rand. May I take it that married life has settled you at last?"

Rand knew that he would have to deal with Helena's ire, but he could not resist goading his grandfather. "I have a wager to win, Grandfather." He did not want the old man in any way to assume he was falling in love with his wife. Or that she cared for him any more than a haphazard fashion.

The old man pressed, looking for a crack to worm wider and discover the truth. "You have been frolicking with your bride, I hear."

Rand wondered if, by taking Helena there, he had revealed his sanctuary in the woods to his grandfather, after all these years. "If by frolicking you mean ensuring that I will soon have a son, yes." No, he thought it unlikely. There was no need to have followed him. They had picnicked in full view of the house. And they had both returned considerably rumpled. Damaging enough details, even if the old man couldn't have yet heard them.

He would hear shortly, Rand had no doubt. Griggson would keep silent until death, but Mrs. Robson had greeted him when he entered the dower house. Her serene gaze had taken in his dishevelment without comment. But her report to his grandfather would be meticulously detailed. The only question to be answered was how his grandfather would choose to interpret those details.

His grandfather's gaze was sharp. Calculating the truth of Rand's answers? The emotion behind Helena's silence? The old man flicked a glance between the two of them. "She draws and you watch."

"I find her ability to capture the essence and dimension of her subjects fascinating. Have you looked at any of her work?" He knew the old man must hate the way Helena guarded her sketchbook so closely. Had one of his spies stolen a sketch from the book? Surely Helena would have noticed. "You must show my grandfather your drawings, Helena."

"Which do you think would interest him most?" she asked smoothly, stirred out of her silence at last. "My sketches of the countryside, or of its inhabitants?"

Rand was dismayed by the threat implicit in her question. He remembered the sketch he had glimpsed of himself asleep—the air of ridiculous innocence her fancy had imparted to him. What would the old man make of such a thing? She wouldn't dare show those sketches. Would she?

"Surely you have grown tired of our landscape by now?" His grandfather was not pleased at the suggestion that Helena might be truly talented. "You must have dozens of sketches of the countryside by now. My grandson accompanies you through the gardens each morning and evening."

Rand was alarmed at the old man's persistence. "The cool of the morning is peaceful. And the evening walk helps to stir her blood." He didn't like the sound of excuse that threaded through his words.

"Stirs her blood, does it?" His grandfather nodded. "Then that is why you retire early with her."

"You watch us closely, my lord." Helena regarded his grandfather with something less than her usual sympathy tonight. Had she seen through the man? He didn't dare hope so. So few ever had. He felt a chill of warning along his spine and drained his wineglass yet again. The few who had were gone. Banished from his life.

Playing the role of overprotective guardian, his grandfather sighed gustily. "Forgive me, my dear. It is a habit I learned long ago, to keep my headstrong grandson from losing his life—or his sanity—in his foolish games. It is a debt I owe his parents."

"I understand." Helena's sympathy was restored. Rand tamped down his chagrin. Helena was safer not knowing the truth of the old man's games.

His grandfather, satisfied that he had once again beguiled Helena, turned his attention back to Rand. "I don't believe you've gambled once since you've been here."

"There you would be wrong, Grandfather. I gamble at least once a day—sometimes more." He winked at Helena, who looked as though she might slay him.

"And you have no care whether you win or lose,

I sometimes think," his wife said sharply. "Or even what the stakes might be." She deplored his behavior once again. Life was good.

Her prim austerity lasted throughout dinner. But Rand was certain he could cajole her out of it with a moonlit walk back to the dower house. Remembering her pique with him last time, he asked her, "Do you mind if I dismiss the carriage so that we may enjoy the night air?"

"As you wish, my lord," she answered stiffly, still without looking at him.

He took the coachman's lamp to light their way. When he turned, he found that she had already started on the path. Worse, she refused his arm when he offered, and strode down the path as if the hounds of hell were after her.

He matched her pace easily, but had no clue how to begin to unravel her anger. She had not been this cold to him when he had forced her to choose between marrying him or exposing the fact that she had taken a lover. What had he done?

Rand had the sense that he had made a grave error in judgment. But he was not certain exactly what the error had been. "I did not mean to fall asleep so soundly. Did you try to wake me?"

Now that they were away from his grandfather's watchful gaze, she did not bother to keep her bitterness from him. "Why would I disturb your rest? Didn't you deserve it after your feat?"

His feat. He tried to puzzle out exactly what had angered her. A suspicion dawned on him, but he found it hard to credit. Helena could not object to having had an orgasm at last. Could she? Perhaps she would have preferred him to wait, until they were indoors, in his bed?

He found the cold silence intolerable. He did

not deserve to be treated so just because she didn't like knowing he had the power to make her lose herself in orgasm. "What is the matter? What have I done but give you a little pleasure?"

"Nothing, my lord. You have done nothing but what you said you would. And so handily, too. Not even a month into this bargain of ours that I didn't want in the first place and you have taken me where I never wanted to go. It is a pity we did not think to wager on the matter, for you would have won handily."

"Wager on what—" Abruptly he remembered what she had asked him in the bower. Whether he had made a wager on how quickly he could bring her to climax. Obviously, she had not spoken in jest, but in true concern.

She stopped abruptly. "I am the fool. I thought it meant something, that you would take me to your secret place." The lamp swung so that the light illuminated her pale face. He could see tears glinting on her cheeks. "Share a part of your past, your childhood, with me."

He was appalled at the depth of her misery. "You look for deeper meaning where it does not exist."

"Apparently so."

He saw in an instant that the wall he had tried to break through—that he had broken through this afternoon—had been meant to guard her heart. And having breached that barrier, what had he done but fall asleep and compound the damage? What a bumbling fool he had been.

He set down the lantern in the pathway and took her in his arms. She stood stiffly in his embrace. "I'm sorry. I didn't mean to hurt you." He could not love her. He could not love anyone. "Remember the bargain we made." He put his lips tight against her forehead and whispered, "Don't fall in love with me, Helena. I couldn't bear it."

*"You* couldn't bear it? What of me? How am I to laugh with you, make love to you, live with you— and not fall in love with you?" Her sad smile might have broken his heart—if he had one.

"Don't mistake pleasure for love. Live in the moment, Helena. Attach no more meaning to what we did—I could be any man in your bed."

"And I could be any woman in yours?"

"Helena, this is new to you, I know. But you will see, in time. You will grow bored with me. You will take a new lover. When you grow bored with him, you will move on. That is the way of things. Unless you make the mistake of letting your heart get involved. Of thinking of love where there is only desire. I would not see you hurt for the world."

She made a choked noise of disbelief.

"Don't fall in love with me, Helena. If you do, you can only be hurt."

She turned away from him. "I won't fall in love with you Rand. I promise." He wished, for both their sakes, that there was more conviction in her voice.

"It is best that way," he said, as if he believed her.

*Don't fall in love with me, Helena.* His voice had not been unkind. But there had been a gentle implacability in the words. As if he knew that coming to her that night would be a final cruelty, he left her to her bed, to her solitary sleep. She told herself not to read meaning into his absence. He still had his wager to win.

Helena had not been an unwitting dupe. She

had accepted the marriage bargain when she chose
not to reveal the truth to Miranda and Simon. She
had known even then that she could escape him
by revealing the truth. And she had chosen to keep
her secret. She must learn to live with her bargain
marriage. To come to terms with it the way he had.
She tossed fitfully in sleepless contemplation. How
had he come to terms with it so easily?

In the morning, a wagon load of supplies were
delivered, to Dibby's delight and Mrs. Robson's
consternation. "What shall I do with all this?" the
housekeeper asked Helena.

"What is it?" Helena, muddled from her sleepless night, disinterestedly surveyed the goods. Her
heart began to pound as the neatly packed objects
became clear to her. Frames. Canvas.

"Where did this come from?" she asked the
delivery driver sharply.

"London, milady." He doffed his cap with an
impatient air, as if he would rather dump the lot
and be on his way.

Helena inventoried the goods again quickly.
Frames and canvas for every size painting she could
wish to do. Oils of every imaginable hue, and
brushes with bristles so fine he must have asked a
true artist's aid in choosing them. Spirit gum. A
sharp set of knives. All that she would need to stock
her own studio was here before her.

Rand had shown her the long-neglected music
room when he finally took her through his childhood home. He had said the room would make a
fine studio, and she had agreed. He had not said
he had ordered . . . She turned to Mrs. Robson. "I
think we will put these things in the music room."

"That room hasn't been used in years." Mrs.
Robson's eyes were dark with disapproval.

"I know. It has the best available light," Helena replied firmly. "If it will not be used for music, it can serve me well as a studio."

"I don't know what his lordship will say—"

"I will speak to my husband, but I assure you now he will let me do as I like."

"I meant the marquess, milady," Mrs. Robson answered stiffly.

"The earl is master here, Mrs. Robson. Best you remember that."

The housekeeper curtsied. "As you say, milady. I did not mean to give offense. Just everyone knows the earl ain't got the sense of a flea. The marquess handles all his affairs so he won't get them in a tangle again, like he did before—" The housekeeper broke off, horrified by what she had said.

"The earl is married now. He handles his own affairs," Helena said firmly, wondering if it were possibly true.

"Yes, I do." He had come up behind her.

She did not turn. She did not know what to say to him. How to act, after their discussion last night.

Mrs. Robson ducked her head and said quickly, "Yes, milord."

When the housekeeper had bustled off to find help to unload, he kissed her neck. "Thank you for your support. I do handle my own affairs, as you can see." He picked up a sack of fine nails. "Have I not handled this affair well?"

Taking her cue from him, she acted as though they had never had a serious conversation about love. "Did you order this for me?"

"I did. It is my wedding gift to you." He cocked his head to the side and regarded her seriously. "Am I forgiven for my clumsiness yesterday?"

"There is nothing to forgive." Helena hoped

her words did not reveal that she had spent the
night coming to terms with the bargain she had
so heedlessly struck with her life. "In fact, I believe
it is I who should beg your forgiveness."

"Never."

"As you noted, I am new at this business of marriage and physical intimacy without love." She hesitated, embarrassed and unsure of what she should
say. "If I could ask a favor of you?"

"Anything."

He spoke so quickly, so glibly. She did not think
what she asked of him would be easy. "Give me
time to adjust. A few months." By then, she hoped,
she could convince her stubborn heart not to hope
for love.

He stared at her in consternation. "I cannot
forbid myself your bed for months, Helena. Not if
we wish a child."

"I am not asking you to forsake my bed," she
clarified. "Only your desire to see me . . . go over
the edge. Just until my heart understands our bargain as well as my head does."

As she had foreseen, he had difficulty coming
to terms with the idea. She stopped his objections
with a kiss and heard Dibby let out a scandalized
gasp behind her as the girl returned from the main
house.

But she could not concern herself with the girl's
shock now. She kissed him again, lightly, twined
her arms about his head so that he could not escape
her gaze. "Please. This gift would mean more to
me than even all this." Her arms swept wide to
indicate the art supplies piled around them.

He stared at her for a long moment and then
nodded reluctantly. "As you wish."

"Thank you." She was tempted to put her arms

about his neck again and kiss him in gratitude, but she thought better of it. Somehow the feel of him made it harder for her to separate love and desire as she must learn to do.

A fleeting sign of sorrow crossed his features. Or was that her wishful imagination at work? For he was deviltry incarnate as he grinned at her and said in a low voice, with a quick glance at the appalled maid watching them, "You'll thank me with that portrait we discussed." His dimple was a deep curve in his cheek. "I will be more than delighted to pose for you in your new studio. But perhaps we should lock the doors for the servants' sake."

"Perhaps," she agreed, thinking of how much safer it was to sketch him from a distance than it was to allow him near enough to touch.

"Excellent. I shall clear a space in the entry for the work, when it is done. Do you think we shall have fewer guests, or more, when I hang in rivalry with David himself?"

"As we have had no guests at all yet, I cannot say." Surely he was not seriously contemplating hanging a nude portrait of himself in the entry? Well, even if he were, she would not paint a nude of him for all the world to see.

The men from the main house arrived to help Dibby and Mrs. Robson unpack the newly delivered equipment. Soon all her supplies littered the floor of the music room, pushing the scratched and out-of-tune piano into one corner and the rest of the neglected furnishings into the others. Helena supposed she would have to supervise a thorough cleaning.

But first she set up her easel and framed a canvas large enough to hang gracefully over an elegant mantelpiece. She had decided what she would do as thanks for her husband's gift. Both his gifts.

Helena set about preparing the canvas for an oil painting of her husband. Not a nude, as he had suggested. Surely he could not want that . . . And even if he did, she did not want other women to enjoy the view that was her right as his wife. He could not object. Her enjoyment had all to do with desire, not love.

She flipped through her sketches, surprised to see how many she had done of him. Ros would have accused her of mooning after her husband like a lovestruck schoolgirl. But, she told herself firmly, no longer.

One sketch caught her eye. She propped it on the easel, imagining the colors she would use to capture the scene. Rand on horseback, racing full-out.

That was how she would paint him, she decided. Not the traditional stately, controlled portrait of a man on the back of a powerful beast. No. A man and beast, wild and paired in a leap over a stile. Hellbent for the thrill and damn the consequences.

He would love it.

He might not love her, but he would love her painting. She was certain of it.

# Chapter Sixteen

Rand listened to the bustle as the music room became home to Helena's art studio. There was a distinct note of joy in the bustle. He was forgiven. The arrival of the art supplies he had ordered for her in London had been excellently timed.

He had bruised her heart unmercifully yesterday, and he had been unsure how long her recovery would take. The set of her shoulders as he approached her had not told him how she would choose to greet him this morning. Cold and punishing, as she had been at dinner last night? Lost and heartsore, as on the path? But no, she had matched his light tone with seeming ease.

She was, in her own way, as brave as Ros. No doubt her heart still ached from the mashing he had given it. But she, and her heart, would recover. Be stronger, perhaps. Looking into her eyes, his own apprehensions for the future had eased. She would adjust to his terms, despite her desire for love and a true family instead of what he offered.

The one wrinkle in the fabric of his future was her request that he not make her climax when he made love to her. His first thought had been to refuse her request outright. Absurd. To refuse the release her body craved because he would not spout lies about love and devotion?

His every instinct rebelled against the idea of taking his pleasure while she remained like an unfinished canvas beneath him. He remembered vividly her expression when she . . . Why would she ask such a thing? To protect her heart, she would deny herself unnecessarily. And in denying herself, she would deny him.

He glanced at the door to the new studio. Perhaps his gift had changed her mind on the matter? Or at least softened her to hear his argument? If he could not give her love, he could at least give her pleasure. . . . No. He had promised.

Still, her request was temporary. All he need do was show her that what she asked for was unnecessary. Unreasonable. Surely, he could find a way around his agreement. Perhaps he could show her that sex and love could be divorced quite successfully.

He thought once more about his promise. He would not break it. But he would find a way to bend it. He told himself she, and her future lovers, would appreciate his efforts in the end. He pressed his lips into a grimace. The abstract thought of his wife making love to another man inexplicably gave him indigestion.

He found her preparing a large canvas that sat upon her easel. Or rather, he found her staring mesmerized at the blank canvas as if she could see a finished painting upon it.

She jumped a foot when he said quietly, "Are you ready for me, yet?"

Slowly, an awareness that she was no longer alone grew in her eyes. She smiled in apology for her preoccupied trance as she realized that he waited for an answer to his question. "Not yet."

He glanced around the room, chaotic still. A room in the midst of transition: half discarded music room, half disorganized art studio. She had ordered the drapes taken down, he saw. The windows were bare and the light shone in at will. The room looked very different from the days when his mother lived here and played the piano. And her harp. Soon Helena would transform it. Perhaps exorcize the ghosts, as well.

A breeze from a wide-open window caressed his cheek. "I might be cold in here without my clothes."

She glanced at him as if uncertain of his response as she said firmly, "You needn't undress for me this time."

"No?"

"I thought my first effort would be along these lines." She showed him the sketch she wished to base her oil upon. There was a hint of mischief in her eye when she added, "As you can see, it would be entirely impractical for you to sit the saddle without proper clothing."

"I suppose," he agreed reluctantly.

"I'm certain the servants, as well as any guests we may have, will thank us in the end," she said encouragingly. "And this will make a magnificent portrait . . . if my skill proves sufficient for the subject."

He studied the sketch she had propped on the easel. He did not recognize the reckless devil on horseback. "Do I really look like that when I take a gate?"

She considered him for a moment and then nodded. "And when you take a woman, too, my lord." She blushed to the roots of her scalp. But she did not look away.

"I look quite capable," he said inanely. How the devil did she imagine he could control himself around her when she spoke words that inflamed him instantly? "Anyone seeing this might mistake me for a man of consequence."

"Though headstrong," she agreed with a smile. She said hesitantly, "I thought perhaps, instead of hanging it in the entry here, we could give the oil to your grandfather, if it turns out well enough."

The idea of a portrait of his in the marquess's possession gave him a chill. "Even if it were poorly done, it would be too good for the old man."

"Rand."

"Helena, you do not know us. I have my reasons for what I do."

"Isn't it time to make amends with him? You are not an irresponsible young man anymore."

He had married a reformer, Rand realized. First she wanted him to love her. Now to be responsible. "Who says I am not irresponsible?"

"You forget—you showed me the difference between an irresponsible lover and one who cares for his partner's pleasure." She thumbed through sketch after sketch of him, and he watched in somewhat horrified fascination at the way she saw him. In all of her sketches he seemed . . . whole.

"You see what you wish to see. I think you were

wise to ask me to pull back. Your heart will get you into trouble.''

She raised her head and gazed at him steadily. ''I see you.''

''Did you see your lover as clearly?''

She flushed. ''I did not sketch him but once.''

''May I see?''

''No.''

He paced the music room restlessly. ''Secrets. We all have them.'' He stopped before her, tilted her head up, and kissed her lips lightly. ''Maybe I don't want my grandfather to see me as a man who has finally outgrown his irresponsible habits and deserves respect.''

Helena watched her husband retreat from her commonsense advice as if it were poison. Could he not see that his own behavior kept his grandfather at odds with him? Even the servants spoke of it.

As she wondered, Marie came timidly into the room. ''Would you be wishing to dress for dinner, now, milady?''

As if released from imprisonment, Rand moved toward the door as he said sharply, ''Yes, go. We do not want to keep his lordship waiting. He might begin to believe I haven't the sense to feed myself or my wife.''

The maid lost all color in her face and shrank away from him as he passed, though he took no note of her. Frustrated, Helena saw that the sun had long since begun to wane. She shook her head. She found it much too easy to lose track of time when she worked. As well as when she was in her husband's company. She smiled at the still-ashen maid. ''Thank you, Marie.''

She swallowed her frustration with her husband's

stubborn pride as she took a final moment to contemplate the prepared canvas. Was she a fool to hope that she could make Rand's grandfather see the good in his grandson?

Perhaps she might broach the subject with the marquess tonight, about the subject for her oil painting. He could hardly object to such a gift, even if he considered her execution execrable.

She sighed, hurrying to prepare for the coming contentious dinner. There must be a way to bridge the gap between the two men. She could not bear a decade or more of these meals.

Rand was his usual charming and lighthearted self on the short carriage ride over to the main house. She wondered where he stored his anger. She could feel it.

She knew that the sharpness of his wit only displayed a thin edge of all that seethed within him. What else but anger and frustration could drive a man to marry a woman he hardly knew to make a child he didn't want?

That question fueled her through dinner. Watching the overbearing marquess browbeat the incorrigible earl. Watching the smiling, laughing, twinkle-eyed Rand tease the footmen and the serving maid. Watching him drinking the brandy until his eyes were glowing from more than good humor.

What secrets haunted her husband that made him certain he could not love? She had given her word not to fall in love with him. But she had not promised not to help him. Not to search for a way for him to live with his secrets without turning to fleeting pleasures of gambling and drink. And bedroom games.

She suggested they walk back, hoping that the fresh air would clear his head. She thought it less likely he would remember and keep his promise to her if he were in his cups. No matter that she thought he was wrong to believe he could not love; she did not want this angry, charming, love-forsworn man to sweep her over the edge of pleasure tonight.

As if he sensed her reason for the walk, he kissed her lightly on the lips. "Do you worry that I am too far into my cups to act the stud tonight?"

"The night is pleasant." She turned away from his kisses. Gazed up at the sky. "The stars are bright in the sky."

He circled his arms around her waist and pulled her close to him, resting his chin on her head lightly. "That is no answer to my question."

"You are the one who made the foolish wager, my lord. What matter to me if you do not visit me tonight?"

"I want it to matter." His hands moved to cup her breasts, his touch warm through her gown.

"Why? You do not want love."

"No."

"Then why does it matter if I am content to be your broodmare or to fall asleep alone, as I please?"

"Because I want you pleased."

His words prodded at the unhappy realizations she had faced last night. "Have you thought that I would prefer not to be pleased by a thing that will soon be taken away from me?"

"What?"

She tensed, but she did not turn toward him. Did not look at him. "When you have performed your stud duties successfully, you will be gone from here."

His caressing hands stopped their movement.

"But I am here now. That is what matters. The now. Not the future."

"I do not mean to complain. I merely wish you to see that, for me, there is no gain in learning what this pleasure is. In coming to accept it. To expect it. To desire it. And then have it taken away."

"You are free to find new partners."

New partners. Lovers. Like William. Or worse, because she would know the words of love were false. "I will not."

"Why not?"

"I find I much prefer to be within the rules of propriety, rather than outside them."

"Ros would not—"

"I am not Ros." No. Ros had been sensible enough to refuse the marriage. To look into the future. "I have always known that. But marriage to you has shown me that truth in a way I had never expected." Helena had lacked the courage to reveal her secret and save her heart.

"I wish I had forced Ros to the altar, then."

"You never could have. I am the weaker of the pair of us. And both you and she knew it." Helena wished she had been stronger. "I hate you both." But the words burned away her anger and left her cold. She didn't hate either of them. They had been true to themselves. She was the one who had betrayed herself into this marriage.

"Hate?" He sighed. "Since you are stuck with me until I am conveniently dispatched by a duel over the fall of a card—or perhaps a riding accident when I am in my cups—you would be better served to turn that hate into a fine disdain. Much like that my grandfather has demonstrated."

She had avoided the question until now, but she

was so angry with him it was easy to corner him. "Why do you dislike your grandfather so?"

He raised a brow and stared at her a moment, as if he might not deign to answer. "Better to ask why he dislikes me."

"He is your grandfather. He wishes you to make him proud. He does not dislike you." Helena was not absolutely certain of that. But the marquess spoke fondly of him at times.

Fondly of when he was a child, at least. "He only wants you to shoulder your responsibilities and not go gambling away your fortune. Or fathering a bastard a year."

She would never have dared to say such a thing to him if she had not been furious.

He was angry. She had never seen him angry before, she realized. His eyes glinted icy-green. His lips were pressed to a thin line. His nostrils flared. "You have no cause to care if I father a bastard a day, as long as I get a legitimate son upon you."

"I have cause enough to worry about children left to depend on you for their welfare."

"My grandfather sees to them well enough."

"I am certain of it. What of their mothers? Once they have ceased giving you pleasure and you have dropped them in the dust? Does your grandfather see to them and their broken hearts as well?"

"They leave no broken hearts. And no broken promises," he said. "Perhaps that should be your lesson tonight. How love and pleasure can be detached, so that you can have your body touched, but not your heart."

"What do you mean?" Blasted man. He had promised, but the look in his eye suggested that he would try to find some way around his agreement with her.

"You will see."

"You promised . . ."

But he was transformed once again, his anger gone into some subterranean depth in his soul. "Don't worry. I'm not going to do anything you don't beg me to do."

Rand enjoyed the uneasy glances she gave him as they moved closer to the welcoming lights of their home. He had made her angry when he referred to Ros. He had meant to. Perhaps he should not have had so much to drink. Perhaps he should leave his wife and her reforming heart to sleep alone tonight.

But even as he had the thought, he dismissed it. He would do as he promised. He would not push her over the edge until she begged him to. But he thought he had a way to get her to beg him. She had not made him promise not to, he told his guilty conscience. And she would be better for learning what he had to teach her. Stronger. Harder. Like he was. He shook away the sadness that assailed him at the thought.

She did not lock her door to him, as he had feared, but when he entered, to find her in only her dressing gown, he could see the apprehension shadowing the blue of her eyes.

"I'm not going to eat you, my dear." He fetched silken cords and dangled them before her eyes. "Or, perhaps I will. Yes. I think I shall feast on you tonight."

She opened her mouth to object. He overrode her. "I know your restrictions. I will honor them. But surely you do not restrict me to the same barren landscape?"

She narrowed her eyes. "Not at all, my lord. I

would not dream of hindering your enjoyment in any way."

"Excellent." He smiled. She would soon find that she would be heightening his enjoyment more than she dreamed possible. He dangled the cords once more. "These should help with our lesson."

He could see anger suffuse color into her face. "What will you do with those?"

As if it were no more than his usual love play, he said, "Tie you, so that you cannot stop me from pleasing you."

The thought horrified her. Or intrigued her. Her eyes widened and she took a step back. "You promised . . ."

"I said please you, not send you over the edge." Her frown told him she knew he was playing word games with her and she would regret letting him tie her up. If he didn't soothe her fear somewhat, she would refuse him. "I have found these to be . . . amusing . . . in bed games. They will not hold you if you wish release."

She came closer to examine the cords. Took one in her hand. Let the silk slide through her fingers as she examined the cord. "How do they work?"

"Like this." He grasped one of her delicate wrists in his hand and used the cord to tie her to the bedpost.

She tugged in a flurry of panic. Nothing happened. "You said it would not hold me—"

"Don't worry. They release with a tug here." He demonstrated and she was free. Before her breathing had regained a normal rhythm he lifted her in his arms, kissed her soundly, and dropped her onto the bed.

She rolled away when he tried to tie her, and crossed her arms tightly as she stared at him with deep suspicion. "I know there is a trick hiding here somewhere."

"I am innocent as a schoolboy." He allowed his dressing gown to drop to the floor and held out his arms. "See? I have nothing up my sleeves."

She rather boldly examined his erection. "Can you blame me for not trusting you?"

"What can I do to convince you?" He threw himself on her mercy. "As you can see, I am eager to gain your consent to play my game."

She glanced rapidly from the ties he held to his erection to his face once, and then again. He strove for an expression with the innocence of a babe. At last she uncrossed her arms and held out one hand, palm up. "I still do not trust you. Toss them to me."

He felt the disappointment cascade through him. She would not play the game. "As you wish." He tossed them with some height and enjoyed the arch of her breasts when she stretched up to catch them.

To his surprise, she did not hide them away. After another brief inspection of the bindings, she looked up to meet his gaze with a smile. One cord dangled in invitation from her outstretched finger. "Let me try them on you."

# Chapter Seventeen

He climbed up onto the bed beside her, watching her carefully. He could not make sense of this change in mood, and it left him feeling uneasy. Not to mention that he did not relish the idea of being tied. "That was not the idea of the lesson, my love."

Inexplicably, she flinched. But as quickly, she recovered and pouted at him, lifting one cord to rub absently along her lower lip. "Fair is fair, my lord. If I tie you, and you escape, then I will let you tie me."

The seductive note in her voice spread heat through his groin, even as he realized with a touch of admiring surprise that she had meant to do so. Evidently he was an excellent teacher, or, more likely, she was the most apt pupil he'd ever had.

Humoring her would not hurt, he decided. In fact, it could lead to a very satisfactory end to the evening. He gripped one bedpost tightly. "Very well."

She rose up to give him a kiss before turning away to bind him to the bed. She turned back to him, dangling the other cord. "Now the other."

Some warning bell rang out in his head, but he ignored it, inflamed by the heat and perfume and sheer seduction she exuded. He moved to grasp the other bedpost, the cord already tied pulling snug around one wrist. In a moment, he lay before her, arms tied. "I'm helpless, now. Are you happy?"

"Yes." Her lips curved upward in a smile that lit a glow of mischief in her eyes.

"Good." He found the loose end of the cords with his fingers and pulled. "Now it is your turn."

When he pulled at the cords, however, they held fast. A quick glance showed him the problem. He smiled up at Helena, who knelt above him, her hand resting warm on his chest. "You've tied them wrong. I can't release them."

"No?" She glanced incuriously at his bonds, but made no move to remedy the situation.

He did not like the look in her eyes. He yanked on the cords once again, fighting the panic that being bound incited. "Untie me, Helena."

She reached for one bound arm, and then halted, her hand hovering scant inches above the cord. She turned her head and regarded him as if he were a puzzle she wished to solve. "What advantage is there for me, should I release you?"

None. And she knew it. He lay back against the pillows, hoping that she would consider him harmless. His shrug was hampered by the position of his bound arms. "I cannot give you your lesson like this."

"Why not?"

"I must be able to touch you if I want to please you."

"True." Her fingers went to the cord and he thought himself on the verge of freedom. Until she paused once again and glanced at him thoughtfully. "Although, we could change the lesson."

"To what?"

She paused as if thinking, her fingers running in lazy circles on his chest. "Perhaps I should learn how to please you." His heart gave an uneven jolt as her smile widened.

Helena watched Rand react to her unexpected suggestion. "Please me?" His eyes flared and his struggle to free himself stopped for a moment.

"Why not? Surely you don't think the idea impossible." One brief glance was all that was necessary to see that his eager reaction to her proposition was in full evidence.

"Not impossible. Some other night. I don't want to play this game tonight." Oddly, considering the straining elongation of his member, his mouth was set grimly. "Untie me."

"But I very much wish to learn this lesson. Tonight." Again, his expression and his nether regions were at odds. Another interesting fact to file. A man and his member sometimes warred over what they desired. Tonight that fact had favored her. Rand, without the influence of his eager member, would not have allowed her to tie him up.

The wine he consumed at dinner, as well as the two brandies afterward, probably had contributed to his agreement, as well. He was not drunk enough to slur his words. Definitely not too drunk to perform his stud duties. She eyed him dispassionately. Now that she had him tied up, what should she do with him?

"Then I will teach you—but I do not need to be tied." He was angry. No doubt he didn't like being tied up. She knew she wouldn't have liked it.

That thought gave her the impetus to ignore his distress, as he no doubt had intended to ignore hers. "What do you like?"

Uncooperatively, he tugged against his bonds and glared at her. "Untie my hands and I'll show you."

Helena could feel the force of his anger. She would rather loose a rabid dog. "I think not." She had tied up a beast. If she released him . . .

She would not. Not until she had tamed him.

At last he realized that she was serious. "You will regret this impulse. I assure you. When you untie me—"

She kissed him into silence, using her tongue as he had taught her so very well.

And then she pulled away, a primitive satisfaction coiling inside at the insensible daze in his eyes. "*If* I untie you."

"If you don't untie me, I won't cooperate."

"No?" A quick check showed that his interest seemed to be . . . diminishing. Had his anger allowed him to win the battle he had waged earlier? Or did bondage itself reduce the desire?

He eyed her grimly as he shook his head. "No satisfaction for either of us."

"Then you will not be providing a very useful lesson, will you?" Seeing that her argument had not swayed him, she added, "Or ensuring that you win your wager."

His gaze was unblinking and his tone curt. "Not tied up, I won't."

She sighed and bent over as if to plant a kiss, stopping inches from his mouth. "I suppose I can always while away the hours until the dawn practicing the lessons you have previously taught me.''

He turned his head into his shoulder, preventing her from kissing his mouth. When she pressed a kiss to his shoulder instead, he twisted away.

She retreated, thinking of a new plan of assault. At last, she scrambled down to the end of the bed and reached for his foot, intending to caress him as he had done her the morning he attempted to convince her not to jilt him.

He snarled at her touch. ''Release me and you can touch me anywhere you wish.'' The full power of his body revealed itself to her as he kicked and twisted so that she could not get a firm grip without hurting him.

''Enough!'' Flushed and panting from her scuffle, Helena left the bed and struggled into her dressing gown. Defeated, she contemplated him glaring at her from the bed. Perhaps she had not been wise. . . .

''Giving up?'' His grin mocked her. ''Do you understand now that I will not be a trussed-up lamb at your table?''

He looked so triumphant she felt a flash of defiance race through her. Perhaps she could not touch him. But hadn't he taught her that touch was not all that inflamed a man? ''I still have one or two more lessons to practice.''

He looked startled, but still certain of his imminent victory. ''I should have taught you to surrender gracefully.''

His arrogance tipped her into certainty. ''You tried. Yesterday. I'm afraid it is a lesson I refuse to learn.'' It was more than time for him to learn a lesson about playing with people's hearts. Timid little Helena would take a page from Ros's book.

She began to back away from the bed, not taking her gaze from his angry one.

"Where are you going?" He followed her with his eyes. Wary. Uncertain again.

Good. The connecting door between their rooms stopped her progress. She went into her room and retrieved the object she sought. For a moment, she hesitated at the doorway. Perhaps she should leave him until the morning. Let his anger cool.

But that was not likely, she realized, as he called to her in his dratted warm voice, "I didn't mean to frighten you, my love. Please untie me." No doubt the sweetness of his words were meant to trick her into believing he was not murderously angry. After a moment's silence, he confirmed this with a low growl. "I will not be abandoned like this."

She thought of Ros and pulled her courage up around her as she came back into the room and stood at the foot of his bed where he could see her clearly. "I will not abandon you, my lord."

"Good. I know you are distressed by these circumstances. I should not have pushed you." He smiled at her, but the dimple did not show and his eyes were still a wintry green. "I hope you have regained your senses enough to release me."

"I have regained my senses fully." She did not take off her dressing gown, but she pulled the sash loose until it barely held the edges closed. She held up the hairbrush. "And they tell me that releasing you before I use this would not be wise."

Outrage warred openly with amusement on his face. "Are you threatening to spank me?"

She decided to appeal to the amused portion of his emotions. "Why? Have you been a naughty boy?"

Before he could answer, she raised the brush to her own hair and began plying it slowly and thoroughly from her scalp to the ends that fell like silk nearly to her waist.

Amusement won the battle and his smile reached his eyes and the dimple appeared. "Do you intend to try to lull me into a safe sleep before you release me?"

Lifting the brush again, she exaggerated the arch of her back and her breasts as her arm rose and fell. She was rewarded for her efforts by seeing his jaw drop. When the sash of her dressing gown slipped loose, she let the gown fall open. Slide down one shoulder. She saw his throat work and felt a flush of triumph.

Slowly and thoroughly, she brushed her hair as he watched and responded involuntarily to the sight. The gown slipped farther to reveal cleavage. Reveal one breast.

He shuddered convulsively and then closed his eyes. "You will not win."

She saw the progress she had made wilt before her eyes. Desperation made her ask softly, "What would you have done to me if I were lying there?"

He refused to answer. Refused to open his eyes and look at her. Stubborn man. Stubborn, dangerous man, now that she had tied him up.

Well, if he had closed his eyes to the sight of her, there was only one chance left. "Let me tell you, then, since you will not tell me." She would use her tongue in one of the ways he had taught her. "You would kiss me."

He did not respond. But the movement of his belly as he lay before her indicated his breath came shallow and rapid.

She closed her eyes, focusing on what she was

saying. "Yes. You would certainly begin by kissing me." What had moved him yesterday? She could not remember. "Where would you kiss me first? My mouth. Yes. My shoulders. Yes. My breasts? Oh, especially my breasts. You would use your tongue. Your wicked tongue."

She opened her eyes when he let out a half-suppressed groan. To her pleasure, she saw that his interest had definitely burgeoned as she spoke. "I love your tongue, my lord. When you talk, when you kiss, when you use me as your canvas."

He opened his eyes with a groan. "You will kill me."

"That is not my intent. I only want to please you. Why do you refuse to teach me? Have I not done well at my other lessons?"

She could see his desire still warring with the last of his anger. "Your teacher wishes he had taught you nothing."

She let her dressing gown slip to the floor and tossed the brush to the bed. "My teacher seems to have lost his courage. If only he would tell me what he wishes me to do. I will see it done."

He lay still, fighting the battle between his mind and his member again. His mind was losing at the moment, but for how much longer she could not guess.

Helena knew which side she wished to win this particular battle. And there was one more lesson of his that she could use against him. "Perhaps I appeal to the wrong part of you, my lord. I should make my case to the lord of pleasure, should I not?" She climbed onto the bed and reached out to stroke him. To wrap her hand—

He leaped at her touch and let out a gasp. "Don't." His voice held a plea. Even his gaze begged her to stop. But he did not fight her as he had before.

He watched her, his breath held. His eyes could not hide the truth from her now. His gaze revealed how her touch gave pleasure, so she stroked him again. Squeezed her fingers and saw the change in him as he surrendered to his desire.

She smiled and squeezed harder. "What do you like, my lord? Tell me and I shall see it done."

Having given in to his desire, his anger was quickly replacced by sensual awareness. He stretched under her hand, moving his hips as if to guide the rhythm of her hand. His dimple flashed deep in his cheek and he laughed raggedly. "I like riding you."

"You do." She leaned close to whisper in his ear and stretch herself long against him even as she kept up the stroking motion of her fingers. "But we are not speaking of how you please yourself, my lord. We are speaking of what I might do to please you."

His gaze was calculating, as if he wondered how far she might dare go. "There are so many ways."

She kissed him. "Tell me." A waterfall of daring seemed to rage inside her. She kissed him again, teasing his tongue with hers.

He turned his head, breaking the kiss gently to murmur against her ear, "I judge you have mastered that pleasure."

She squeezed him again. "Then what is another?"

"Your hand . . ." He blew out a harsh breath. "More."

She squeezed him harder. "Like this?"

He moved beneath her hand, restless. "Harder."

Harder? Was he certain, or had he lost all sense? "I don't want to hurt you."

"Use your thumb," he ordered, his voice husky.

She squeezed harder with her thumb. "Like this?"

He nodded, his gaze fastened on her face intently. "In circles. Across the tip."

She watched for every nuance of expression as she followed his direction. He closed his eyes as a shudder ran through him. "Yes."

For a long moment she gave herself up to her caress, studying his face carefully to gauge the effects of her work. His breathing became rapid, though he did not close his eyes again.

His gaze unsettled her and she turned her own away to focus on giving him pleasure. In a moment she saw that two hands would be better than one. His lingering groan confirmed her decision. She glanced up to find him watching her with a dazed approval that lit a fire in her depths.

After a while, she kissed his navel as he had kissed her in the bower. His shocked intake of breath sent an answering shock of remembered pleasure through her groin. She pulled away for a moment, startled at her own reaction.

He watched her with knowing eyes. "Do you see the problem now? Pleasure given is pleasure received, as well. Untie me and I can show you what I mean."

She shook her head. If she untied him, he could still be angry enough to seek revenge if she were within reach. A sensual revenge, but she greatly feared she would not survive it nonetheless. It would be wisest if she did not let him go until she had brought him to his climax and he succumbed to the drowsiness that overcame him then.

She bit his ear lightly. "What else?"

Frustration tinged his words. "Nothing you would dare."

"Try me."

His grin twisted and his eyes lit with challenge. "Use your mouth."

"My mouth?" She hesitated. Could he mean . . ? She almost refused, until she saw that he expected her refusal.

She bent low, brought her lips near his rigid member.

And then, just before she touched him, she turned her head, brushing the tip of his member lightly with her cheek, her hair.

She looked into his passion-hazed eyes. "Do you mean that I can kiss you here, as I kiss you elsewhere?"

"I do." Rand felt the silken brush of her hair and fought to retain what little measure of control he could, trussed like a Christmas goose. He didn't believe she would do it. Not proper little Helena. Of course, he hadn't thought she would keep him bound like this, either. Or touch him with the skill of a first-class courtesan.

"I want to please my teacher." She smiled, the knowledge of what she was doing to him clear in her eyes.

He gave a halfhearted tug at his bonds. "Don't let me stop you."

She turned her attention back to her lesson. Her hair brushed over him once more in a silken torment. Her lips touched him, light as butterfly wings.

She was killing him. He would be dead before morning; he knew it. He would wager on it if the room weren't spinning so wildly.

Her tongue.

He was never more glad that he had taught her to use her tongue so well in other areas. She applied what she had learned from him before to this new lesson. He groaned.

Her mouth was hot and wet. Her breath blew against him as she asked again, "What else?"

Afraid she would bring his release before they joined, he urged her, "Ride me, Helena, as I ride you."

"Ride you?" She looked curious at the suggestion.

He wanted more than curiosity to light her face, he realized. "Straddle me. Ride me. No sidesaddle here." He bucked his hips, making the delicious pressure of her hands nearly unbearable.

She climbed on, hesitant and then bold.

"Up and down," he coaxed. "As I would do if I were riding you."

She moved obediently, every move delicious to him. But there was no pleasure in her face, only concentration.

He didn't want her like this. He didn't want to be the only one caught up in the moment. He needed to convince her to free him. "I want to touch you. To please you. Undo the cords."

A wary shake of her head made him want to curse. "Not yet."

What could he say that would convince her? "If you will not untie me so that I can touch you, you must do it for me."

"What?" He saw her blush. Could he shame her? Push her past her willingness to explore and convince her to release him that way?

"Touch yourself."

She ceased her rocking motions. He was not

certain she still breathed until she let out a rush of breath. "No."

"No?" A certain disappointment shuddered through him, though he had not really expected her to be bold enough to follow his suggestion. He only wanted her to release him so that they could finish this dance properly. He gave her a mocking smile meant to infuriate her. "You're not ruthless enough, my love."

Her expression changed, and he felt her body tense over him, felt her clench around him in some angry parody of orgasm. She left him then. Gone from his bed. Gone from his room in a space of time so short he thought he might have dreamed the whole encounter. Except that he was still bound. And he ached for release in more ways than one.

# Chapter Eighteen

She returned and he ceased trying to free himself. She glared at him, and he realized he had tapped a beast he had not perceived lurking beneath her sweet exterior. "I *am* ruthless enough for you, my lord." She was as angry as a goddess scorned. "And I am *not* your love."

"It is just an expression." An unfortunate expression, he began to realize. "I did not mean it."

"I am quite certain you did not mean it." She climbed back onto the bed with a silk-wrapped bundle. "I know that I am not your love."

Apprehensively, he eyed the bundle, wondering what it held. Knives? Was his sweet Helena a torture master in disguise?

"You have convinced me that I will never be your love." She placed her warm palm against his chest. "But I *am* your wife. Sworn to obedience, although you have released me from such any such vow after I give you your son and heir. Am I correct?"

He nodded obediently, as he might have done for his governess. A feeling he had never had before in bed with a naked woman. And hoped fervently never to have again.

"You wish, beloved—" Her eyes lit with anger. "No. Let me begin again. You wish, Husband, for me to touch myself so that you will have pleasure?"

"If you will not let me touch you, then you must do what I would do, if I were not bound." Despite the oddity of their situation, or perhaps because of it, he felt a dizzy rush of pleasure at the thought she might do as he asked.

"Tell me where." Using his bare chest as a worktable, she unrolled the silk to reveal several paintbrushes. She took one with a fat head of soft bristles and lifted it as if she would paint upon a canvas. Instead, she plied the brush lightly over her lips. "Here, my lord?"

She moved the brush to tickle her ear. "Or here?"

"Your breasts." His throat was dry and his interest had returned.

"Very well." Without warning, she straddled him, encompassed him slowly. Clung to him.

While he was still mastering the shocking pleasure, she waved the brush. "Here?" She skimmed the brush across the tops of her right breast, around the perimeter, down into her navel and back up over the left breast.

As it it were his own fingers, his own tongue that touched her, his breath came harshly in his throat. He forced one word from his tight throat. "Nipples."

She frowned. "This brush is not right for such a delicate task." She caressed his cheek with the fat-bristled brush she held and dropped it to his chest.

She tested the bristles of another, more slender brush and then dropped it back as well.

"How is this, then?" She took a brush with what looked like only five or six long whiplike bristles and grazed it across his lips.

"Perfect." His breath caused the bristles to tickle his chin.

"If you say so, my lord." That brush she teased across her nipples. Circling. Twirling.

Again, he could see that she took little pleasure in her actions. All because she clung to the hope that love was not a foolish myth and denied herself the pleasures of the flesh. "Bend down to me. My tongue is the best brush of all for your canvas."

She smiled and shook her head. "Not tonight. Tonight I use my brushes on you."

"And what do I do?" He had never felt this helpless surrender to pleasure before. Though it was undeniably enjoyable, it was frustrating as well. He wanted to please her, but he could not.

She smiled and clenched her muscles tightly around him as she arched her back. "Enjoy the ride." Her eyes were as dark as sin, and he thought she might have had more pleasure than she'd expected from the movement because they widened as if in surprise.

He moved himself against her, hoping to catch her unawares. "How can you look like an angel and turn into such a devil?"

She clenched tight around him again. This time he was certain she did so involuntarily in reaction to his movement. But instead of letting herself give in to pleasure, she grew angry with him. "Is that not what you mean for me to become?"

"You could never be a devil."

"No?" She dropped the brush that had been teasing her nipples and picked up another. "Do you not teach me these lessons for your pleasure—and mine—and that of my future lovers?" Lightly, she ran the brush across her collarbone, down between her breasts, and played it around the depression of her navel.

"Pleasure does not make you a devil." Was there any possibility that her twenty-three years of social drilling could be breached by his sensible yet unromantic words tonight?

Her pain and anger scalded over him, then. "What will it make of me, then, my lord? When I can take and give pleasure with any man. But not love." With one hand she pushed aside the silk and paintbrushes. He heard them clatter to the ground as she clenched tight around him and drove his hips into an ageless rhythm his body would not deny.

He groaned, knowing that soon it would be too late to convince her this was not the way it had to be. "Helena. If I could love anyone, it would be you."

His words had the opposite effect of his intentions. Angry and clear eyed, she moved against him. Her breath came hot and fast, but not from arousal. From anger. "And if I could hate anyone, it would be you, my lord."

The revelation of how deeply angry and hurt she was made him struggle once again against the cords that held him. He wanted to embrace her, comfort her. To reassure her that life was not as dark as she thought it. At that moment, however, his body betrayed him, his hips pumping up against hers again and again until his orgasm shook him and he cried out hoarsely.

She stared down upon him coldly. Though she was slightly out of breath from her exertions, he saw no sign of passion or arousal. "I think I have mastered the lesson of pleasing you, my lord. Would you agree?"

He shook his head, unable to speak for a moment. When he regained his breath again, he tried to explain. "You should have untied me. I could have pleased you. What we had in the bower, we could have had again."

She stared down coldly at him from her great height. "No. We could not. This afternoon, I thought I loved you. Tonight I have accepted that I must see you only as my stud."

He could not help the fleeting thought that she might have spent her anger in an orgasm if only he had found the way to show her such pleasure was strength, not weakness. "Helena—"

She waved away his explanations. "Your grandfather told me that you could not love me on our wedding day. I should have believed him."

Rand, his emotions still raw from the climax she had so dispassionately wrung from him, felt a punch of anger burn in his gut. "It is not wise to believe everything the old goat tells you."

Her eyes lit with an unholy light to have made him angry. "I hope you do not intend for me to be as disrespectful of the marquess as you are."

"No." He didn't bother to hide his contempt. "I expect you will treat him as if he were your own grandfather."

"Why do you make that sound as if it is a crime? He is an old man. Frail. And he is aware of it; see how often he speaks of his own mortality." Her

anger made her tense around him, bringing the
blood rushing back to his cock. He saw her mouth
open in surprise as he leaped back to life inside
her.

Rand goaded her. "He's too stubborn and mean
to do me the favor of passing on." He twitched
his hips beneath her. Maybe her anger would over-
ride her caution and this time she would find
release with him.

Her nostrils flared in anger and she clenched
around him again. "How can you speak like that.
He took you in when your parents died and played
the part of mother and father to you. It is not his
fault that you spurned his efforts to make a decent
man out of you."

*Decent man.* Her words rubbed his already raw
emotions bloody. "No? Who should I blame?" He
twisted up against her when she would have moved
away from him, capturing her hips with his knees
and holding her to him. "Never mind. No doubt
you believe it is my flaw that prevents me from
being a 'decent' man. May I remind you that no
decent woman binds a man and then straddles him
like a fishwife. Or would that wound your ladylike
sensibilities?"

"How dare you speak to me of decency? Do you
deny that if you had your way, I would be the one
bound to this bed and you would have been deaf
to my pleas?"

"If I were in your place, you and I both would
be too sated from pleasure to be arguing." He
emphasized his words with several more thrusts of
his hips, lifting her into the air with him.

She struggled to escape the grip of his hips as if
she didn't realize that her movements would bring

him to release again. "If you don't like my terms, take yourself to London."

He recognized defeat as another, much less satisfactory climax coursed through him by surprise. Angry that she could affect him while remaining untouched herself, he released his grip on her hips and let his legs fall slackly away. "I will, as soon as you cooperate and begin breeding, *my love.*" It was too far. He should not have said it.

The silk cords prevented him from enfolding her in his arms. He could only watch the hurt consume her.

The words, he knew, could not be called back.

She slid away from him with boneless ease as he fought a wave of drowsiness.

He struggled against his own torpor. "Stay with me."

"I can't, Rand," she said softly. "For both our sakes, I can't stay with you."

He heard the click of the latch, and the sound abruptly brought him alert, driving all desire to sleep from his exhausted body. "Helena." No answer. He was alone in his room. In his big bed that had been his father's before him. Even the comfort of sleep after sex had deserted him.


Knowing that he slept like the dead after a bout of lovemaking, Helena crept back in to untie his bonds in the dark. She did not light the lamp for fear of waking him. The fear of seeing the expression on his face haunted her as well. What had she done? What had she become, to have been so angry, so vengeful? He had always made love to her, though he professed not to believe in the emotion. She had brought him his release in anger. Twice. Could he ever forgive her?

As she untied the first cord and laid his heavy arm gently beside him, he grasped for her clumsily. His voice was clear, alert. "Helena, I am sorry. . . ."

He was awake. With a squeak of alarm, she backed away and ran into her own room. She locked the door and stood, heart beating frantically against her ribs, listening with her ear pressed against the wood. And then she remembered that she had only untied one of his bonds. Dare she go back?

As she listened, though, she heard him groan. He cursed softly, and she jumped, startled. She pressed a hand to her mouth to stifle any other sound she might make. Pressing her ear to the door again, she listened to the sounds from the other room. Her name. Once. Twice. A sigh. The creak of the bed as he moved about. Of course, she realized. With one hand free, he could release himself from the other bond.

She closed her eyes against the tears of relief. She would not have to go back to face him; he had freed himself. The muffled thud as his feet hit the floor sent a shiver down her spine. The door latch rattled by her ear as he tried the connecting door. He cursed. Locked.

She sagged against the door. He would give up now.

Instead, her heart pounded at the sudden soft scratching noise. "Helena. Let me in." She didn't answer. She didn't dare. And then, blessedly, there was silence.

She jumped when his voice came again after several minutes of quiet.

To her surprise, he sounded sad, not angry. "I

know you are there, Helena. I can hear you breathing. Let me in." Had he forgiven her so quickly? Impossible.

She was tempted to speak, but dread held her silent.

After all, what was there to say but that they had nothing to say to each other? He wanted passion without love, and she could not seem to accept those terms gracefully.

"Helena . . ." This time his voice betrayed bitterness. Anger. The door thumped under her head. Had he hit it? With what?

For a moment she waited, expecting him to break it down. Or find the spare key.

Instead, after several more minutes of silence, he thumped the door again, much less forcefully than before. "I know you're there, Helena. I suppose I can't blame you for not wanting to see me." He sighed. "Perhaps we both need time to think. We married so hastily. . . ." The door latch jiggled again, and Helena leaped away from the door in shock. After another silence in which she neither moved nor breathed, he said, "I will be back in a few weeks' time. If you are not breeding then, we can try again. On your terms."

She wanted to open the door then. Wanted to throw herself into his arms and beg him to stay.

But she would not be a fool again. After all, her terms, as he meant them, said nothing of love, only pleasure. "I hope I am breeding."

Her voice sounded too reedy, too sad. She said more harshly, in an urge to drive him as far as possible from her vulnerable heart, "For then I might not have to witness you destroying yourself to prove your grandfather right about you."

The door thumped again. His anger was there,

too, just under the surface, as she suspected. "I hope it, too. I am done with this place for now. Focus your artist's eye on something or someone else for a while. I am tired of how you see only what you wish, instead of what exists."

Helena listened to the creak of the bed as he returned to it. The sounds of him turning restlessly, cursing softly. But he did not come back to the door. And she did not go to him.

Instead, she curled up against the door, her arms embracing her as if to give comfort where no comfort was possible. Unable to unlock the door, unable to return to her bed, she slept.

Marie found her there the next morning.

"Master's gone." The maid spoke cheerfully, as if of the passing of a bad storm and the dawn of blue skies and warm breezes.


Helena took a sip of her morning tea, and turned when she felt a chill at her neck. No one hovered in the doorway to her room, but she could have sworn . . . She shook her head. She felt the eyes of Mrs. Robson upon her even when the woman herself was not to be seen. No doubt Marie had told her how she had found her mistress curled up asleep against the door to her husband's bedroom. The locked door.

In the three weeks since Rand had gone, the feeling that she was being spied upon was ever present. Did they feel pity for her? Or did they think she had made her bed and should lie in it with a little more grace?

She sighed. It was time to stop mooning about, wishing to see him ride up the pathway. He was not likely to be back for a few weeks, at least. If he returned at all. She needed to go about her business. Stop giving the servants reasons to gossip over her.

Perhaps she should return to her painting? She had not been in her fledgling studio since that night. When she had retrieved the paintbrushes. Even now the thought of what she had done made her body alternately hot and then cold. Had she truly tied him up and . . ? She had no words for it. Only images that flashed unbidden through her mind. How could she have done such things? Without even, as Rand had had, the excuse of strong drink?

She picked up her sketchbook and thumbed through her drawings, trying to interest herself in resuming work. She had attempted to sketch scenes of her family from memory. Of Ros.

But somehow Rand always appeared on the paper. Smiling at her. Holding out his hands to her. Whenever she realized what her pen was drawing she stopped immediately, turned to a fresh page, and willed herself to find another subject.

More than once she had dropped the sketchbook and pen to the ground vowing never to draw again. But she always retrieved them within a few hours. That was how she knew Mrs. Robson kept a close eye on her. Several times she had found her sketchbook disturbed, the sketch showing not the one she had been working on.

Helena sighed. He has been gone three weeks, she told herself sternly, as she focused on the drawing she had just done: a tiny Rand down on one knee, holding an even tinier flower, like the one he had plucked from the grass. It was time to move on with her life.

Today she would clear out the studio at last.

Begin to paint. Since she seemed to be obsessed with him, she would work on her husband's portrait. Perhaps when he returned—No. She would not look any further into the future than today.

She thought of what the painting could do, if he would only let it. Stubborn man. And then it occurred to her, that in his absence, she could present the painting to his grandfather without interference. He might complain, but he would never take it back after it had been given to the marquess.

The thought made her eager to resume her painting. After all, Rand was in the wrong, not she. It was perfectly proper for a wife to wish harmony in her family. She was not asking the moon of him, though he seemed to think it.

Why was he so set on thwarting his grandfather? The marquess had done his best by his grandson. If he was a bit on the imperious side, that was to be expected. Indeed, her husband had certainly inherited that aspect of his grandfather's personality.

She surprised Marie with the announcement that she would dress in her oldest gown today. "It is time for me to get the cobwebs out of my studio and get to work." Maybe work would clear the cobwebs that plagued her mind, as well.

Dibby fetched two men from the main house to carry the piano upstairs. Helena sorted through the other furniture to see what else should be stored in the attic. It was then that she found the harp.

She had just moved aside several painted chairs, delicate and worth restoring for a quiet contemplation corner in her studio, when she saw the dust cloth-covered object.

"I'll take care of that, milady," Mrs. Robson said

hastily, distracted from her supervision of the men carrying the piano.

But she spoke too late. Helena whisked away the dust cloth to discover a harp. All its strings were cut in half. Cleanly. Deliberately. She let out a cry of dismay. "Whoever would have done this?"

# Chapter Nineteen

Mrs. Robson turned back to the men moving the piano as if she had not heard the question. But Helena had seen the housekeeper's face whiten in panic.

"Mrs. Robson." Patiently, she asked her question again when the housekeeper had reluctantly glanced her way. "Who cut these harp strings?"

It was obvious that the housekeeper fought an internal struggle for a few moments. Helena wondered what dreadful secret was about to be revealed. Or hidden. But Mrs. Robson told her the truth. "The earl."

She looked down at the mangled instrument, puzzled. "Why would he do such a thing?"

The housekeeper dipped her gaze to the floor. "I don't like to gossip, milady."

Gossip. As if Helena were some stranger asking out of idle curiosity. "Surely it is not gossip to tell me how this harp came to be so savagely damaged? I am mistress of this household, am I not?"

"The earl was angry." Mrs. Robson's words came through clenched jaws. "He didn't want to go to the main house. He was furious that his mother was gone."

What an odd way to talk about his mother's death. But the destruction became understandable. Not quite so horrible. "I suppose that is natural, then. A child in the throes of grief when his mother died."

Mrs. Robson looked as though she would object, but then she subsided. "As you say, milady."

Helena ran her fingers lightly over the destroyed harp. In her mind's eye she could see the scene. Rand, in a fit of mad grief, destroying his mother's favorite instrument. Not able, at his age, to understand why his parents had deserted him.

Her own parents had died when Helena was just about the same age as Rand had been at his parents' deaths. She remembered her utter lack of understanding. Of death. Of the change in their household: Money had become scarce; servants had left.

She had not thought of those times in many years. If not for Miranda holding their family together . . . Her sister had rocked them, and told them stories with happy endings to distract them from the sad truth of their own lives. To give them hope for the future. She could not imagine the marquess comforting a frightened, angry, heartsore little boy.

But she could not ignore Mrs. Robson's certainty that the problem was not grief, but madness. Helena watched the woman as she asked tentatively, "Perhaps he was simply anguished over his parents' deaths?"

"I couldn't say, milady. The doctors seemed to think it an instability of the mind."

Doctors. "So long ago. He was a child, then," Helena temporized, not wanting to believe what the housekeeper told her. She had seen no signs of madness in him in their brief time together. And Ros would have known—wouldn't she?

"Perhaps, milady." Mrs. Robson would not dare say otherwise, Helena realized.

Although her expression indicated she held to her own opinion. "I just know what I saw. And there was not sorrow in his eyes; there was blood and madness."

Helena thought of the man she had spent a month living with and learning to know. She said firmly, "He is not mad now."

The housekeeper's eyes flickered to Helena's face and then back to the floor. "Only because he is afraid to go back."

Back? Helena felt a cold dread seize her. "Back where?"

Mrs. Robson's small black eyes were lit with cold satisfaction. Apparently she felt she could vindicate her own opinion with facts. "Back to the madhouse."

"He—" He had never told her. But, then, that was not something a desperate man would tell his reluctant bride, was it? Especially if he wanted her to bear a child. His child.

"Rand was put away?" Still, a madhouse seemed excessive. Had the marquess overreacted? "For cutting the strings of a harp? When he had just lost his mother?" Helena was stunned at the cruelty.

Mrs. Robson shook her head. "No, milady. He

just got a proper beating and sent to bed without supper for that. The marquess didn't have to have him locked up until later—when he turned eighteen." The woman shook her head with patently false grief. "I was there, so I'm not carrying tales, milady."

As if she relished Helena's horrified attention, the housekeeper nodded, her eyes flashing as she remembered the details. "Mad as a hatter, he was. Ranting and raving. He didn't just destroy a harp that time, milady."

Helena was afraid to ask what Rand had ruined at eighteen. A man nearly grown, no mere child. A man who didn't believe in love. Or had he, then? She sank into a nearby chair. Afraid to hear the rest of the story. Afraid not to know the truth.

The housekeeper no longer seemed reticent. In fact, she seemed to relish telling Helena the truth about the man she had married. Her dislike for her new mistress had been for the most part concealed before, but now it was on full display. "His grandfather had to put him away. Took three big men to carry him out."

In the face of the housekeeper's undue elation at her news, Helena strove to keep her tone calm and without judgment—or horror. "How long was he . . . away?"

As if she thought the punishment not nearly enough, the housekeeper said dolefully, "Only for two weeks, mind you. And then he came back meek as a lamb."

"And he has been fine since then? No hint of . . . anger?"

"So it would seem, milady," the housekeeper agreed reluctantly. Her mouth tightened a moment before she added, "But no matter; we all knew."

"Knew what?"

"Knew he could do it again."

Helena felt a sense of dread even as she asked what she knew she must ask. "What did he do that was so horrible?"

But the housekeeper was no longer forthcoming. Helena was not certain whether she truly felt the need for discretion, or had decided it would be more satisfying to torture her mistress with the limitless possibilities. "I think you'd need to ask the earl himself for the answer to that, don't you, milady?"

There was a loud bang from above and Mrs. Robson hurried to the doorway to peer upward. "Is that all, milady? I need to keep an eye on those men."

"Thank you for your honesty, Mrs. Robson." Helena nodded.

She had not needed to think another minute before she knew who she could ask about what had happened when Rand was eighteen. And it would certainly not be her husband. Or his grandfather. Both of those men had ample reason to tell her a fairy story meant to ease her fears, whether they were justified or not.

As she dressed for her dinner with the marquess, she contemplated how she should ask her questions. At last she decided a direct approach would be best.

"Marie. Mrs. Robson has told me the earl was sent away when he was eighteen."

"Yes, milady." Her cheerful countenance took on a wary cast.

She kept her voice gentle so that the girl would

not become alarmed and uncooperative. "Is that why you are so afraid of him when he is home?"

The girl began a wailing excuse. "I don't mean to be—"

Helena waved her to silence. "What are you afraid of, exactly?"

Marie sniffled. "That he'll do it again."

Helena wanted to scream, but she didn't think it would make the girl any more quick to answer her questions. "Do what again?"

At last Marie told her what she needed to know. "Hurt a girl from the village, milady."

"He hurt someone?" Helena did not want to ask any more than she already had. But it was too late. "Are you certain?' "

"Yes, milady. Jenny Bean. He killed her, he did." Marie's face shone with conviction, but then darkened. "Well, it was suspected so. There was blood in her cottage and her not to be found to this day."

Blood. Still, there were many explanations for that. "He gave no explanation? No reason?"

Marie looked at her blankly. "What docs a madman need with reason, milady?"


The marquess paid her an unexpected visit one afternoon. Mrs. Robson did not announce him. Helena might not have known he was there for hours, except that she had just finished a particularly exacting hour's work on the leg that gripped the horse's midsection in her painting.

As she took a moment to stretch her aching back, she caught movement out of the corner of her eye. She turned, thinking . . . hoping . . . that she would find Rand there, offering to sit for her again. Offering to answer the questions that swarmed in her mind about the things she had learned since he had been gone. She managed a smile of welcome when she saw that it was not her husband, but instead his grandfather.

He was seated in one of her delicate chairs even though he was much too large a figure for the chair's thinly curved legs. She had no idea how long he had been there and she was not aware he had been watching her paint until he said abruptly, "My grandson did not exaggerate your talent, I see."

She looked at the nearly complete painting, trying to see it objectively. "Thank you, my lord." At times she thought it captured her husband perfectly. At times she was tempted to burn it and start over.

Despite his praise, his expression indicated an aversion to the painting itself. Was it the subject? Rand was a handsome man, and she had let his reckless joy in life show in both his pose and his expression. Had the marquess noticed a slight hint of madness about the mouth and eyes, or had Helena herself imagined the effect because of the story she had pried from Marie's reluctant lips?

The marquess, true to form, returned to the subject dear to his heart. A subject that she had heard nightly at dinner for weeks. "Mrs. Robson says you have not taken care of yourself properly since that irresponsible husband of yours took himself off to London."

Knowing that he had taken the trouble to visit out of concern, Helena answered without showing the uneasy irritation she felt. "I sometimes forget myself when I paint."

He snorted. "You don't eat. You don't sleep. Are you expecting?"

"It is too soon to say," Helena answered evasively. She was almost certain that her painting was not the cause of her tendency to eat and sleep less of late.

She knew he waited for her to confirm his suspicions. Instead, she began to clean her paintbrushes. "I have given the matter little thought since there is nothing to be done. It is either true, or not." She thought she would find in a few weeks that she carried a child. But she did not want to say until she was absolutely certain. A few more weeks. Perhaps when Rand came home. If Rand came home.

"We'll see about that." The marquess snorted again and departed with a shake of his head.

A week later, he returned with a stranger in tow. A small, round, white-haired woman with serious brown eyes and pink cheeks.

Helena was at tea. Mrs. Robson announced them properly, this time. But a proper entrance did not make the marquess display any more than his usual abrupt manner, after he had kissed her cheek.

"You're pale as milk, girl." He pulled her to her feet. He fixed her with green eyes so eerily like Rand's, and yet with less warmth . . . or was that her imagination taking liberties with her memory?

"I'm healthy as a horse." She made the comparison knowingly, since he was eying her in the same manner he eyed his acquisitions for the stables.

He said brusquely, "Twirl around, girl." When she executed a quick pirouette, he shook his head. "Slowly. Twice."

Helena did so, feeling as if she were six years old again. The only thing missing was having Ros to wink at her as she turned.

He turned to the as-yet-introduced woman. "Well? What do you say?"

The woman did not look at Helena as she spoke. "I believe you may live to see a great grandson, milord. In the very near future."

He nodded in satisfaction. "Good enough."

"My lord?" Helena felt as if she had been stripped naked. "Who is this?"

"What?" He turned to her, confusion dimming his broad smile. She wondered for a moment if he remembered that she was still in the room. "Oh. Nanny Bea."

Then he turned to the woman again. "I'll have the coachman bring in your bags. Mrs. Robson has gotten your old quarters ready for you."

The older woman regarded her with a frank and appraising stare. There was no pretense in her assessment. But no unfriendliness, either. "So you're the one my little Rand picked for a wife, hmm? Little on the thin side. Have you been having trouble keeping your stomach settled?"

Helena nodded, wondering if Nanny Bea would approve or disapprove of the sickness that had kept her from eating much these last few weeks.

"Well"—the woman took her hand and patted it gently—"we'll take care of that. I promise you'll be eating and sleeping better now that I'm here to look after you."

Helena waited until the woman had bustled away before addressing the marquess. She worked hard to suppress the quiver of rage that threatened to display itself to him. "Have you added to my staff?"

He blinked, as if surprised she was able to speak. "Nanny Bea. For the child, of course."

She looked at him in astonishment, although she couldn't have said whether it was more for his hiring a nanny for her without consulting her, or being certain there was a need for a nanny. "There is no child."

"There will be soon. Nanny Bea knows these kinds of things." He reached out and pinched her cheek.

"My lord, if I am to have a child, it will not be here for some months." Helena hesitated before she added, "And I do not mean to doubt Nanny Bea's abilities, but it is early yet to know for certain—"

He patted her cheek to silence and comfort her in a single gesture. "Bit soon, I know, my dear. But with all this painting you do, you need someone to keep you fed and rested. Marie's barely got the knack of dressing you. You need someone who'll make you eat."

Helena knew that he meant his actions in kindness. Didn't he? "I hardly think—"

"Blood means everything to me, my dear." His gaze pierced through her. "I trust Nanny Bea to do what is necessary to ensure my blood line carries on into the future."

Nanny Bea entered the room once again, her eyes shrewd on Helena. "I'll be off to freshen up and unpack, if that suits you, milady."

"Certainly." Helena could think of no way to refuse her. To send her packing. The marquess would only send her back. "Please take as long as you need to get adjusted. I really don't need any help right now."

Accepting the marquess's dictates as gracefully as she could, she smiled at the woman who had raised her husband. She had the sense that the other woman had been as helpless to deny him as she had been. The marquess knew how to get his way. Perhaps that was what had driven the wedge between he and his grandson?

Nanny Bea smiled back cheerfully. "We all need help sometimes, don't we?"

But Helena did not miss the quick appraisal. Did she wonder if Helena would make a good mother? Or were her concerns more for Helena's rather woeful abilities as wife? After all, the woman had been Rand's own nanny.

Somehow, Helena found the thought cheering. Nanny Bea was a female who could tell her much about this household. About what she was bringing her child into.

Perhaps even whether Rand truly suffered from bouts of madness. Had his destruction of the harp been done in childish grief? Had he really been responsible for the death or disappearance of the woman Jenny Bean? She knew the questions themselves frightened her. What would the answers do?

Somehow, Helena felt that Nanny Bea would not give her answers couched in suspicion or a truth tinged by some old grudge. There was a calm competence about the older woman. And, despite her snow-white hair, she was not ancient. There were lines on her face, but not the deep grooves of advanced age.

She sighed. There were months yet for her to decide if the woman was competent to care for an infant or not.

No doubt a nanny the marquess trusted had much wisdom to impart to a woman in Helena's condition. A woman abandoned by a husband frightened of any responsibility, and smothered by his grandfather who had no idea what it required for a woman to bring a life into the world and raise it safely.

* * *

Rand stumbled home in the early hours of morning. He had won every hand this evening. That made a week of winning nights at the table. He could go to Avonmeade with gifts this time. He liked to bring presents. He'd only been to Avonmeade once, directly after leaving Parsleigh. He'd brought no gifts that time. He'd not even made a good job of being cheerful, and he'd left too soon.

But now he could return in a proper good mood. His luck had shifted. Since leaving Parsleigh, he found the cards had favored him amazingly well. Perhaps marrying Helena had brought him luck at last. That thought cast a dark pall over his joy. If only he didn't know the cost to her, he could be happy at last.

His mood darkened further when he poured himself a brandy and noticed that Griggson had left the note from his grandfather on the side table. A discreet method of indicating that Rand should not ignore his family any longer.

Apparently the valet thought that two months was too long to leave his bride alone. Perhaps he had money on that blasted wager, like everyone else in London who seemed to be cheered to see him in town and not rusticating with Helena.

The glossy crimson seal on the note flickered in the lamplight. Three days Griggson had been silently reminding him that the note waited to be opened. Three days he had been ignoring it. He had either won the bet. Or lost it. And blast it all, he didn't know which he would prefer.

Rand cursed and opened it. After perusing the two short sentences, he downed his brandy in one swallow.

"Griggson," he called, his heart pounding. "Pack my things. We are going home."

"Home?" The valet queried after a moment of silent, sleepy cogitation.

Rand cursed. "To Parsleigh."

# Chapter Twenty

Rand arrived in the middle of the night. The moon had been high and bright, so he had ridden hard. When he came into her room no smell of sickness, of imminent death, assailed him. The room's scent was of Helena and her oranges and cinnamon.

Had she taken a turn for the better as he traveled home? Opening the drapes to allow the moon to bathe the room in a cold light, he went close to the bed, dreading what he might see.

He glanced around, looking for cold baths or medicines. Plasters, perhaps. Nothing. He saw no sign of Marie or Mrs. Robson by her bed, keeping a vigil.

She seemed peaceful enough. What he could see of her. The pale curve of a cheek. The wing of hair smoothed back against her scalp. She braided her hair, he remembered, when he was not there to insist she let it free.

He checked his impulse to touch her, reluctant to wake her if she was in the midst of recovering from her illness. If this might be the first deep, healing sleep she had found in days.

As if she sensed him somehow, even before she woke, she stirred and called out his name. Was it some stray noise he had not meant to make, or something more? He held himself still, holding his breath so that even that small sound would not disturb her.

Whatever instinct had roused her though, stirred her again. She came fully awake and opened her eyes wide. Her glance darted to the open drapes.

After a few moments of stillness, she turned her head to stare directly into the shadows by her bed, where he stood. She could not see him; he was bathed in the deepest of the shadows. But she did not sound doubtful, only wary, when she spoke. "Rand. I wondered if I would ever see you again."

He stepped into the shaft of pale moonlight by her bed and laid his hand on her forehead, kissing her there, gentle as he thought a nursemaid might do. "Are you well?" He detected no fever, just the warm skin of a sleeping woman.

"Your grandfather wrote to you, didn't he? I asked him not to." She tried to sit up, but he would not allow her to.

"I did not mean to wake you. You need your rest."

She protested. "I am fine."

He searched her, seeing no signs of illness. But his grandfather's note had been clear. "Are you certain?"

"Of course." She smiled, a gesture of puzzled amusement.

The illness must have passed while he refused

to open the envelope. While he gadded about London as if he had no responsibilities.

She must be furious with him. "I came as soon as I realized."

"Why?" Suddenly, her receptive mood changed to one of reserve. Her words were tinged with bitterness. "You have what you want. You needn't come from London until the birth."

"Birth?" For a moment the exhaustion from his hard travel and the overwhelming relief to find her alive and well clouded his brain so that he could not understand her words. Did she mean death, then? Had she thought he would not return until she died?

"Of your child, my lord." When he still stared at her stupidly, she twisted her hands in the sheets and babbled as if to hide some shameful secret from him. "That is the reason you married me, is it not? For a child? I can't promise there will be a son, but I hope you don't hold that against me. I think you will agree that I cooperated fully with you in your desire to make a child."

Full comprehension took him a moment and he felt himself relax with relief. "Then you have not been ill?"

"What did your grandfather say to make you think that?" She shook her head and raised a hand to caress his cheek as if just now understanding his worry. "I have suffered from dizziness and my appetite is gone, but that is all to be expected, I am told."

"I am glad." He climbed into bed and took her into her arms. She was not dying. She was not even ill.

His mind believed the truth. His body wanted confirmation, wanted her safe in his arms. "I missed you." He hadn't meant to say it. "I'm sorry for the way we parted. I shouldn't have pressed you."

"You don't have to lie. My behavior was wicked and there is no excuse for that. I will never behave so shamefully again." She wanted to believe him. He could see the desire to believe that he had come from London out of concern for her lighting her eyes.

He was careful of his words, not wanting to end up with the same dispute between them. "How disappointing. I had thought you might consent to try the game with you captive this time instead of me." *Pleasure*, he told her silently. *Not love*.

The light of hope in her gaze died quickly. To be replaced by wariness, as if she were no longer sure of who he was. "I assure you that I am not the same little fool you left in the dust two months ago, my lord. I have learned much since you left." Her words would no doubt have had more starch, but it was the middle of the night and sleep had robbed her voice of much of its power. She stiffened in his embrace, but did not pull away from him. "Enough to wonder if you meant to come back."

Jenny. She had heard about Jenny from that fainthearted maid of hers. He shouldn't have left her alone. But he had had no choice.

He ignored her words and concentrated on the fact that she had not pushed him away. He reached out, past her stiffness, past her harsh tone, and touched her cheek softly. "Confess. You missed me."

"I did not." Reflexively, she turned her face into his shoulder and rubbed her cheek against the smooth linen of his shirt.

He kissed her. "Liar."

In a moment's time she relaxed into his arms, returning his kisses as passionately as she ever had.

When he turned from her and put out the lamp she said softly, "Why is it that I cannot refuse you, even this? I know you have no heart. And yet—"

He sighed, and the bed shifted as he removed the remainder of his clothing. "What need have I of a heart, when I have all other means to please you, Helena?"

She pressed a hand to his chest, which somehow slid up to his shoulder. "Not all other means."

Rand understood that her pride had been wounded. No doubt, despite her apology for tying him to the bed, she was like all other women he had ever known and thought he should be begging her forgiveness. Which perhaps he should. If Marie had told her about Jenny . . .

But he had traveled hard to reassure himself she was well and he had no intention of being thrown out of her bed now. "No?" He reached for her, certain that he could convince her otherwise before dawn.

And then he stopped as full realization struck him. She was pregnant. It was done. The wager all but won, his future all but secured. And yet . . .

"Are you certain you carry a child?" He rubbed his palm across her flat belly. A child. His child. The very idea was too much to comprehend. More intimidating now that becoming a father loomed as a reality rather than a theoretical avenue of escape.

She put her hands over his. "The signs are all there."

"When do you think the child will be born?"

"Who can say? I have not"—her voice drifted to

an inarticulate sound and then regained clarity—
"since we married."

He hardly dared believe it. How long since he
first touched her? Nearly three months? Was that
long enough to know for certain? "You thought
. . . with your lover . . ."

She stiffened and pushed his hand away. Sharply,
she said, "Time will tell, but Nanny Bea says there
is no question, and your grandfather will entertain
no doubts."

"Nanny Bea is here?" What was she doing working for his grandfather again? He fought down
his sudden surge of anger. Helena would want an
explanation and there was none he wished to give
her concerning his old nanny. Or Jenny, if it came
to that. He wanted her to take him as he was and
not dredge up the past. That job could be safely
left to his grandfather and the villagers around
Parsleigh.

"I know it must seem odd to have a nanny before
there is even a child." Helena's own puzzlement
was clear in her voice. "Your grandfather arranged
for her to come to take care of me and ensure he
has a healthy great grandchild."

"Of course." At least the old man had worked
against himself this time, did he but know it.

"He has been very good to me, Rand. He says
that Nanny Bea will make certain that I eat and
get proper rest. I think he might have forbidden
me to paint, but Nanny Bea told him it would do
the child no harm."

Do the child no harm. What about the child's
mother? That was no doubt a secondary concern
to his grandfather. "I wish you had waited to tell
him until we were certain."

She laughed, relaxing at last into his arms again.

"I did not tell him. He told me." And then, with just a touch of accusation, she added, "And I could not ask your opinion, since you saw fit not to come home."

His grandfather had told her that she was pregnant. Typical of the old man. He shuddered, imagining the scene. "I'm sorry I left you at his mercy for so long. But luck was with me."

He kissed her. "You have brought me luck, my lady. And I will stand guard against the old lion for you, now that I am home. No doubt he will make his will known again regarding our child. He can be like that when something important to him is at stake." As when he summoned Rand with a fabrication guaranteed to make him return without question.

"He has not been so horrible. At times I think he might be classified as indulgent." Tentatively, she said, "I think he is pleased with you, despite the fact that he might lose Saladin to you."

The wager. Was that why the marquess had summoned him from London with the imperious lie that his wife had suffered an illness and was lying near death? Or had he merely wanted to test his grandson's indifference to his bride? His stomach clenched with an old fear and then slowly, he smiled.

For once, he realized, he need not worry for Helena's safety, even if the old man guessed that Rand cared for her more than was wise. She carried his heir. The old man would not dare hurt her.

He pulled her against him, kissed her. He would find out the old man's reasoning tomorrow. No doubt it had something to do with taking up his responsibilities. Every conversation with his grandfather seemed to revolve around duty, responsibility, and sacrifice.

For tonight he would lose himself in his wife. Celebrate his coming freedom. He pulled back the covers to kiss her abdomen through the linen of her nightdress, ignoring her protests.

They would have a son; he could feel it in his bones. Freedom. God, he had waited so long for it.

Though he had slept little, Rand did not want to put off the confrontation with his grandfather. He strode up the path to the main house, thinking that he was glad to be home for once in his miserable life. He had a wife who welcomed him into her bed, though she ought more probably guard it from him. He had a good chance of being master of his fortunes in no more than seven months at the most.

He wasn't really used to being as cheerful as he appeared, but he liked the feeling. The best part of all was knowing there was nothing the old man could do to ruin things, unless he wanted to consign his title to die out. And that the Marquess of Markingham would never do.

Folkstone showed him to the library as if he were expected. No doubt he had been. He did not waste time with pleasantries that he knew would only irritate his grandfather. "Why did you send me a note saying that Helena was ill?"

For once, he felt he had the upper hand and didn't mind showing his true feelings. Irritation. Anger.

The old man chose to respond with innocent surprise. "Isn't she?"

He thought of Helena as she had been last night. This morning. "Not in any sense that can be helped within the next eight months."

"I see you have talked to your wife, then. Did you wake her, thinking her ill?" There was a faint undertone of disapproval.

Rand refused to allow himself to be put on the defensive. "She woke when I checked on her. She is most definitely healthy."

His grandfather seemed unduly interested in his words. The green eyes scanned his face with the fierce attention of a bird of prey. "So you shared her bed. Why? You have already secured your wager."

Not understanding why the old man showed such interest, Rand strove for a matter-of-fact tone. "I wanted her. My wife is a beautiful woman, Grandfather."

"Yes. And you are not one to resist a taste of beauty, are you?" There was mockery in his grandfather's words. Rand had a foreboding sense that he had missed some detail and things were not as secure as he had believed.

Rand stripped the defensiveness from his tone, seeking simple lechery in its place. "She is my wife, Grandfather. I don't see the need to deny myself. Even if my wager is as good as won."

"Yet you have stayed away two months, and would have stayed longer if I had not seen that you made your way home." The old man scrutinized him, much as he had when Rand was a boy and had caused some trouble or other. "Are you pleased about the news?"

"Delighted." He knew his tone was too bitter, but he wasn't sure what face to present to the old man. He was tired. He had slept very little.

Perhaps he should have waited to confront his grandfather. There was an uneasy undercurrent that threatened bad tidings, if he were not too exhausted to avoid whatever mistake he was on the verge of making. And he was beginning to realize that what had seemed simple not so very long ago, was more complicated and fraught with dangers than he liked to think.

"We should drink to the increased likelihood you will win the wager you made in London, should the child not be a girl, of course." The marquess poured them both brandies.

Rand raised his glass. "And the increased chance that Saladin will be mine, as well."

His grandfather halted the glass at his lips and peered over the rim at Rand. There was a calculated gleam in his eye. An all-too-familiar gleam. "I'm not so sure of that."

Rand braced himself for the blow. "What do you mean?"

His grandfather's tone was congenial, as if he were confiding his own weakness. "I don't know about your London cronies, but I'm not willing to accept just any mewling brat to satisfy our bet."

Rand knew that his grandfather enjoyed his discomfort, so he strove to look puzzled but not concerned. "A girl does not satisfy the wager, I know. But surely a son does. He needn't be born with a golden spoon between his lips, I hope."

"No." The marquess sat back, took a sip of his brandy. "He just needs to be born from your seed."

Rand allowed a small measure of his profound shock to show. "Besides the fact that there has been no other man around her while she was at Parsleigh, I assure you that I made my bid for an heir daily."

"Did you know she had a lover before you married?"

Rand again chose not to hide his surprise, although the sick feeling from the last blow intensified. "How the devil could you know that?"

The old man waved the question away as if it were of little consequence. "I have my sources. I see you are not as big a fool as I thought you. Did you know before or after you married her?"

Sources. His grandfather always had sources. But who . . . Her lover. There was no one else.

Helena had only told Ros, and Ros would never have told another soul. Only the fool who had taken advantage of her could have spoken of it. In jest? In confidence? In his cups? Did it matter? His grandfather knew.

He sighed. "It was over before we married."

"Over, but perhaps not forgotten."

Rand froze, realizing the quicksand he walked upon. He had not cared if Helena had her lover's child. His grandfather would find such a thing intolerable. "The child is mine."

His grandfather leaned forward, all pretense of geniality stripped from his features. "How can you be certain?"

"I am." Even as he spoke the words firmly, Rand knew his grandfather would require more than the word of an irresponsible rake on a matter of such importance.

As if to confirm his thoughts, the marquess sighed gustily. "This is not a matter for a careless wager, Rand. You are speaking of my heir."

His heir. As if Rand had played some middleman in a tradesman's bargain. "My heir's paternity is in no doubt. Anyone who dares say otherwise will meet me at dawn, I assure you."

"Ah, yes. A duel." His grandfather looked as though he had smelled something unpleasant. "I know you have had your share of such foolery. But what have they ever proven but the lunacy of men who would risk death to prove nothing? I'm sorry, but I don't find a dead fool any more or less worth believing than he was when he was alive."

Lunacy. Rand felt the threat. He tasted bile. "My child. I have no doubt."

His grandfather sat back, as if willing to hear him out. "Then ease my mind. Tell me how you are certain."

Reluctantly, he said, "She began her menses before we married." He added detail for veracity, knowing how his grandfather prized detail. "That is why I was in no hurry to find my bed on my wedding night."

"Women have been known to lie about such things, Rand."

"Not Helena."

The marquess's gaze was pitiless. "Has she command of your brains then, as well as your cock?"

Rand stared at him, burying his horror. He had thought Helena was safe as long as she was carrying his child. But with this turn . . . He took the only retreat he could think of. Standing, he slammed his brandy on the desk. "I would no more be fooled by a beautiful face than I would allow a cuckoo in my nest. The child is mine, Grandfather. I will listen to no more insinuations."

He turned on his heel and left, trying to erase the image of the mocking smile forming on his grandfather's lips. He wanted to be sick. He wanted to rage against the unkind hand fate had just dealt him. Again.

If the marquess doubted the child's paternity,

Helena was in danger. The truth mattered little if the marquess could not find some way to confirm it for himself.

As Rand walked to the dower house where his wife was waiting, three thoughts repeated in time with his steps: Helena carried his child. She was in serious danger. And he did not know how to protect her.

# Chapter Twenty-One

Helena dappled a final bit of green for the eyes and sighed. Finished. She arched her aching back, knowing that soon she could no longer take the hours of standing required to do a large portrait such as this one. Fortunately, she had planned nothing for the immediate future but a small watercolor of the dower house to hang in the nursery.

She glanced at the man in the portrait. She had captured him as she saw him. Would the subject be pleased or displeased? She knew she had done a good job in bringing the essence of the man she knew to the canvas, but would he agree? Or would he think she had idealized him beyond necessity?

A glance at the window confirmed that the light was nearly gone. And Rand was still not returned from speaking with his grandfather. Had they fought? Two strong-willed men battling over what? Names? Schools? Surely it was much too soon for those battles. Though she did not doubt that they would come in time.

"You've done a good job capturing the earl." Nanny Bea spoke softly, as if afraid to startle her.

"Thank you." Helena could not suppress a yawn. "I find that my work tires me much too easily of late."

Balancing a small tray of tea and biscuits, Nanny Bea hesitated, and then nodded as if she had made a decision. "Only natural, milady. Why don't you have a lie down before dinner? I'll bring your tea up with us, then."

"That would be lovely." Helena went willingly up the stairs. A lie down seemed the perfect thing for her exhausted and aching body.

Once in her room, the nanny bustled her into bed, plumping pillows and fluffing covers.

"I'm not ill, you know."

"Of course not, milady." Nanny Bea set the tea tray on her lap. "Now drink your tea."

"I'd really rather just sleep, I think."

"Nonsense. You must keep up your strength. Drink your tea for me and eat a biscuit, and then you can sleep all you like."

"Perhaps when I wake?"

"Do I know what is good for you, milady?"

"Do you?" Rand's voice cut across the quiet of the room and Helena was suddenly wide awake.

"Rand." She sat up, careful not to upset the tea tray. "I did not know you had returned. I finished your portrait today, and I wanted to show it to you. How did your talk with your grandfather go?"

"Fine." He moved across the room and took the tray from her lap.

"It is best if she have her tea, milord."

"She does not want it."

Helena watched the conversation over the tea and knew that somehow they were discussing more than tea. The undercurrent of tension was palpable.

He stood, holding the tray as if he might dash it at Nanny Bea should the woman dare cross him.

"Don't be a goose, Rand. I am not so tired as I was. Bring me the tea and I will drink it."

"As you wish." He smiled, but there was a clear flash of fury in his eyes. Somehow, as he moved toward her, the tray slipped from his hold, spilling the teapot, mug, plate, and biscuits to the floor. Everything shattered into a thousand pieces.

There was a moment of silent horror as they all three surveyed the damage. And then Rand sighed. "I am more exhausted from my travel than I thought, if I could be so clumsy."

"No matter, milord. I can brew her another cup." Nanny Bea smiled, but there was sadness in her gaze, Helena was certain, before she bent and began to gather the shattered remains into her apron.

"Leave that for Dibby." Rand frowned at the bent figure of the woman, who ignored him. He turned his gaze up to Helena, shrugged, and smiled. She could sense that the smile was an effort. What had gotten into him?

He sat beside her on the bed and kissed her forehead. She hoped for a moment that he might join her, but he only said, "Rest now, Helena. All will be well when you wake."

Her fatigue returned in a crushing wave as the drama of the last few moments faded from her blood. She wanted to ask him why the sadness of his voice belied the comfort of his words. But she was too tired to form the words.

Rand watched her fall asleep right before his eyes. He could sense the exhaustion in her heavy-lidded gaze. He knew she fought it, but the battle was lost in an instant. Was this what he had done to her?

"I said leave that for Dibby," he whispered as forcefully as he dared without waking Helena.

Nanny Bea stood, bundling her apron around her burden tightly so that the shards made little noise. "I've taken care of the mess now, milord. No need to trouble Dibby."

He followed her out into the hall. He was not pleased that Nanny Bea had joined the household. "Why are you here? Did your other position not pay as well as this one?"

She didn't offer excuses. Only reasons. As always. "Your grandfather called upon me and asked me to come to look after your wife. He trusted me."

He reminded himself that Nanny Bea had been loyal to him always, even through the worst. "I know why he called for you. I asked why you came."

She looked at him steadily, her tone a nursery-room scold for a child who was not seeing what was right before his eyes. "Would you rather he hired some other woman you neither know nor trust to see to your wife?"

He wanted to believe her. Wanted to believe she would not hurt Helena. "What's in the tea?"

"Nothing that will hurt your wife." Her gaze flicked away from him as she spoke, though she brought her eyes back to his almost before they left his face.

Nothing that would hurt his wife. His stomach began to ache. "And the child?"

Her hands fidgeted, making the broken pottery

click together erratically. "He thinks it too soon for you to have a child."

Too soon. Rand thought for a moment of telling her the truth behind the marquess's motives. But Helena would not want her to know. So he settled for a half truth. "He just doesn't want to lose his bet. Eleven months would delight his black heart."

Her eyes full of sympathy, she spoke slowly, as if afraid her words might hurt him. "He has good reason to believe the child may not be yours."

Damn. His grandfather had spilled Helena's secret to Nanny Bea. "He told me. I assured him she had been the victim of a libertine of the worst order and that there was no chance the child was not mine."

She seemed surprised. Her mouth curved up in the enigmatic smile she had tormented him with when he was a child. Never knowing if he had pleased her or come too close to disappointing her. "What would you have me do?"

"Protect Helena and the child from him." He wondered if the frail woman was up to the challenge of besting the marquess right under his very nose. She had done her best when he was a boy. But she was older now.

"Have you thought of the consequences of opposing him?" She sighed. "It might be wiser to let him have his way."

Perhaps better for himself, but not better for the innocent woman he had dragged into their battle by benefit of marriage, Rand was certain. "I've let him have his way so often that I don't even know myself anymore. Not this time. Even if you won't help."

"I never said I wouldn't help." She raised a wrinkled hand to his cheek. "But your grandfather won't give up. There's really only one way to protect her. And only you can do it."

"What? Take her far away and never look back?"

She frowned, as if she thought he was being deliberately obtuse. "Tell her the truth."

The truth? No. She was the first person since Jenny to look past his glib exterior and see a man worth loving. That they had both been wrong was beside the point. He would be damned before he'd tell her that he wasn't the man she thought him. "I've told her all the truth she needs to know. That I am not a man to love a woman." He tightened his fists. "Or a man any woman is wise to love."

She patted his cheek with a sharpness just short of a slap. "How you can bring yourself to hurt that sweet creature, I never can guess, my lord."

Rand looked at Nanny Bea with a pained expression.

She never called him "my lord" unless she was greatly put out with him. "If I don't, she could end up drowned like Silky."

She scoffed. "Silky was a puppy. Your wife is a woman grown."

"A wife, Nanny. Not a gamekeeper's son to be sent away. Or a tutor to be fired at a moment's notice. Or Jenny. She has a family. She cannot easily be got rid of. Do you want to test his limits?"

"Perhaps he's softened some in his old age?" There was a strain of hope in her voice.

"You've been away from him too long if you think that."

"If there is a chance . . ."

Rand shook his head. "You think I should test him with my wife? And if he hasn't softened with age? What will become of her then?"

Nanny Bea shook her head. There were tears in

her eyes. "You can't do this alone. You're right about her being your wife and not being so easily dismissed. There's only one thing you can do. Tell her."

"I can never do that."

"You must."

She meant well; he knew it. But no one, not even Nanny Bea fully understood his grandfather. He didn't want to argue any longer. "She would not believe me, anyway. She thinks he is everything he seems to be."

He moved down the staircase blindly, wanting peace. The door to Helena's studio was open and he entered. She said she had finished the portrait of him and he was curious to see it.

The room had changed greatly in the two months since he had left here. The old musical instruments were gone. The rugs had been rolled and no doubt carted to the attics. There was an airy feel to the room. Not entirely workmanlike. Dainty chairs grouped around a table made a feminine rest area.

He admired the neat way she had organized her supplies. The easel she had placed to catch the best light. The painting she had just finished still rested upon the easel. He walked around to take a look, his stomach clenching in anticipation.

The portrait itself struck him like a blow. Just as she had promised, he was dressed. Like the sketch she had showed him, he and his horse were caught in midleap over a stile. But the color and the size and the detail made everything plain to him. She thought him a hero. Or perhaps she had only painted him that way, which was almost as bad.

He closed his eyes, fighting the rage that threatened to spill out at last. He would not let the demon in him free in this bright and hopeful room. He would not damage her work. He would not. No matter how much he wanted to smash the portrait of himself as she saw him. As he could never be.

Helena woke abruptly to find it was full dark. Groggily she realized that Marie must not have awakened her for dinner. She sat up and saw the napkin-covered tray, the pitcher of lemonade, a favorite treat of hers.

She glanced at the closed connecting door between her room and Rand's. He must have told Marie not to wake her. Had he also thought her too tired for a visit from her husband? She hoped not.

The rest had done her good, she realized. She must thank him for his concern. If only the marquess would not take it amiss that she had missed dinner. Did not consider it a mark against her. Think it showed some weakness of the younger generation. She sighed. She would have to tell Marie not to let her sleep through dinner again.

A thud from his room brought her fully alert. She realized that a matching thud had been what pulled her from her exhausted slumber in the first place. She rose and pressed her ear against the door. She heard only silence.

Without giving herself a moment to be afraid, she opened the door and went through. Rand sat slumped in a chair by the fire, a nearly empty bottle of brandy clutched in his fist.

Unbidden, the stories Mrs. Robson and Marie had told rose up in her mind. Madness. Murder. She dismissed the suspicions. He was drunk. She had seen him drunk before, though she wished never to do so again.

And then she took in the state of his room. The mattress had been torn from his bed. The bed hangings ripped and shredded into ruins. A mirror hung shattered and crooked upon the wall. How had she slept through this destruction?

He was awake, she discovered, as he said, "You should be asleep, Helena. Walking about in the middle of the night is not good for the child." His voice was raw. From drinking so much, she supposed.

The child. She did not think he cared a fig for the child. He simply wanted her to leave him alone. "Why have you done this?"

The painful sound of his voice made her throat ache in sympathy. "I saw the painting. You are more talented than even I expected."

Did he consider that an answer to her question or a change of subject? "I am pleased with it." Was he too drunk to hold a sensible conversation with her?

"You should be." His words carried brutal accusation. "You created a miracle with your brushes. You turned a weak and infinitely flawed man into a hero ready to ride to the rescue of his fair damsel."

"I painted what I saw." Had her painting turned him to drink? Had she allowed the stories from Mrs. Robson and Marie to color her work? Did Rand spy a hint of madness in how she saw him? The thought horrified her.

She had fought believing such a thing of him. But the evidence of this room . . . "Have you gone mad?" From where she got the courage to ask him outright she couldn't have said.

A stillness came over him. But not surprise. She thought he must have been expecting the question. "What do you mean?"

"Marie told me. And Mrs. Robson. About the harp." She did not dare bring up the village girl. That was rumor. Unlike the harp she had seen with her own eyes.

He didn't look at her, although he raised the bottle to his lips and took a drink. His arm fell back to the floor limply, the remaining brandy sloshing in the silence. "They told you about Jenny, as well, I suppose. And you believed them, of course."

"If you tell me differently, I will believe you."

"Then you are truly a loyal little fool." He raised his head to look at her and his eyes were not unfocused, as she had expected. They blazed at her. Terrified her. His voice rasped ominously, like a rusty hinge. "I'm not fit company tonight, Helena. Go back to your bed."

She wanted to comply. Her legs were rubbery with fear. But she was his wife. And her painting had somehow helped to cause the incomprehensible pain that visibly wracked him. "Can I not help? A pot of tea? A cold cloth for your head?"

He laughed. "Help? There is no help." His laughter halted in a fit of coughing.

She wanted to go to him, but her feet were too heavy to command. "Surely there is something I can do."

His look pinned her and he smiled. A terrible parody of his usual smile. The dimple jagged like a crazed scar down his cheek. He seemed to know the fear that choked up inside her. "There is."

"Name it." Her voice sounded reedy and thin, even to her own ears, but he showed no signs that he noticed.

"Go back to bed."

"But . . ."

"I want to win my wager, Helena. I am more likely to do so if you have a healthy child, am I not?"

"Yes."

"Then go back to bed and we will both be better off."

She managed to force herself to walk steadily out the door. But once it closed behind her, she could not help herself. She turned the key in the lock. And then she leaned against the sturdy oak bonelessly, trembling like a leaf in a gale wind.

# Chapter Twenty-Two

Rand woke with the sun shining in his eyes. His drapes were opened wide. No doubt Griggson's subtle reminder to him that he was expected to rise at some point in the godforsaken day. He groaned and commanded himself to get out of bed. But the pounding in his head and the sudden bile that rose in his throat convinced him to do so would be much too much effort just now.

No matter what Griggson thought, there was absolutely no good reason for Rand to go to all the effort to rise, wash, dress. This day would be like every other day for the last two weeks. Sheer hell.

Two weeks of wanting her and the absolution she hoped to give him. Two weeks of not taking what she offered him bravely each night. Because he did not want to hurt her. And he did not know how to protect her. He sighed. If he was not already mad, he soon would be.

She was afraid of him now. She knew about his past. And she, like everyone else, thought him mad. Although, with courage he could only admire, she had not chosen to desert him. No, worse than that, she wanted to rescue him.

Even a solid fortnight of drinking and a constant crashing hangover had not erased the sight of her from his memory. Wanting to run and yet offering him help. He had craved to tell her to stay. He had longed to bury his troubles in her soft body and pretend that all would be well in the morning. But even with a bottle of brandy in him, he had known that would only be a lie.

He felt trapped like a butterfly in a jar. Unable to leave for fear of what his grandfather might do to her. Unable to face her without brandy burning warm in his gut. Face her courage. Her questions. Her hope. Haunted by her, he rose at last, ignoring the pounding of his head. He rang for Griggson, and when the valet came, he demanded a bath be prepared. "I'm done rusticating, Griggson. It's back to London for us."

"As you wish, sir." The valet nodded impassively.

Dressed, shaved, feeling better than he had since he had faced the portrait, he cornered Nanny Bea in the hall. "I am leaving, for my sake. For hers. Promise me she will be safe."

She looked at him sternly. "I can't promise such a thing. Already your grandfather is impatient that the tea I am supposedly giving her has not worked."

"I can't leave her unprotected. But if I stay I will go out of my mind."

"Tell her the truth, then. She's not so softheaded as you think, my boy. Give her a chance. Her heart is loyal and she loves you."

Helena was most definitely loyal. To the point

of lunacy, perhaps. "Loves me?" It was his turn to scoff. "She wishes me to Hades and no doubt about it."

"So? All wives should wish their husbands to Hades when they behave as badly as you have. First you leave her alone two months and then you come back and treat her like she's a flame and you're an icicle."

"You know why I must keep her at a distance." She was perhaps the only one who truly understood. "Grandfather must not believe Helena is more than means to an end for me."

"You cannot keep fighting this battle alone."

"I'm not." He would not bring Helena into it. "I have you beside me, and I am grateful for all the years you stood between me and the monster. I hope you will do the same for my child."

"I am too old—"

His head ached. Why would she not just agree so that he could leave this accursed place? "Who else can I trust? Who else would believe the truth?"

"Your wife."

"Helena is too innocent. Too good." She would never be able to paint him the same way again, if she knew the truth.

"She has a child to protect. You must give her the chance to do so. The chance your poor mother never had."

His mother. He fought the frustration that threatened to boil over inside him at her stubborn insistence. He wanted to end this discussion. Leave for London. "I will never tell her."

She blew out a breath of frustration and gave him a look he had not seen since his puppy Silky had been drowned by his grandfather. Sad and purposeful at the same time. "Then I may give her the tea. To protect her from your grandfather's folly—and yours.''

Pain exploded behind his eyeballs as his anger flared. She wouldn't dare. He grasped her arm tightly. "If you do, I will see you in hell."

He heard a gasp behind him. Sharp as glass, Helena commanded, "Rand. Let Nanny Bea go. Now." He turned his head. To his chagrin, her pale face was lit with righteous anger. His reforming angel was in full-winged glory.

"I'm sorry." Sorry that he had not left for London yet. Sorry that he had given her one more reason to doubt his sanity. "I let my concern for you overcome my good sense."

His good sense? He had been a moment away from doing Nanny Bea bodily harm. Helena stood stunned by the violence she had so narrowly averted. "Perhaps you should show your concern for me to my face, rather than behind my back."

He looked at her. One minute anger blazed from his eyes, radiated from his tensed body. The next he stood calmly. Smiling. Reasonable. "I do not want to overtax your health."

"Speaking to me more than three words at a time will prevent me from having a healthy heir for you?" She allowed her scorn to show. "Nanny Bea says it is not unwise—"

His expression darkened, with concern, not anger. "If something should go wrong . . . If you should lose the child . . ."

Was that it, then? Did he fear she would have a miscarriage? Did he think her sister's barren state a bad omen for the fate of his own child? "Do you believe me incapable of bearing a healthy child?"

He seemed truly astonished. "Of course not. So

much rests on this one thing going well, Helena. You cannot imagine."

"I cannot imagine? How can I not know how much this means to you?" She laughed. "You coerced me to the altar, made love to me every night for a month, abandoned me for two months, and now don't speak to me for fear you will ruin your prospect for a healthy son and heir."

He touched her cheek gently, but there was a restless ferocity in his gaze. "I will see that you don't regret it, Helena. When the child is born, you will have everything you wish for and more."

That was patently false. "I doubt it. What I want is a loving husband and a healthy child who means more to his father than a winning wager."

He closed his eyes. "I cannot be that man, Helena. Why won't you see that?"

Why? Why wouldn't he even try? She appealed to his reason. "Your grandfather wishes this. He might even give you the control you desire so badly early, in anticipation of the child, if you changed your ways."

"Changed my ways? To be what? My grandfather's puppet on a string?" His anger scalded over her, and then again, abruptly, he calmed. "And if I like my ways?"

She tried to match his calm. "You don't have to change everything about yourself." She waited for him to erupt again in anger.

He only laughed. "How fortunate."

She sighed. "If you showed him, now you are a husband, now you are to be a father, that you understand you must put aside your reckless ways and become the responsible heir he has wished for all these years . . ."

There was a sheen of panic in his eyes. "Responsi-

ble? How tedious. I have told you before not to try
to reform me, Wife."

"I don't speak of reform. Just—maturity."

"Maturity?" His laughter sounded tired and
forced. "Surely you do not think that simply
because I was able to get you with child quickly my
heart and soul have been polluted with a need for
my grandfather's approval—or yours?"

Polluted? Was that how he saw the need for love?
A poisoning of the soul? "I don't understand you.
You want an heir. And when I tell you that you will
have one, you seem to hate me for it. What do you
fear?"

"Fear?" He said the word as if it were a curse.
"Perhaps I fear knowing the child you carry is not
truly mine."

She felt as if a fire had been lit in her veins. And
then she felt impossibly cold. Through numb lips
she said, "Perhaps it is best if you leave, then."

"The first words of sense you have said in weeks."
His words were formal, without a hint of humor.
He bowed as if she were someone he had just been
introduced to at some formal event, and then disappeared into his room.

From the window, Helena watched him stride
out of the dower house without saying good-bye.
She felt numb. She had tried for two weeks to reach
him. And all she had managed was to send him
away.

"What have I done?"

"Nothing you shouldn't. He needs to be shaken
up a bit. He's gotten too used to thinking he's
alone in this world." Nanny Bea patted her shoulder. "Go after him, child."

"How can I? You heard what he said." His words
still echoed in her ears. She still saw his anger. Saw

the pain in his eyes. The retreat. The fear. Fear of what? She searched for an answer in the nanny's calm features. "He treated you horribly—after you raised him. Why should I expect more?"

"He had his reasons." Nanny Bea nodded enigmatically.

"There is no excuse."

Nanny Bea nodded in agreement. "Not an excuse. But a reason all the same." She sighed. "But you'd have to ask him for it."

Helena turned away in frustration, to see him ride out. Nanny Bea's words echoed in her head. Perhaps she should go after him and ask him all the questions she hadn't yet dared ask. A sudden, crushing fear squeezed her lungs. She couldn't let him leave like this. She might never see him again.

She ordered a horse saddled for her and followed him swiftly. Elated, she saw him after only a few minutes' hard ride. She called after him, hoping that he would not take her pursuit as an excuse to spur his mount away from her.

He turned and reined in. His frown was thunderous. "What are you doing?"

She pulled up next to him, suddenly uncertain of what to say to him. "Come back, my lord. I should not have sent you away."

"Indeed you should have."

"Nanny Bea says that I must ask you what devils haunt your sleep. And I agree with her."

"Go home," he said impatiently, slapping her horse's withers.

The horse rose in protest at being treated so poorly. Helena felt herself lurch the wrong way and begin to slide. And then her girth snapped with a sharp sound and she felt a rush of air. She braced for the impact of hitting the ground, and instead was crushed around the ribs by strong arms and held dangling safely a few inches off the ground in her husband's arms.

Rand held her against him, reeling with the events of the last quarter hour. Only minutes before he had watched her courageous front crumble in front of his eyes when he accused her of a crime he knew her innocent of.

He had expected a cry of outrage. He had been fully prepared to ignore angry protestations. But he nearly broke when he heard the quiet little gasp. And the long heavy silence after that one sound made him wonder if he had finally succeeded in pushing her away so far that he might never see her smile again.

After all that, she had followed him. Was she a fool? Or was he? And then, a more pressing concern than the fact that his wife had unfortunately fallen in love with him caught his attention. Her girth had snapped. He had heard it clearly before she had catapulted from her saddle and he had made his frantic grab for her.

He lowered her to the ground and dismounted. Seeing that she stood shaken and pale, but unharmed, he moved to examine the failed saddle. The girth had not been worn through. It had been cut nearly clean through. His heart seized as he remembered turning at the sound of her voice to see her riding hellbent for him. If the girth had broken then . . .

She came up beside him. He knew she saw the same thing he saw. There was not much room for mistake. The girth had been cut. She had been meant to fall.

He had been beside her because she was a stubborn, loyal, and courageous woman. He had not been meant to catch her. If he had not been in a position to catch her as her saddle gave way, she might have fallen. A fall that would no doubt have been bad enough to cause her to miscarry. To be badly injured. Perhaps to die.

She threw herself into his arms, and he held her shaking body close, his heart beating rapidly. His hand pressed tight against her back, feeling her heart beat in the same staccato rhythm as his against the palm of his hand. He had to do something. But what?

He left her at the dower house in the care of the maid and Nanny Bea and went directly to speak to his grandfather. He did not mince words. "Helena has had an accident."

Apparently, the old man had decided to pretend surprise. His grizzled brows rose. His jaw sagged. "Has she?"

Rand played along with the old man's game. He'd be caught out soon enough. "The girth of her saddle snapped."

The old man nodded wisely, as if he thought over what was said. Tried to make sense of what had happened to Helena. "I've seen that happen before."

Rand said bluntly. "She wasn't hurt."

His grandfather did not quite hide his disappointment. His surprise. "Good. Good."

"Yes." Rand leaned forward, knowing the old man understood him, whether he admitted it or not. "I don't want this to happen again."

"Do you care so much for her, then?"

"She is my wife, Grandfather." It was bad enough that his grandfather didn't believe she carried his child. If he thought Rand had fallen in love with his wife, she had no chance at all. "She carries my child."

His grandfather was not willing to make the concession. "Or she carries her lover's child."

Desperation made Rand more reckless than he had ever been in his life. "I'm willing to wager on it. Are you?"

His grandfather blinked twice. The offer had shocked him as much as it had Rand. "What will you wager?"

*My soul,* he thought but did not say. "I am willing to give up gambling entirely if I lose."

"You must be sure of yourself."

No. Sure of Helena. "I am. I will not lose. The child is mine."

The old man frowned, as if considering all the ramifications of their wager. "There is no foolproof way to be certain of such a thing."

Reckless again, knowing he could be condemning an innocent child, but gambling for the time to protect them both. Helena and the child. "If he or she has green eyes like mine, or yours, surely you cannot doubt it."

"Agreed." His grandfather was not finished with him, though. "On one condition."

He checked his impulse to flee. To take Helena and run to the ends of the earth. His grandfather would find him. Would lecture him on duty and responsibility and strip him of all chance for love and affection. As always. "And your condition is?"

The old man leaned forward as if to enjoy every nuance of Rand's expression. "You are not to live with her again until the child is born."

He shrugged as if it would be no hardship to leave Helena. "I accept your terms."

He walked back to the dower house, wondering what he could tell her. That he had made a wager about the color of their yet-unborn child's eyes. And on that wager hung her welfare, the child's welfare, and his own sanity. That he must go to London and leave her alone. Alone with the old man who thought she carried a bastard who would sully his impeccable lineage.

Could his grandfather be trusted to keep his word and not make any attempts to cause her to miscarry until after the child was born and the wager settled? Or was he, like Rand, using the wager as a blind to give him time to achieve his true goal?

One thought drummed through his mind. She would have to go back to London. To the duke and duchess. They could protect her as he could not. She was not safe here, even with Nanny Bea to guard her food and drink. He could not protect his own wife when he was hundreds of miles away from her. So she must be brought to London. Near enough that he might protect her, in case his grandfather did not mean to keep his word.

# Chapter Twenty-Three

Helena had not expected to see London again until after her child was born. But Rand had accepted no argument. He had seen Helena and Nanny Bea packed and off to Miranda and Simon in a day's time. He had accompanied them, as well. As an outrider only. She had not been alone with him during the swift trip. Not even when he took his leave from her abruptly at the duke's door.

Fortunately, Helena had several days to herself in London; until Miranda arrived home to discover her in unexpected residence—without her husband.

"I'm sorry I wasn't here when you arrived. Why didn't you write? When did you get here?" Miranda's worry was obvious.

"Welcome home. Is Emily's new baby healthy and . . ?" Helena dissolved into tears. "I'm sorry. I don't know what's wrong with me. Ros would never forgive me, if she were here."

Miranda smiled sympathetically. "No doubt your condition excuses you."

Helena choked back her tears. "How did you know?"

"Your husband does not strike me as a man who does anything half measure. The news of his wager had been *on-dit* for months."

"I had hoped . . ."

"Such delicious gossip is hard to check. Simon has tried."

Helena could not strain all the bitterness from her voice. "Tell him not to bother. Rand will see that it spreads."

"So. Not that I'm not delighted to see you, but why are you here instead of at Parsleigh? And where is that blackguard husband of yours?"

"He is in London, as well. Although he prefers to stay well out of my way. He says I've tried to reform him once too often."

"Have you?"

"I've been trying to understand the answer to that myself," Helena admitted. "He claims he cannot love. He wants us to go about our separate business."

"Separate lives are not unusual. And few husbands wish to be reformed, even if they should be."

"He does such scandalous things. And yet, when I think of how he has treated me, I must admit that he has been more than kind to me." The studio equipment. The tedious nights posing for her. The tenderness in his every gesture.

"Why, then, has he tossed you back to your family like a discarded plaything?"

"Some secret fear of his. He will not tell me what it is."

"Then you'll have to ask him more forcefully, won't you?"

"How can I, when he won't see me?"

"Well, he cannot avoid you at an affair like Lucinda Cavendish's ball, can he? The gaming will be heavy there."

"But I am . . ." Helena gestured at her still-slim waist.

Miranda looked at her skeptically. "You have a few weeks yet, I think. Better now than when there can be no doubt."

"True." She was prepared to launch herself out the door as soon as she resolved to act. But then she decided wisdom required her to get advice from Miranda on the best way to win a husband's heart. Although, what useful advice could the wife of a paragon of virtue give the wife of a paragon of sin?

Miranda hadn't offered assurances, but she had offered encouragement. And a ball gown for the largest ball of the season. Unfortunately, the duchess had not been able to offer to accompany her. A touch of some illness had kept her sister abed.

Helena surveyed the guests at the fashionable party. She saw no sign of her husband. He had given her a choice. And she would take it. She was safe in London. Safe with her family.

But she could not remain apart from him, no matter the risk. She must see him. Must find out what secrets were so terrible that he would turn his back on her to protect them. She was resolved. Resolved to wage a war for her husband's heart, even though he swore he did not possess one.

She knew that he must. For she had fallen in love

with him. And she would not dismiss her feelings simply because he dictated she must. She loved him. She needed to look in his eyes and tell him that, no matter what he said or did, she loved him.

But now that she was here, she saw no sign of him. She could not ask anyone here; there would be gossip about her trailing after her husband before the end of the hour. Where was he? She half hoped not to see him and half hoped that when she did he would take her in his arms and declare that he had run mad and only now regained his senses.

Before she could think up some excuse to ask, she saw coming toward her the last person in the world she wanted to see. William. She wanted to pretend she did not see him in the crush, but he took her hand and exclaimed over how well she looked.

"Thank you."

She would have gotten rid of him, then, if she hadn't seen Rand at last. Rand, looking at the pair of them like a thundercloud about to burst. Helena tensed as he approached. He had already thrown the question of whether her lover had fathered her child in her face once since she told him she was pregnant. Would he suspect that William was the one?

Maybe, she thought, he already knew? She studied her husband's face but could not see beyond the mask of casual indifference he displayed to the world.

Just as William opened his mouth, no doubt to ask her to dance, Rand said, "I believe this is my dance." Within a moment he had swept her away to the dance floor, far from William, who stood pouting as he watched her. She pretended she did not notice him as Rand swept her around in an exuberant waltz.

"Have you something to tell me?"

"I love you." Horrified, she heard what she had blurted out even as his eyes narrowed with shock.

*I love you.* The words sent a numbing paralysis through him. His step faltered and then recovered as he moved her swiftly away from the dance floor and dragged her down the hall into the blessedly unoccupied library.

She glared at him. "What will people think?"

He crossed his arms. "That I'm scolding my wife for being out in public when she should be safe at home."

"I had to see you."

"To tell me you love me. Are you fool enough to believe that such words will make me eager to reform?"

"No." She flushed. "I married you, so I suppose I am a fool. I just wanted you to know. And since you don't visit me, and I shall soon be stuck home getting fat with your dratted heir, I came here tonight to tell you—"

She broke off as someone entered the room. Her former lover. Rand fought an impulse to kill the man. It was a simple and primitive need. But a foolish one. A duel would cause more talk, and Helena did not deserve that. He gave the man a frigid glare, expecting that he would take the usual course and back out of the room with an apology.

The clod merely came forward with a hearty grin. "My lord. Congratulations. I hear you are close to winning your wager." The cad had the audacity to leer at Helena. "Perhaps even closer than you suspect."

Helena was pale as she answered equably, "I

cannot perform miracles, Baron, though some have accused me of such. The outcome of the wager will be decided with no more than the usual expedience."

"But how can you be certain?"

She smiled. "My husband is a patient man, Baron. He does not act without . . . shall we say, without utter conviction?"

"But without certain facts . . ."

Helena raised a regal brow and Rand was tempted to applaud her as she said, "My husband and I have a sophisticated marriage, Baron. He has all the facts."

At that, the weasel turned a bright pink and glanced at Rand with decidedly more wariness. "Indeed."

But it was not Rand he needed to be wary of, for Helena leaned close and said confidentially, "And I must tell you, he has taught me something I feel you must know, Baron."

"What is that?"

Her gaze fixed on Rand as if he were the only man in the room. "Women can have pleasure, too."

As the baron muttered some unintelligible comment and scurried from the room, Rand laughed. "Your way was much more satisfying than the duel I was about to propose."

"Speaking of satisfaction . . . I need to ask a favor."

"What?" His mouth dried suddenly. She couldn't mean . . .

She moved to the door and turned the key. "First, no more interruptions, I think."

She leaned against the locked door and tapped her bottom finger with her lip. "Second, remember that silly promise I made you make? The one about—?"

"I remember." Too well.

"I want you to break it."

"Helena—"

"Now."

No, his mind said sternly. Unfortunately, he was in thrall to a stronger-willed part of him at the moment. He crossed the room. Lifted her into his arms. Kissed her. In an instant her skirts were around her waist and her legs were locked around him.

"If you want pleasure, we should take our time," he whispered against her neck, even as he freed himself and slid into her.

"Hurry," was all she said, her breath hot and fast against his ear as his movements pressed her back and up against the door. Her urgency drove him; his fingers found and stroked her until she moaned against his lips. As his climax thundered over him, he thought he might disappoint her, and then he felt her convulse around him as she, too, went over the edge.

Regret flooded over him in the next moment as he realized what he had done. He pushed away from her. To his surprise, as her skirts fell to the floor she looked almost untouched. Except for the flush in her cheeks and the dazed light in her eyes.

"You'd be a fool to love me."

"I know. It doesn't seem to matter."

"No. You can't." A gate he had not been willing to open in years, one that he thought rusted shut, swung open inside him. The unvarnished truth escaped him. "My grandfather tried to make you miscarry the child." He could see she doubted him already, but he gave her only truth. If she condemned him, she would do it with all the facts. "He knows of your relationship with William and fears the child is not mine."

She gasped. "You told him?"

"No. He was a spymaster in the years we fought Napoleon. He has a network, still. Spying on me . . . and those who love me." He closed his eyes. "All my life he has taken care of me. But there has been a price. Anything . . . Anyone who loved me . . . who I loved back, he took away. A puppy, a tutor, a . . . friend."

"The village girl? What happened to her?" Her face twisted as she began to comprehend what he was telling her. "You were there that night. That is why you are afraid for me. But you don't fear what you will do. You fear what *he* will do."

"Jenny Bean? She was sweet, Helena. Like you. She didn't approve of me. She'd heard stories . . . but she liked me. Tried to reform me."

"What did he do?" Her voice twisted with bitterness. "What did he do that Marie and all the village thinks you did?"

"She had a reputation in the village. For going out with the young men. . . . She wasn't a whore, Helena. But she liked her pleasure—"

She closed her eyes. "What happened to her?"

"We were in her cottage, just talking. Three men came in. Two of my father's men. And a former beau of hers. My father's men held me while her beau—"

She interrupted him, her eyes full of horror. "Held you?"

"They had to beat me unconscious. When I awoke, I was in a madhouse. Jenny was gone. My grandfather told me that I needed to cut away my sentimental streak or I would always be a weak man."

"My God!"

"I left for London. Sent him a fortune in debts to pay. Let him believe I no longer cared about Jenny. About anything. I vowed never again to care for someone. To make them vulnerable."

"Not even me." It wasn't a question.

"You most of all." He had to make her understand. "Don't you see? If I care for you even a little, he will see you hurt. And the child with you."

"But . . ." Her face drained of blood, and she sagged against the door. Finally, he saw, she understood.

So he told her the last. The worst. "And now, somehow, he has guessed how I feel. Perhaps because I fought so hard to convince him the child was mine." He caught her gaze, held it. Willed her to understand. "If I do not stay away from you until after the child is born, he will see you both destroyed."

He could see the knowledge in her eyes. Could see her fight it. At last, she asked, "So what are you saying?" He knew she only wanted him to say it aloud.

He moved to hold her tight to him. He pressed his lips to the top of her head and closed his eyes, striving to embed the feel of her like this in his memory. "That we must not do this again, if we want our child to live."

Helena finished gluing the whiskers on her cheeks and turned to her anxious audience. "How do I look?"

"Like a prime noodle." Nanny Bea shook her head.

"I should have tied you girls to your beds." Miranda shook her head in time with Nanny Bea. But then concern shadowed her face. "Are you certain you are well enough for this? Perhaps you should wait a week or two more?"

"A month recuperating from a birth is enough." Despite the gravity of the situation, she could not suppress a smile. "As you will find out soon enough, Duchess."

Miranda did not smile, although the placid way she moved her hand over her slightly rounded abdomen indicated she had only anticipation for the event. But she was not distracted from her worries. "A few more weeks can hardly matter."

"I'm strong enough." Physically, at least. The birth had been relatively easy. It was the aftermath that had taken all her strength. "I can't wait any longer to find Rand. The marquess has already sent a note demanding that I come back to Parsleigh. To try again."

"Where will you go?" Her sister's concern deepened her voice.

Where would he be? A gambling hell? A club? Certainly not Parsleigh, but anywhere else in London. "I don't know. But I have to find him."

"He ought to have come to you, after what you'd been through."

Helena laughed without amusement. "Rand never does what he ought." His note, sent right after the birth, had said he'd set her free. He'd give her a divorce. She'd wanted to see him. To convince him there was no need for a divorce. But Griggson had steadfastly said he was out of town.

Despite Simon's best efforts, no one had seen her husband in a month.

Nanny Bea took a folded paper from her hand. "You'll find him here, milady."

Helena looked at the older woman in puzzlement. "How can you be sure?"

"You'll see when you get there." The woman patted her hand and tightened it around the map. "Just see you don't let appearances fool you."

"Another one of his secrets?"

"The last of them. And the biggest of all." There was more than worry in the nanny's expression. There was outright fear. "If the marquess were to find out . . . You mustn't let one of his spies see you."

That was the last of Helena's worries. "In my disguise, I will be just another young buck to them, no doubt." Convincing Rand that together they could face his grandfather and defeat him was the challenge she didn't know if she could manage. But she was determined to try.

Miranda embraced her. "Ros would be proud of you."

Helena brushed the tears from her eyes brusquely. "Stop it, or I'll give myself away before I've found him."

# Chapter Twenty-Four

The house, at first glance, looked abandoned. Helena had a strong urge to turn around and leave. But Nanny Bea had said not to let appearances fool her. She entered apprehensively and her apprehensions were not calmed by the appearance of the main hall.

The chandelier hung in cobwebbed splendor. The marble floor was chipped and stained and looked as if it hadn't been cleaned in several decades.

For some reason the chipped floor made her remember Rand's story about his mother and her diamond ring he had used to mark the floor. The thought heartened her, and she moved forward with more hope than she had since she began her journey.

From somewhere above her came the sound of a harp. A haunting sound. Was the somber harpist Rand? She followed the music to a narrow hallway that looked at though it had, at one time in the house's youth, led to the residents' bedrooms. Clearly, the music came from behind the first door on the left.

The door was closed but unlocked. She could hear the music clear through the solid oak of the door. She turned the latch and pushed the door slowly open.

When she heard no objections, she entered. The room she entered was clean. The wallpaper fresh and new, the paint and furnishings new as well. How this room had come to be in the midst of chaos and decay she could but wonder.

The sound of the harp came from the far corner of the good-sized bedroom. The harpist, she saw, was not Rand. Instead, the music was made by a woman who reclined on a couch. Rand knelt at her knee, enraptured by the music. He was smiling up at the woman with love in his eyes. The sight took her breath away.

Questions filled her mind. What was he doing here? How had Nanny Bea known he would be here? How was it he could look like that when his grandfather . . . Dread touched her, but she would not be a coward now.

He had promised her nothing but to lead her own life, she reminded herself. He owed her nothing but a child, and that he had given her, though he did not know it yet. Would he be glad or angry when she told him her own secret? It didn't matter. He must know. And he must help her defeat his grandfather.

He heard her approaching and turned. "Jenny, more tea if you please. Her appetite is—" He broke off, gaping at her.

The woman's pale blue gaze focused on her and

the delicate features wrinkled in a frown. Her voice was thin, like she was. "Whatever is that young man doing here? Have I a visitor? I thought I wasn't allowed visitors."

Helena saw the woman Rand loved clearly. Her long hair was white and pulled back in a fashionable chignon. The eyes were hollow and innocent as a child's as she stared at Helena.

"I believe this visitor is for me, milady." He stood as he spoke.

"What is the world coming to when a butler has visitors in my parlor?" The woman smiled as she spoke, apparently more amused at her own confusion than frightened by it.

"I cannot say, milady." Rand's gaze fixed on the door behind Helena. "But I see Jenny has come with the child. Are you ready for them?"

The woman sat up. She vibrated with enthusiasm. "I'm always eager to see my son. Send them in."

Helena moved aside for . . . Jenny? Could it be Jenny Bean? She carried in a child no more than six months old. He was beaming and holding his arms out to the woman, who reached out for him.

Not knowing where to begin, Helena looked at Rand and said simply, "Nanny Bea sent me."

He led her out of the room as the invalid cooed to the infant. "My latest bastard." He smiled absently as the child let out a carefree laugh.

Helena stopped, turned, and glanced at the child. As she had thought, his little head was crowned by a mop of red hair. His eyes were a deep, bright blue.

And Jenny, whether Jenny Bean or not, was glaring daggers at her. "Who's that fine gentleman?" she demanded of Rand.

Just as Helena remembered that she was dressed

as a man, Rand said, "My wife." He shut the door, blocking their view of Jenny's gaping jaw.

"I'm sorry. I thought my note was clear." He looked at her with no expression on his face. Was he glad to see her? Furious? Indifferent? He shoved his hands deep in his pockets. "I suppose you want an explanation?"

More than that. "Yes."

"My mother," he said. "Or what is left of her after she threw herself from the window of the asylum my grandfather committed her to."

"That woman is your mother?" But his mother was dead. Helena caught herself. Nanny Bea had said she would find Rand's biggest secret. It didn't take a minute's thought to understand that Rand's mother was better off with the marquess thinking her dead.

"How long has she been here?" She couldn't tell how he felt. What he thought. His face was blank.

"Since I was eighteen." He rubbed a weary hand over his eyes. "The old man made a mistake. He committed me to the same place he'd put her, years ago. After I found out what they'd done to her . . . I hired someone to steal her from there."

"No one told your grandfather?"

His smile was bleak. "They didn't even care. She had thrown herself from a window by then and couldn't walk. Her mind wasn't right. They just told my grandfather she died. And he believed them. He told me. Told me not to grieve for her; she'd been flawed. Not a good mother. I knew he was lying, but I didn't argue. Because I knew she'd be safe here."

"Why here?" She didn't add, *in a run-down aban-*

*doned manor house,* but she suspected he knew what she left unsaid by her tone.

"This is where I should have been born. It was my mother's house. We used to visit. But my grandfather wouldn't let my father live here. He wouldn't release the funds to keep this place up. He wanted my father close. He wanted me close."

He said softly, "I thought, once I had my son, that I would move here. Raise him here with the money that was mine, by right." He took her hand. "I'm sorry, Helena. So very sorry for what my arrogance has cost you."

She squeezed his hand. "That's why I came. To tell you it's safe now. Safe to fight him. Together." She leaned against him, suddenly trembling, and he put his arms around her in needed support. She had still not recovered all her strength.

Rand kissed her. As he did so, Jenny opened the door, carrying the child away, and they were exposed to two pairs of startled expressions. The child merely blinked sleepily at them.

His mother gasped. "Why are you kissing that young man, you wicked thing? It is entirely improper."

"This is not a young man, milady," Rand said gently. "This is my wife."

"First visitors and now a wife. Society is not what it used to be. But you are a good butler, all the same."

"Thank you, milady."

Jenny bustled back in, without the child this time. "I'll see to her," she whispered to Rand. "You've got business to sort out." She shut the door, and the harp began to sound its haunting tune again.

"Why have you come?"

"The marquess is ready for us to try again."

She knew he would be angry. "He sent me a note demanding I deliver him a great grandson as soon as possible."

"After . . ?" His eyes blazed as words failed him. "The marquess can go to the devil. I have no doubt he'll find him a companion soul."

"My bargain with you was a living heir. I returned to see to keeping my end."

"Helena—"

"You must be free of him. There is no other way. He will have you in the madhouse, otherwise. He wants an heir. It will take time to give him another one. He will be patient. And we can plan. Perhaps find some other way."

"He won't be patient." He shook his head, his face set. "And you'll be in the same position as my mother. I won't do that to you . . . again. We'll divorce. The old man won't be interested in you then."

"But he'll still be interested in you. And your mother. And what about Jenny?" Helena argued with all her heart. She held his cheeks and stood on tiptoe to kiss his resisting mouth. He was close to shutting her out, not because he didn't care for her, but because he didn't want her hurt.

Adamant, he moved away from her violently. "I won't touch you."

She moved to wrap her arms around his waist, clinging to him as if they were in a storm that threatened to rip them apart. "We can win. I'm willing to wager on it. Aren't you?"

"No more wagers." He shook his head. His hands moved restively across her back. "I won't make love to you, Helena."

She closed her eyes and loosed the final argument she had marshaled as she traveled to find him. "Then I shall find someone else to father your child."

Her words thrummed through him, bringing an ache deep in his bones. "You wouldn't." But he wasn't sure. She was not the same woman he had married ten months ago. And he had only himself to blame for that; he was the one who had brought all the pain and loss into her life.

She looked up into his face. Still his reforming angel, but harder somehow. "You told me when we married that you would acknowledge any child of mine as yours. Was that a lie?"

Damn her. Of course it had not been. But now? Now he would kill any man who dared touch her.

As if she saw the answer in his eyes, she smiled and refined her torment. "Besides, I find I can't live without that pleasure you have taught me to enjoy."

He buried his face in her neck, inhaling the sweet scent of her. "I don't deserve you."

"Or I am your just reward. Have you thought of that?" She kissed his ear.

He shuddered. "Perish the thought, Wife."

His joy was momentary, interrupted by a voice he had hoped never to hear again. "Glad to see you were able to track him down."

His grandfather stood watching them. Watching him. As if he didn't realize he was not welcome, he said warmly, "You're better at the game than I'd thought, boy. I'd never have found you without her."

He peered at Helena and said imperiously, "You don't make much of a man, if you don't mind my saying so, girl. Change into skirts, if you thought to bring some."

Rand felt as if time had stopped. He had had

nightmares about this day for so long he was not completely sure he would not wake in a cold sweat. Meeting the old man's gaze head-on, he was at the same time completely prepared and completely unprepared.

The time had come for him to protect his family from the threat the marquess posed. He put his arm around Helena. "You are not welcome here."

"Why? Because you're afraid I'll find out you brought your mother here and put her back in the madhouse?" The marquess must have seen his surprise because he laughed. "Coin will always free a tongue, boy. I thought I taught you that."

His answer was a rasp, like a terrified boy about to be caned. "You will not put her back there."

"Her mind is gone. And her legs." His grandfather shrugged. "But I will not insist. You keep her as best you can. Just don't ask me to support any of your bastards."

Rand reeled at this new blow.

"Clever of you to have me pay for your bastards and then use the money to give some poor girl and her child a start while they nursemaided that broken lunatic." The old man leaned against the wall. There was a touch of regret in his voice. "Are none of them yours?"

Defiant, Rand answered sharply, "They all are." But he did not mean that he had fathered them.

"You were always a disappointment to me."

"No man . . . no child . . . could ever please you, Grandfather. You are looking for perfection. And I am far from perfect."

"You could have been. If you weren't so weak and sentimental."

"It is not weak to love or to be loved, Grandfather. My wife has taught me that truth, and I am

grateful for it." He was not strictly lying. He knew
that it was the truth, though he was not certain the
hollow shell of his heart could be revived.

"Truth." His grandfather spat out the word as
if it were a vile taste in his mouth. "Truth is what
we make of it. Come home. Home to Parsleigh
where you belong, and get a child I can be certain
is your own on the girl. Come home, boy, and I
will see to your mother's care. I will provide servants
to clean and maintain this hovel for her."

"He is no boy, he is a man, my lord. Perhaps it
is time you recognize that." Helena, he saw, had
no intention of backing down. She was loyal to the
end—even to a madman who would never be able
to return her love.

"What would you know of it? A pair of trousers
and fake whiskers doesn't make a man out of anyone." His grandfather glared contemptuously at
Helena. "I am leaving. I expect you to follow immediately. Both of you. Or Lydia will go back where
she belongs."

He turned on his heel and left them before Rand
could think of a reply.


Helena watched the marquess go, wondering
how Rand had survived his grandfather's care for
so many years without losing his gentle nature.
She realized she was trembling. But she forced her
limbs quiet and gazed up at her husband. "We will
win this time. It is just for a little while—"

He glanced down at her, his gaze hopeless. "Do
you think I haven't said that to myself a hundred
times before?"

"You've never had me to fight with you, before."
She smiled and reached up to twine her hands

around his neck. She pulled his head down for a kiss. "Remember, I am Ros's twin, and not nearly so fainthearted as I sometimes seem."

"True. And we wouldn't want the old man to think we were meek mice, would we? To be disappointed in us? So we shouldn't just dash out the door, now, should we?" As if his heart had been unlocked, he returned her kiss with a passion that left her breathless. He rubbed his nose along her fake sideburns. "I've never made love to a man before. I think I'd like to try it."

She laughed as he propelled her backward into an empty room, grateful his grandfather had not managed to kill this wickedness of his. "I'm afraid you'll be disappointed once you've got these clothes off me, then."

"Perhaps." He gazed at her appraisingly. "But these clothes themselves call for an appropriate position."

"And what is that?"

"Down on your hands and knees, of course."

Obediently, but a trifle uncertainly, Helena knelt down and brought herself into position. "How—"

But she had not gotten her question fully formed before Rand knelt down behind her and reached to unfasten her trousers and slide them down to expose her suddenly very vulnerable nether regions to the air.

He patted her bottom, and reached to stroke a line of heat through her belly with his finger. "Not truly disappointing, I think. Just unexpected, considering the garb."

He brought himself over and into her in one fluid motion. She supported his weight with her hands as he slid a hand under her loose linen shirt and fondled one breast idly. "What do you think of the position, my love?"

For a moment she wondered if she would hurt his feelings if she were honest. She twisted her head to look over her shoulder, but could not see his face. Diplomatically, she said, "There's a certain friction missing from this angle."

He laughed and moved his free hand to supply what was needed. A burst of sensation shot through her, leaving her dizzy and breathless. "Better."

"No." He curled up against her back and shifted his weight so that they landed on the floor cradled together. "I don't want you to bear my weight. I'm too heavy a burden for any woman."

"This is more comfortable." She wiggled against him. "I could fall asleep."

His fingers twisted just as his mouth clamped over a sensitive spot on her neck, and she gasped. Heat and want enveloped her without warning.

Dimly, through the dizzying rush of blood in her ears, she heard him say, "Not just yet, I hope."

# Chapter Twenty-Five

Curled together on the floor, they had made love and then fallen asleep. Rand never was to know whether it was the smoke or the noise at the door that woke him. But whatever brought him awake told him at once that there was danger.

One deep breath filled his lungs with acrid smoke and he coughed out Helena's name even as he drew his discarded shirt over his nose and mouth and drew a cleaner breath.

She came awake quickly. "Fire." In an instant she was fully alert beside him. They struggled haphazardly into their discarded clothing and he led her at a crawl to the door. It was hot to his touch.

As he paused, she moved, tugging at his arm, pointing to the window. He shoved the dilapidated sill upward, and they both gasped for a clean breath for a moment before staring silently down at the ivy vines that had overrun the expanse of stone wall under their window.

The climb down was daunting, but not impossible when compared with the smoke and flames they might face inside.

He took a deep breath, and before Helena could realize what he intended, he lifted her into his arms and lowered her slowly out the window. When he could go no lower, he said, "Grasp hold of the vines and work your way down. If you fall, bend your knees to ease your landing." And he let her go.

She fell a foot, but then gained a hold in the ivy. Looking up, she grinned at him triumphantly. "You forget that I grew up following Ros on her adventures." Like a monkey, she quickly made her way down.

The door behind him burst in and a tongue of flame shot out the window above his head. Her expression was anguished as she looked up at him and urged, "Hurry."

"Move out of my way." He leaped, reaching out for ivy and feeling the vines shred and rip through his hands. But they served their purpose in slowing his fall at least, his landing only hard enough to knock the wind out of him for a moment.

Frantic, they raced around to the front of the manor house. Flames could be seen coming from the upper windows, although the lower floors seemed untouched by fire as of yet.

Jenny and the hysterical red-haired mother of his latest bastard were huddled against the side of the well, their children watching wide-eyed in terror.

"Where is my mother?"

Jenny left the weeping woman and said sorrowfully, "She's still inside, milord. She would not leave her harp." She handed him a bucket of water and went back to draw more.

"How could you abandon her?"

There was apology in her voice, but no shame. "I had to get the boy to safety. I tried to bring her, but the harp got stuck on the railing, and she wouldn't let go." She didn't say what he knew had been her thoughts—that an eight-year-old boy with all his wits about him was worth more than a broken old woman who didn't know her own son.

"I'll go." He ran toward the massive front doors, as smoke began to boil out.

Helena followed him. "Then I will come with you."

He waved her back. "I know this house; you do not. I cannot risk being separated from you and having you lost."

"Rand . . ." He could see her fear naked in her eyes that she would lose him. But he could offer no assurances. Only . . . "I'll wager you a new gown that I'll be out with my mother in under a minute."

She stopped, closing her eyes. "Hurry."

Jenny came jogging up with two buckets and handed one to Helena. "We need you to help us see to the buckets, milady."

Rand fought through the roiling smoke, sensing his direction by years of familiarity. Still, he might not have found her in the hellish chaos if not for the sounds of the harp cutting through the din of the fire.

He found her lying on the floor at the foot of the stairs. She had tried to crawl for safety, but the harp had caught in the railings and was wedged tight. She played it where it wedged, as if there were no fire around her.

He bent down to shout in her ear above the

crackle of the flames as they ate through dry wood and years of dust and debris. "Milady, we must leave at once."

"My harp," she cried, clutching the unwieldy instrument to her as he tried to lift her.

"You must leave it."

Stubbornly, she wrapped her arms around the instrument.

"No. My son loves it so."

Desperate, he coughed and promised blindly, "I will get you another. You must leave it."

She seemed no more concerned than a curious child. "Is there danger?"

"Yes." Again he tried to lift her, again she resisted.

"Is my Rand safe?"

"Yes." He cursed, realizing that he had wasted time with the harp when he should have used the baby as a lure. "Don't you want to calm him? He is very frightened right now. He needs his mother."

"I must go to my little boy. He needs me." She released the harp without further protest. He carried her from the burning building.

He grinned at Helena. "I know. I owe you a gown."

She didn't smile back. In fact, she looked grim.

"You were supposed to be gone. Headed back to Parsleigh." His grandfather stood staring at the ragtag survivors as if he were sorely disappointed.

"I'm sorry to have dissatisfied you yet again, Grandfather." He put his mother down gently, against the well so that she could lean back against the stone wellhead for support.

His mother bleated in alarm, whether because of the fire, or his grandfather, he could not say. Jenny hurried to put the redheaded child in her arms, and his mother soothed the baby's fears and calmed herself, with a crooning, "There, there. It will all be fine in a moment, Rand. Mama won't let the bad man hurt you ever again."

Moving as fast as a snake, his grandfather plucked up the boy and stared into his face for a moment. "Not my blood," he said at last, and would have tossed the child to the ground if Jenny hadn't leaped to catch him by the arms.

The air was suddenly full of infant screams. Before Rand could move, his mother let out a scream and threw her battered body at the marquess's legs, unbalancing him. He would have tumbled harmlessly against the side of the well, but the untended stones crumbled under his weight and he fell headlong into the well, disappearing from view.

His mother leaned against the crumbled wall, staring at the spot of gaping stone where the marquess had disappeared. After a moment, she held out her arms to the baby. "Everything is fine now, Rand. The bad man is gone. He'll never hurt you again."

Helena came awake suddenly and opened her eyes to see Rand leaning up on one arm, watching her. He smiled lazily at her. "I wish I had a paintbrush."

"What would you do with it?"

He teased a strand of her hair, playing it across her lips. "Create a masterpiece, of course."

She sat up, remembering how they had arrived last night, a filthy, tired group, all still stunned from the sudden death of the marquess. "We haven't time. We have to deal with our displaced householders before the duke thinks we've dropped them in his lap permanently."

"Your sister seems unsure of me."

"What should she be? Remember, you did bring me back covered in soot and dirt, dressed in men's clothing . . . or should I say, half dressed in men's clothing." She smiled when he seemed to take her teasing seriously. "She will come around. You have a way with women, my lord."

"Do I?" He pulled the sheet from her slowly, exposing her breasts, and then her abdomen. He stopped, examining the faint pink scars that marked her there. He leaned down to kiss across her belly and then rested his cheek against her there.

She patted his head and would have spoken then, but he rose, startling her, to pronounce, "We must always sleep together in the same bed."

"As you like." She kissed him lightly on the lips.

He rolled away. "You are too accommodating, considering the bargain you made with me." Though his tone was teasing, his eyes were serious.

"What bargain is that?" She stroked her fingers along his ribs, and watched the gooseflesh rise on his skin. "That I should be able to do as I wish?"

"Exactly."

"But I am."

He traced the scars on her belly again. "I'm sorry I couldn't protect you. I'm sorry my grandfather succeeded in making you miscarry the child."

She raised his head with her hands. "He didn't."

He looked at her with a touch of fear, as if she might have turned as mad as his mother had from her grief. "Of course he did. If he had not been set on tearing us apart, you might have a healthy son in your arms right now."

"Rand—"

"We can try again."

She didn't know how to prepare him for the shock. Was there a way to ease into it? "If you like. But there is no hurry."

No hurry? He could see the wary expression on her face. Was she afraid he couldn't bear the guilt of what his arrogance had cost them? No hurry. He didn't believe her for a moment. She hadn't been certain she wanted to be a wife, but she had known she wanted to be a mother. But he humored her. "I don't know how good a father I'll be. Or even how good a husband. So if you wish to wait, there are ways to arrange it."

"New lessons?" Her eyes lit with mischief.

He couldn't understand her light mood when what they discussed was so serious. "Would you rather not? I did promise you a child."

"As I recall you saying once, you always keep your promises. Though you make few."

"You listen altogether too well. The question is, do you know me better, or do I know myself better?"

"I have a secret." She rose from the bed. Though she seemed worried, she could not suppress a smile. "I would have told you sooner, but your grandfather interrupted my plans."

Another secret. He had only a moment to suspect what it might be before she returned and confirmed his suspicion with the swaddled bundle in her arms.

"I didn't want to lie to you." Her gaze followed him nervously as he sat up. "But Nanny Bea thought it best if the marquess not know."

"She was right, Helena." He could see the guilt she felt. He knew what that crushing vise felt like and he wanted to erase it from her completely. "Do you think I could have hidden my mother away for eight years and not understand why you might keep my son away from my grandfather?"

She smiled then, wholeheartedly. "Let me introduce your son to you. I hope you don't mind that we've named him. But it would have been unfortunate to let him go all this time addressed only as 'Boy' or 'Baby.'"

Rand held his breath as Helena handed his son into his arms. "What have you called him?"

She touched the tiny cheek. "James Randolph." The boy slept deeply, not stirring at the exchange.

"After my father. He would have approved." The small body lay trusting and pliant in his father's hold. A father whose forehead was rapidly beading with sweat. "Take him back," he pleaded with her.

"No." Helena only smiled. "I want to capture this moment."

He began to groan at the sight of her sketchbook, but broke off when the child stirred restlessly in his arms. "I might drop him."

She looked at him for a moment, consideringly, not as an artist but as a mother. Then she shook her head and pulled her pen out of her basket. "You never would."

His son's body was warm against his bare chest, one tiny arm free of swaddling curled against his shoulder. He reached a tentative finger to be instinctively grasped by the sleeping infant's fingers.

Helena was looking at him now with her artist's eyes.

He realized that she might fall into one of her near trances and leave him with the child. He

looked down at the boy, suddenly worried. "I don't
. . . I never . . ."

She settled easily at the end of the bed and found
a clean sheet for her drawing. And then, as if belatedly hearing the panic in his voice, her artist's gaze
cleared for a moment, to that of a wife who loved
her husband despite his myriad flaws. "A baby's
head is sweet to kiss," she said softly.

"I . . ." He looked down at the sleeping child,
afraid to move too much lest he wake the beast
that lurked in every infant he had ever seen. He
had seen relatively few and all from a distance,
but even so he knew the terrible power of their
displeasure.

"You know I am likely to make a hash of being
a father. A husband. I have no experience with
responsibility. Duty. Love."

Her artist's eye appraised him. "Tell that to
Jenny. To your mother. To those eight bastards of
yours." Her wife's eyes blinked. "Are any of them
yours?"

"Not a one. The first was Jenny's son. I thought
the old man should pay for that one, even if he
wasn't my blood. And then my mother was so happy
with a baby. So certain that he was her son. When
Jenny's boy turned one, though, my mother
seemed to know he wasn't really her son. So I found
another baby for her to love."

"Then you have more experience with infants
than most fathers."

He shook his head. "No. I left that to Jenny and
my mother."

She laughed at him. "Kiss your son's head."

When he hesitated, she crawled up to him and
leaned over to press a kiss to his lips and one to
the top of the infant's head.

And then she settled back at the end of the bed with her pen poised. "Well? Your turn."

She didn't seem to believe he could do much damage. Perhaps she was right. Cautiously, he bent his head and pressed his lips to brush over the infant's scalp. There was so little hair that his lips felt the firm resilience of his son's skull.

He breathed in the scent of an infant . . . his son. Helena's child. The boy slept now, but soon he would wake and cry to be fed. Soon he would walk, run, be old enough to be given a puppy.

The enormity of the responsibility settled on his shoulders. With an acknowledgment of the depth of his cowardice, he realized he would never have dared father a child if he had realized the awesome duty embodied in one small human being.

As if sensing his father's insecurity, the boy woke and opened his eyes to gaze into Rand's face. After a moment of exploration, the little lips pushed out and the little body began to squirm with a force that shocked Rand. He appealed to Helena. "I don't know what to do."

Helena lifted the child from his arms and the incipient squall turned into an angelic smile as the boy turned to gaze at his mother's face.

"I see the boy has taste. He must get it from his father."

Helena laughed as she nuzzled her son with casual affection. "He will know you soon. And love you."

"As long as he has you . . ."

She unswaddled their son with swift practiced movements and placed the squirming infant, clad only in a nappy, on Rand's bare chest. "He needs you."

Rand might have argued further, but his son

pushed up against his chest with his small arms,
raising his head to look in wonder at his father's
eyes. And he smiled.

"See?" Helena rubbed her hand along the
infant's back, encouraging the exploration. "He
needs you. I need you. And you will come in time
to accept that we always will."

He watched her retreat again to the edge of the
bed and wanted to call her back even as he struggled to accept what he knew to be true.

He was a husband. A father. A man who took
care of his responsibilities. But what if he failed?

He knew so little of how to care for those one
loved. How could she be so certain that he could
learn?

As if she read his doubts in his expression, Helena leaned over and kissed him lightly on the lips.
She touched his cheek gently as she said, "One
lesson a day, from now until you beg me to stop."

If you liked THE NEXT BEST BRIDE, be sure to look for Kelly McClymer's next release in the "Once Upon a Wedding" series, THE IMPETUOUS BRIDE, available November 2002, wherever books are sold.

Rosaline Fenster, Helena's twin, never had any intention of marrying into the aristocracy and suffering a life of boredom. So when she left her intended the night before her wedding, she sailed to America, determined to live on her own terms. Dreams of the untamed wilderness in the fabled West lead her to a wagon train heading for California. Unfortunately, only married women are accepted into the group. So when Rosaline meets the gruff but undeniably attractive Rob Lewis, she asks him to pose as her husband. . . .

Look for the other books in this chaming series!

### THE FAIRY-TALE BRIDE

### THE STAR-CROSSED BRIDE

### THE UNINTENDED BRIDE

### THE INFAMOUS BRIDE

# COMING IN MAY 2002 FROM
# ZEBRA BALLAD ROMANCES

## __JUST NORTH OF BLISS: Meet Me at the Fair

by Alice Duncan    0-8217-7277-5    $5.99US/$7.99CAN

Belle Monroe is considering letting a handsome stranger at the World's Columbian Exposition take her portrait to publicize the fair. Although she's terrified of posing, the persistent photographer's tender advances soon make Belle wonder if this brash Northerner and a proper Southern girl like her could actually be meant for each other.

## __A PRINCESS BORN: Of Royal Birth

by Sandra Madden    0-8217-7250-3    $5.99US/$7.99CAN

When Edmund Wydville returned to his country estate, Kate Beadle was fully grown—and uncommonly beautiful. She had loved Edmund since childhood, but understood that nobility had no business wooing women of uncertain origin. Edmund would find that love was far less concerned with noble blood than with the way Kate made him feel.

## __FLIGHT OF FANCY: American Heiresses

by Tracy Cozzens    0-8217-7350-X    $5.99US/$7.99CAN

Hannah Carrington had been whisked off to Paris by her mother. She was glad to explore the City of Lights, but husband-hunting was another matter, for Hannah dreamed of studying science. Marriage would put an end to all that—unless it was to a man as inclined to scholarly study as she was, namely Lord Benjamin Ramsey.

## __SUNLIGHT ON JOSEPHINE STREET: The Cuvier Widows

by Sylvia McDaniel    0-8217-7321-6    $5.99US/$7.99CAN

After her husband's untimely death, Marian Cuvier felt determined to find a new place in the world. That led her to Louis Fournet, Jean's former business partner. When the darkly handsome man awakened feelings Marian found unfamiliar, she discovered that convincing herself not to fall in love again would be the most difficult task of all.

---